The Lying Tree

SUNDAE LEIGHTON

Published by Sullen Press, 2022.

The Lying Tree
Available in these formats:
ISBN 978-1-7376181-4-0 (Paperback)
ISBN 978-1-7376181-8-8 (Ebook AZW)
ISBN 978-1-7376181-9-5 (Ebook EPUB)

This book is a work of fiction. Name, characters, places, incidents or otherwise are written from imagination only. Any resemblance to actual persons, things living or dead or events is coincidental.

This book is intended for mature readers 18 years and older. It contains sexually explicit and graphic scenes and language that might be offensive to some readers.

All characters are 18 years of age or older.
All sexual acts are consensual.

About this book

This book contains dark themes that might be triggering. It contains self-harm, drug and alcohol abuse, mental health issues, as well as some LGBTQIA+ hate that some readers may find troubling. Please read at your own risk. This is a love story first and always between two troubled boys who found one another at a time when they needed it most.

For my fellow dark romance writers...tell me how you keep your sanity because I nearly lost mine while writing this one.

Playlist[1]

Something in the Way - Nirvana
Come Back...Be Here - Taylor Swift
Chainsaw - The Band Perry
Sour Girl - Stone Temple Pilots
No Surprises - Radiohead
Take Me to Church - Hozier
Slither - Velvet Revolver
I Know - Fiona Apple
Wrecking Ball - Miley Cyrus
Heaven Can Wait - Meatloaf
Illicit Affairs - Taylor Swift
Bi-polar Bear - Stone Temple Pilots
Loving the Alien - Velvet Revolver
Superstar - Taylor Swift
Always Remember Us This Way - Lady Gaga
Demons - Imagine Dragons
Sweet - Cigarettes After Sex
Love in the Dark - Adele

---

1. https://spoti.fi/3O2gkMJ

Prologue

Matthias

Four years ago

I shrugged my backpack up over my shoulder as I stood by my locker, waiting for my best friend, Helena Hampton, so that we could head home. I kept my gaze down, away from everyone else, pretending to be busy on my phone and hoping no one would bother me. I only had a few more months left here before I could leave to run off with Killian, Helena's older brother. It would be just like he promised, and we'd never look back. It was his words from two nights ago that kept me going. His whispered confession, the look of lust in his eyes. Killian cared for me, and maybe one day he might even love me the way I did him. I knew it was only a matter of time before he admitted it.

I gazed down at the one photo I had of us on my phone, taken on Saturday night. Killian's arm was wrapped around my shoulder as we both gave sleepy smiles to the camera. His dark curls were a mess, and my own dirty-blond hair wasn't much better, but I didn't care. I was happy in that moment, and it was written all over my face.

It was the snickering and hushed whispers of my classmates that finally caused me to drag my eyes over to where they stood, watching me. Wait, why *were* they all staring at me right now? People had their phones in hand, and they were pointing and smirking as if I was suddenly the latest Canfield gossip.

"We have to go." Helena suddenly hooked her arm through mine. "Now, Matty, no time to waste." she hissed, but there was something in her voice that had me pulling away.

I tilted my head as I stared at her. "What happened? What's going on?" I could feel all the eyes of Canfield High on me. "What is everyone watching, Helena?" Fear began to claw at my mind. On second thought, maybe I didn't want to know the answer to that question.

"There's...there's no video." Helena sank her teeth into her bottom lip. "Just sound. It's you, and Killian." She gripped my wrist, but I shook her off. "Don't do this, Matthias, please," she begged.

I felt all the blood rush from my head. "What do you mean it's me and Killian?" Nausea started to creep in as I processed the situation.. Did someone record us in the treehouse? Record us having sex? Jesus Christ, that would ruin him. No one knew about us except Helena, and she would never tell anyone.

"Let's go." She tried again to get me to move.

"Hey, Fuller!" Evan Combs shouted, but I refused to look in his direction. "You really think that Killian Hampton could actually love someone like you?" Obnoxious laughter followed as panic struck my body.

"I don't think he knows about this yet," Ruth Collins pointed out. "We should play it for him."

"I love you, Killian," I heard myself say. "I've always loved you, and I hope that someday you can love me back. Do you think that's possible?" More obnoxious laughter followed.

Tears stung my eyes. There was no way someone could have been in there. We would have seen them, or heard them, unless...*no*. Killian wouldn't have, would he? When I met my best friend's blue eyes, the ones that matched her brother's, I already had my answer. I shot off down the hall toward the front door without looking back, ignoring Helena calling out to me. I didn't care that it was sleeting outside, that it felt like sheets of ice beating against my skin when it made contact with me. All I could think about was that Killian had used me. Had begged me to tell him how I felt, only to turn it all against me. I found myself running until I was at the house, and then I was climbing up into the treehouse, sobbing and screaming like a complete lunatic. I only stopped when I saw everything from that night still there.

The mattress. The twinkle lights, which were now off but still hung around the room. The empty bucket that he had put the champagne in. I dropped down onto the bed to cry, feeling as if my entire soul was leaving my body. How could someone be so horrible? Had Killian been using me the entire time?

"Matty, I'm coming up," I heard Helena say, but I didn't bother to answer her. *Everyone knew*. Everyone at school, probably the entire town now, and they all thought I was a fool. I couldn't agree more.

I heard the sounds of Helena as she climbed inside the treehouse, her feet thumping against the floorboards as she moved closer. When her hand touched my shoulder, another sob escaped from my throat.

"How could he?" I whispered when I met her gaze. "How could someone be so cruel, so horrible?" I tried to catch my breath, but my lungs couldn't seem to absorb enough air. "You know he wanted me to tell him?" I coughed out a bitter laugh. "Killian begged me to tell him that I loved him. Said he wanted to hear it from me before he left, promising me he would come back when I graduated in June so we could be together. And for what? All so he could ruin my fucking life." I felt another wave of tears slipping down my cheeks. "I hate him." I wanted to curl up and die. I wanted Killian to find me here, to know that he did this to me, but he wouldn't care. He never did.

Helena squeezed my shoulder. "You don't mean that, Matty. You've been in love with Killian since you could understand what that word meant," she whispered. "I'll talk to him, and he can fix this."

"Fuck him, Helena!" I shot up off the floor. "Did you know he pursued me?" When her brows shot up, I continued. "That's right, that asshole brother of yours kissed me first. He said he knew I liked him, could see how much I wanted him, and he played me like a violin." I wanted to hit something, I was so angry. "I was his dirty secret, but I was always there when he wanted me. In the middle of the night, in the closet while I was supposed to be working, in his bed or mine while we were supposed to be sleeping, it didn't matter. Killian said jump and I asked how high." I slammed my fist into the wood, feeling the pain as it ripped through my arm. When I did it again, I screamed so loud I was surprised someone didn't call the police. The pain in my hand didn't mask the pain in my heart.

Helena wrapped her arms around my waist, pressing her frame against mine. "You're going to break your hand if you keep doing that." She tugged lightly. "Please, Matthias, you're scaring me," she whispered.

"I want to die."

"Don't say shit like that."

I spun around to face my best friend. "All this time, all this *fucking time* I kept thinking things would get better, that Killian would get over his fear of people finding out he was with me, only to have him break my heart. What am I supposed to do, Helena? He ruined my life." I felt a new batch of tears slip down my cheeks.

"I can talk to him. He cares about you; I know he does. I've never seen Kill act the way he does when he's around you. You calm his demons," she reminded me.

I shook her off. "I calm his demons, Helena? Killian *is* the demon. Do you actually think he would do something that wouldn't make him look good? He's been making everyone else the bad guy for years. You, his friends, your grandmother, me. Everything is always about Killian." I slumped to the floor, my bones useless to support my weight any longer. "My life is over." I gasped.

"Fuck this town." Helena got down onto her knees so she could be next to me. "They're all a bunch of closed-minded pricks. They wouldn't know true love if it jumped up to bite them in the balls." She cupped my face with her hands. "Killian loves you. He just doesn't know how to express himself like that."

I shook my head. "He doesn't, and he never did. If he loved me, he wouldn't have given that recording out to anyone." The nausea from school hadn't subsided. "Oh god." I groaned before dragging myself to my feet and reaching for the empty champagne bucket. My stomach clenched and roared, but nothing except dry heaves escaped me. Sweat covered my body like a second skin. "I'm never going to recover from this. You know that right? I'll never be able to get a date in this town because of him. I'm going to have to move as far away from here as possible. I was supposed to..." More dry heaves began to wrack my body as I remembered how Killian promised to come back for me so that we could be together. More lies from his mouth.

"Matty, tomorrow people will be talking about something else that they don't know shit about. You know how Canfield is," she soothed.

I closed my eyes. "I don't believe you," I whispered in response. The thought of going back to that school tomorrow made me shudder. Maybe I could fake being sick for a few days.

"You'll get through this. I'll be here with you one hundred percent of the way. I love you, Matthias, doesn't that count for anything?"

"Thank you." I didn't know what else to say.

Things didn't get better at school though. People tormented me as often as possible. Pictures of Killian were constantly shoved into my locker and stuck to the door. Flyers for his band, Mulligan Downtown, were always around, even though he wasn't. I spent the next few months just trying to keep my sanity so I could graduate high school, and the next four years trying to forget I had ever met Killian Hampton. Until he came back into my life to shatter the walls I had built to keep him out.

Chapter One

Killian

Present Day

I glanced over my sunglasses as my Uber driver drove insanely slow down Main Street. Jesus Christ, what was with this dude? I told him that I was in a hurry, but here he was, moving at a snail's pace as if I had nowhere to be. Did he not understand what I meant when I told him to drive like Dale Earnhardt once I gave him the address? Maybe I should have told him there was a huge tip in it for him so it would light a fire under his ass.

I ran my hand through my hair as I caught a glimpse of the local ice cream shop. I hadn't been back here in over four years, and I suddenly wished I hadn't waited so long. Maybe if I had come sooner, helped more, given back, things could have been different, and I wouldn't have had to return to Canfield for my grandmother's funeral. Shit, this was too much. I could already feel the anxiety clawing at my brain, and I knew the moment I locked eyes with him that—.

All the air disappeared from my lungs when I saw the two-screened movie theater where Matthias had worked. The memory of stolen kisses while he was supposed to be working hit me so hard that I thought I might suffocate. The promises I broke the second I crossed over state lines and stepped foot in L.A. tormented me. The lies I told myself to feel better about what had happened came flooding back to my mind.

Shit, I was an unimaginable bastard.

I was surprised when the hot tears stung my eyes. *Get yourself together, Kill,* I shouted at myself. *That was then, and this is now. You're a goddamn rock star. Millions of people fucking love you. Your songs are played on the radio all over the world, and your tour is sold out for the next two years. You can stick your dick in anyone you want, so why think about Matthias?*

Only Matthias...shit, he was different. My little sister's best friend was always there. He'd had a shitty home life, so Gram let him hang out with us whenever he wanted, which was all the time. At first, I'd pretended it was annoying. Like I didn't have time for some nerdy pest like him, until that night I had kissed him and changed everything.

I couldn't help it. He was just so perfect. He had been hiding in the treehouse covered in his own blood, and looked scared to death. I hadn't expected to find him there, but the anger that ripped through me when I'd realized who had hurt Matthias scared the shit out of me. I wasn't gay; I liked chicks with big tits and a perfect, peachy-shaped ass. But at that moment, I had begun to question everything I knew about myself. Matthias had stared at me with those hazel eyes that I had noticed for the first time that night, and I'd wanted nothing more than to claim him as mine.

"Sir?"

I hadn't realized the car had stopped, but suddenly I was sitting in front of my childhood home. "Shit, sorry man." I raised my hip to slip my wallet from my pocket. I planted the hundred in his hand. "Keep the change," I added before he could say anything else, and quickly climbed from the car.

The cold winter air hit me and whipped through my bones. I cursed myself for not bringing a coat; when I had left California, it had been a balmy seventy-two degrees. I grabbed my bag from the open trunk before I noticed my sister watching me from the porch. I gave her a small wave before heading her way.

"What did you do to your hair?" Helena asked as she raised an eyebrow.

I instantly touched my head. "You don't like it?" What if the fans hated it, too? Cutting it last night had been impulsive, but it was so much easier to deal with now.

"Your curls, Kill. They're gone. You had the most amazing curls. You know how much I envied them." She wrapped her arms around my waist in a hug. "I've missed you, big brother," she murmured into my shirt. "How are you not frozen right now without a jacket?"

I chuckled. "I am. We don't get weather like this where I live," I reminded her. "Let's go inside so I can defrost."

The smell of the house hit me hard when I stepped inside. The faint scent of roses filled the air, as well as some combination of cleaning supplies that I had tried to get my housekeeper to figure out, but she never could. I felt like I was a kid again, running through the hallway with my friends, kicking the soccer ball around despite the fact that Gram had told me to take it outside. We never listened, and she never really enforced the rules.

"Killian?" Helena touched my arm. "Are you okay?"

No little sis, I am pretty fucking far from okay. Only I didn't say that. "Well, I wish I was here under better circumstances." I ruffled her pin-straight hair, causing her to slap my hand away. "How are you holding up? You've done all of the arrangements yourself, which can't be easy. You must be exhausted. Did you have enough money? Let me know if you need anything else. What can I do to help?" I rambled on without stopping, hoping I didn't sound as nervous as I suddenly felt.

"I'm surprisingly calm, Kill, but we need to talk before you get too comfy."

There was something in the way she spoke that instantly brought my guard up. "What aren't you saying?" I narrowed my eyes at my sister.

"Nothing, relax." But as she turned to head into the small living room, I saw it. The way her lips turned up into that smirk she'd used when she'd lied to Gram about something and thought she'd gotten away with it. Spoiler, Helena never got away with anything.

I dropped my bag on the floor before I marched after her. "Helena Kristina Hampton..." My voice trailed off when I saw who was in the living room. Dirty-blond hair, hazel eyes, and was still hot as all fuck.

Matthias Fuller.

He shot up from the couch with his phone in hand. "You told me he wasn't coming!" he exclaimed, pointing at me, but he kept those fuck-me eyes on my sister. "What the fuck, Helena? How could you lie to me like that?" he cried.

"You really thought my brother wasn't going to come to our grandmother's funeral?"

"Matthias."

"Oh no, you don't." He cut me off before I could apologize. Not that it would fix things. "Go fuck yourself, you piece of shit." He reached for the dark coat that was lying on the chair and shoved his arms in before he yanked it up over his shoulders. "Just for the record"—Matthias licked his lips, a nervous tick he always seemed to have around me—"I really did love you. I wasn't using you to get off, or whatever you thought you might get out of me. I genuinely cared for you." He pulled up the zipper then tried to shove past me, but I grabbed his elbow.

"You don't get to speak to me like that, Matthias," I growled, shoving him against the wall and caging him in. He stared up at me, and I waited for the fear to appear in his eyes. Instead, the only things I saw were hatred and anger. Not once did he flinch away. "Someone grew a pair." I ran my palm over his thick chest. Someone had been working out, too, but I kept that to myself.

His lip curled angrily. "A lot has changed since you left, rock star," Matthias hissed through clenched teeth. "You're not the boss of me anymore, but I'm sure you can go find some useless groupie to play with while you're here."

"Killian, stop it!" Helena tried to pry me off her friend, but I ignored her. She weighed one hundred twenty pounds, tops.

A cruel smile slipped over my face, and I knew the dimples Matthias loved so much were showing. It was rare I ever allowed them to appear these days. "Oh babe, who told you I wasn't your boss anymore?" I resisted the urge to capture his lips with mine.

"Killian, I'm fucking serious!" Helena's fists pounded against my back. "Stop being this alpha dickbag, right now!" she cried.

I stared down at Matthias, who held his chin up defiantly without breaking eye contact with me. "We're not done," I warned, releasing him to take a step back. Helena had barely moved out of the way in time to avoid me crashing into her.

"We are so fucking done," he grunted before shoving off from the wall. "Thanks for nothing, Helena!" Matthias called out to my sister, and then the front door slammed shut causing my sister to turn around to glare at me.

I closed my eyes so I didn't have to face her. "Jesus Christ, Helena," I sighed. "You told him I wasn't going to be here? What did you think was going to happen? That I'd see him again and realize I need him? That I'd discover he is the person that could fix all of my problems?" I opened my eyes to find her blues dark with anger.

Helena had her arms folded over her chest. "What the hell was that, Killian?" she demanded. "You just manhandled...stop smiling." She shook her head when I tried to stifle a laugh at her words. "Maybe I thought the two of you could talk about what the hell happened that night in the treehouse? Matty won't tell me, and you're not talking." Her eyes filled with tears.

Crap. "Hey." I pushed the hair from her face so I could look straight into her eyes. "You know I love you, right?" I folded her against me, wrapping my arms around her slim frame.

"Did you ever love him? Even a tiny little bit?" Helena asked, causing me to tense. "Kill, he's my best friend."

"I'm your brother. I'm your damn blood."

Helena untangled herself from my grip. "I still don't understand why you hurt him like that. Forcing him to tell you that he loved you. Why? He worshiped the ground that you walked on. It was so cruel, especially when you knew how he felt about you!" she exclaimed. "You really are an asshole." Her eyes simmered with hatred.

The things I had said and done with Matthias were private. I had meant everything I'd ever said to him when no one was around. Only I was afraid, even now, to admit that. Why was this happening already? I hadn't wanted to get into this so soon and definitely not with Helena. "You don't understand, I..." I what? I loved him? I wanted him, sure, but I knew that I couldn't have him because I wasn't gay. Or at least that's what I tried to tell myself instead of facing the facts that were right in front of me.

"Make me understand why you hurt him," Helena ordered. When I didn't say anything, she let out a bitter laugh. "Typical Killian. You keep everything bottled up and never let anyone see the real you because you want to be this tough badass that won't crack," she hissed.

I had let Matthias see me.

I dropped my eyes to my feet. "I don't want to fight with you, Helena," I whispered. "Not with the funeral coming up. I want to grieve with you." I glanced back up to see a little compassion on my sister's face.

She rolled her eyes. "Fine, but promise me you'll stay away from him. Don't go into his room or engage with him tomorrow at the service. Leave him alone. He's suffered enough." Shit, I'd forgotten he still lived here.

"Is he..."

"Oh no, you don't." Helena held up her hand. "You don't get to ask any questions about him. You wouldn't let me talk to you about Matthias when you left, and he locked himself in his room for weeks without talking to me. You're done with him," she declared.

I chewed on my lip. "Sure, okay." I nodded, but it was a lie. I would never be done with Matthias.

We would always be unfinished business.

Chapter Two

Matthias

After what Helena pulled yesterday, I seriously considered not coming to the memorial service today, but I wasn't that type of person. Not only was she my best friend's grandmother, but Barbara Hampton had been one to me, too—when my father had decided the bottle was more important than his own son. She'd fed me, clothed me, and let me live in her home rent free without a second thought. A warm feeling settled over me when I remembered the night, she'd told me I was welcome to stay as long as I needed. Of course, then I remembered it was Killian's idea, and that feeling disappeared.

"I was afraid you weren't coming." Helena threw herself at me when I approached the church. "You didn't answer my texts," she whispered into my coat. "What happened to you last night? You never came home." She sounded scared.

That's because I turned off my phone, I thought. I had to get myself, and I was afraid that Killian might try to reach out to me. If someone gave him my new phone number, that is. "Sorry, I was stuck in my own head." *Meaning, your asshole brother and how he ruined my life.* I didn't have to say that for Helena to figure it out. "I crashed at Cam's." I knew she didn't like my ex, but it was better than going home to fight with her. Or worse.

She scrunched up her nose when she pulled back to look at me, shielding her eyes from the morning sun with one hand. "You hate me, don't you?"

"No, I don't. I'm just disappointed." I didn't have to remind Helena what Killian did to me because she had been there to see the aftermath. "You're the romantic, not me. Unless you want me to castrate him, though, don't try that shit again."

Helena's eyes looked pinched as she glanced behind me. "Speak of the devil," she whispered.

I turned, despite my better judgment, to find Killian standing there with one of his old friends from high school. I remembered Evan Combs well, considering he used to torture me, but Kill was all I could see. Dressed in a long, dark coat and dress slacks, I'd have been a liar if I said he didn't take my breath away with those blue eyes that pierced your soul, paired with a face that was chiseled perfection, like a fairy-tale prince. Killian was sleek and powerful, with untamed pride and muscles that went on for days. The tattoos that he'd added over the years only added to his sexiness, but I had to admit, I didn't like his new hair. I missed the dark-chestnut curls that were forever an untidy mess on his head. He used to let me run my hands through them for hours. The curls were gone, leaving behind shaved sides and short strands that looked too plain for the Killian I loved. Wait, no. Had fallen in love with. I couldn't still love someone that burned me the way he had.

I had followed his career as it took off. Mulligan Downtown were played all over the world, topping the billboard charts and winning every Grammy they had been nominated for. His Instagram was full of happy smiles, sexy models and actresses on his arm, beers with his bandmates, and all the things I would never get to share with him. An emptiness I had thought I would never feel again filled me, and I hated it. The promises from that night began to invade my mind, making me realize I was still hung up on him, and probably always would be.

"Let's go inside." I squared my shoulders before I turned back toward the church.

"Well, look who it is. Matthias Fuller," Evan called out as he and Killian drew closer. Goddamn jocks. Did they ever grow up, or were they forever stuck in high school? Did they even know there was life after that? He chuckled. "Still into dick, right?"

I swung around to face him, clenching my fists at my sides. "Still a massive asshole, right?" I wasn't the wallflower I had been in high school. I didn't want to start a fight here, but if push came to shove, I would knock Evan into next week.

"Relax." Killian pressed a hand to my shoulder. I glanced down, noticing the colorful ink that spun over his fingers, before I met his blue eyes. They looked so different now. "Say you're sorry, Combs." He glanced back at his friend.

Evan looked surprised. "I was kidding, man, relax." He tried to play it off, but when Killian continued to stare at him, he held up his hands. I'd been the victim of that look before, and it wasn't something you could ever stand up to. "Sure, fine. I'm sorry, I didn't realize you were so sensitive, Kill."

"This is my grandmother's funeral, show some fucking respect. She treated Matthias like her own grandson," he hissed. His hand was still on my shoulder, and when it tightened, I hated how it made fire roar through my entire body. "Let's go inside," he suggested.

I resisted the urge to shove Killian's hand away, and instead moved back from him and reached for his sister's hand, lacing our fingers together. I really wanted to know what was going on with his hair. Also, why did his eyes look so odd? Was he not getting enough sleep at night? But he didn't deserve any kind of small talk or consideration; he deserved nothing from me.

Evan excused himself to sit down with a few of Killian's other friends from high school, who looked more than eager to catch up with the rock star, but he made no move toward them. As we moved to the front of the church, I suddenly felt it. Killian's warm hand was on my back, causing my entire body to go rigid. I wanted to shove him away. I wanted to yell at him to never touch me like that again because it was too intimate, but I couldn't. Not without drawing attention to us, which was something he would never want. Sparks flashed in my mind, memories of what we did came rushing back, and it took all I had to not start screaming.

The three of us sat down in the front pew, where I moved to make sure Helena was in the middle, next to her brother. I had to put some space between us. Just being in the same room as Killian was suffocating me. I felt fingers brush my shoulder and when I looked over, his hand was right there, his arm stretched out across the pew behind Helena's back.

"Tell him to stop touching me," I whispered into Hel's ear.

She rolled her eyes before turning to her brother. "We talked about this." She slapped his arm, but I saw the smirk on his face. The way he stretched his arm over the back of the pew and over Helena's shoulders was just casual enough to look like he was comforting his sister, yet also enough so he could easily let his long fingers graze my arm.

"I mean it," I growled before I knocked his hand away from my shoulder, since Helena's slap wasn't enough motivation for him to reposition himself. "Aren't you afraid your friends will see? We wouldn't want that, would we, Kill?" I cocked an eyebrow.

Killian instantly moved his arm away, his hands in his lap instead. The perfect, innocent altar boy who would never touch a man in *that* way. He dropped his gaze to stare at his hands now resting on his thighs.

I felt anger race through my body. That was the one thing he had always been scared of—someone finding out that he *liked* it. Holding hands with me. Kissing me. Having me suck him off, or the way I jerked his cock just the right way. Even worse, Killian loved to reciprocate. He couldn't keep his hands off me when we were alone. Did they know Kill liked to wake up with his arms and legs wrapped around me, like he was afraid I would disappear if he let go? Or how terrified he was of thunderstorms? How he used to beg me to make them stop, sobbing so hard he nearly made himself sick?

I wondered if the groupies and models that Killian brought back to his hotels on tour were as kinky as he wanted them to be. The things he would tease me with until I thought I would come apart at the seams. Was he like that with everyone? Did anyone know the Killian I did, the one who would cut himself just to feel something because he was so manic he thought he was going to lose his mind? Or that he even suffered from bipolar disorder? My guess was no. No one knew him the way I did because he kicked them out before they got too close. If I kept this up, I was going to let Killian drown me all over again.

I turned my attention back to the giant portrait of Barbara Hampton in front of us. She had always been such a friendly, helpful woman, and everyone in town had loved her. This would be the only service for her since she was cremated, and there wouldn't be a burial of the ashes at the cemetery. It was going to be strange not having her around town anymore. She got sick so quickly, and the progression happened so fast that we hardly had a chance to think about it before she was gone. Helena did the best she could, as did I, with taking care of her. But right up until the end, she insisted she was fine and we didn't have to worry about her.

I felt a warm body move in next to me. "Helena looks like her, don't you think?" Killian's voice made the hairs on the back of my neck stand up. When I didn't respond, he tilted his body so that his face was right in front of mine. "Matthias are we going to do this the entire time?" His tired eyes searched mine.

I hated him. I hated him for what he did—embarrassing me in front of the entire school, the entire town like he did—and I hated myself for falling for his lies. I pressed my lips together before slowly bringing my left hand up to scratch a nonexistent itch on my face with my middle finger.

Killian sighed. "That's mature in church," he muttered, just as the priest walked out to start the service. He leaned back in the pew but made no move to get up.

I tried my hardest to ignore Killian. I wanted to pay attention to the service as the priest talked about the amazing life of Barbara Hampton, who had lived her life to the fullest. I had never met Helena and Killian's grandfather, who had died before they were born, but she had never looked at another man after him. It was hard to concentrate at times with the heat radiating from Killian's body. He was sitting so close, his leg nearly pressed against mine. I wondered why he didn't go back to sit with Helena. She was quietly crying next to me, and I tried to comfort her as best I could, but Killian was her brother, not me.

There had been a time when I was stupid enough to believe Killian wasn't playing me, and I thought we might have been able to get married right here in this exact church. The more I thought about it, the more it hurt, and then my vision blurred. It was all my fault because I was the one who thought he'd cared for me. He was the one to blame in all of this. I had been just a kid then, barely eighteen years old, and Killian had been twenty. He was the adult. He should have known better.

"The service is over, Matthias."

I was on my feet before I even realized what I was doing. "I need you to leave me alone." I had just moved past him without saying goodbye to Helena before the tears fell. I heard the snickers from Killian's friends who were waiting outside the church, probably from the rest of the town too, and I wished I could go back in time. I would stop myself from meeting up with Killian on the night that had changed everything. Back then, I would have done anything he wanted, and he knew it.

I locked the door to my car after getting into it, and grabbed my cell from where I had left it so I could text Helena. I had just left her there, but she had to know how much this hurt me. I watched from the driver's seat as Killian came out while holding Helena against his chest, stopping to talk with his friends for a moment. I knew he would invite them back to the house for the reception. He might want them there, but it was the last thing I needed right now. I would go to help my friend, but once it was finished, I had no plans to sleep under the same roof as Killian ever again.

Chapter Three

I knew Matthias hated me, I just didn't think that he would try so hard to prove it, or to show me how strong he was. Only a couple of years ago, I had known him better than my own sister, but this version of Matthias was acting like we were complete strangers. I could understand his feelings toward me—after all, I used the words he told me to ruin his life—but I needed him to know that it was the biggest regret of my life. I wasn't proud of what I did to the boy who loved me.

I could take everything he wanted to throw my way, but not today. Today we were saying goodbye to my grandmother, the woman who not only raised me, but also Matthias when his father wouldn't step up. Maybe if Matthias stopped to remember the good times we shared. Like how I would sneak into his room just to steal another kiss or how he used to be the only that could calm me when my mind waged a war inside my head. He was always the first person I went to when I had written lyrics to a new song because he got so excited. I would sit there watching his facial expressions as his eyes moved over the paper, eager for his approval. Matthias had been more than just my sister's best friend.

He had been the love of my life.

Everything Matthias had suffered after I left was directly because of me. I heard from my sister, and my grandmother, about the horrible depression he sank into. I had never intended to let anyone hear those recordings. It had all been my friends' ideas. They had known the way Matthias felt about me, but they wanted to hear it from his mouth. When I had said I could get him to tell me he loved me, well, they ate it up. They just didn't realize I felt the same way.

I had hoped that coming back home four years later, Matthias would have moved on. However, the way he looked like he wanted to throttle me, and burn me at the stake if he could, was enough for me to realize that he would never feel that way about me again.

Right now, I was standing outside my childhood home, freezing my ass off while taking drags off my cigarette. My old high school friends were trying to make it seem like we were still that. Friends. The more I stood there listening to them, the more I realized I never liked them the first time around.

"Here." Evan Combs passed a bottle of clear liquid to me. "You look like you could use it." He shoved his hands into his pockets. "So, you get a lot of tail now that you're famous?" He grinned.

I took a swig of the vodka. "Sure, loads." The burn of the alcohol did nothing to warm my bones. It was true, but lately I was bored with all the women throwing themselves at me. They didn't make me happy, and the sex was never as good as I wanted it to be. The fake tits, the fake sounds, everything about the entertainment business was so damn fake.

Michael Morgan snorted. "I saw you on Instagram with that chick from *Ted Lasso*. Tell me you tapped that, because she is hot." He grabbed the bottle when I held it out to him.

"Yeah, I hit it." No, I did not. She was much too good for me, very polite. Even though we had presented an award together at the Emmys, I never once hit on her.

Evan let out a holler. "British girls are hot as hell." He shifted on his feet. "Shit, is that Fuller?" He jutted his chin toward the front of the house. "You know, I honestly can't believe he stuck around after what happened with the two of you. Dude was an absolute basket case. Do you think he actually thought you loved him back?" he asked.

I watched wide-eyed as Matthias paced back and forth on the porch. He had on a dress shirt rolled up to his elbows, and the dress pants from the funeral earlier, but no coat, hat, or gloves. With the wind chill right now, it was hardly ten degrees outside. I felt myself mesmerized as Matthias stopped, looked down at his phone, and then wrapped his arms around himself to keep warm.

"Is he okay?" Michael asked. He tried to hand the bottle back to me, but I waved him off. "Did he finally go off the deep end this time? Maybe having you back here triggered him."

Matthias had to be freezing. He was lucky I didn't take him over my knee for not dressing for this weather...and now my dick was getting hard. My mind was so focused on the boy I had ruined that I didn't realize that Michael and Evan were waiting for me to say something. "I should make an appearance." I muttered. "It was good to catch up with you," I added, even though I didn't mean it. Those idiots were hangers-on when I was in high school, and they hadn't changed at all.

I was halfway up the stairs to the house when I realized I had taken my coat off. "It's freezing, Matthias." The words slipped from my mouth before I could stop them, and when he turned to look up at me, I felt that old, familiar smirk tug at my lips. "Put it on," I instructed as he began to shake his head. "Either put it on, or go the fuck inside," I growled.

Matthias's eyes narrowed into angry slits. "I thought I made it clear that you're not the boss of me anymore, Kill." He sucked his fat bottom lip into his mouth before he spoke again. "I have an idea, why don't you crawl back under the rock you came out from?" He shot me the middle finger.

"Get your ass inside the damn house before I throw you over my shoulder and carry you there myself." I watched the way his eyes went wide before desire flared bright. I waited for Matthias to fight me again, but instead he did just as I had instructed, making sure to slam the door in my face before I had the chance to follow him. With a loud sigh, I reopened the door and entered the house behind him, only to find myself in a sea of mourners there to celebrate my grandmother's life. Matthias was nowhere to be seen.

By the time I had untangled myself from the entire town of Canfield, I found myself in the kitchen, and Matthias spun around with a handful of dirty dishes at my presence in the room. We both watched as one of the glasses slipped from the top and shattered the moment it hit the floor.

"Jesus, fuck, thanks a lot," Matthias grunted before he placed the stack in the sink and bent down to pick up the broken pieces.

"That's my fault?" I got down beside him to help, and when he looked at me, I saw a flicker of something I hadn't in a long time in his hazels—*want*. Was it possible he didn't hate me as much as he was letting on?

Matthias's cheeks turned pink before he quickly looked away from me. I heard him mumble something under breath, that I couldn't quite make out, before he stood up. I watched the way he wobbled once before his legs gave out beneath him. I reached out to catch him without even thinking about it before I eased him into one of the kitchen chairs.

"How much have you had to drink today, babe?" I leaned in to get a look at his face, and when Matthias tried to turn away my hand came up to grip his chin between my fingers. Electricity crackled under my skin, but I refused to let go. Instead, I forced him to look at me.

"None of your business, Killian. Let go of me. And don't call me babe."

"When did you get so stubborn?" I kind of liked this new version of Matthias, because the one I knew would let me do whatever I wanted, when I wanted. It made my dick jerk in my pants. With my other hand, the one that wasn't currently glued to his face, I grabbed onto the chair Matthias was sitting in so that I could pull him closer before I dropped the other hand to grip the back of the chair to pin him in place. "I ruined everything, didn't I?" I tilted my head as I watched for his reaction, but he kept his expression smooth as stone.

"You fucking ruined my life, but I've moved on. I'm happy now," Matthias growled from between clenched teeth.

I leaned closer so that our noses were nearly touching. When I opened my mouth to say something else—what, I have no damn clue—the sound of the door opening behind us made me jump away so fast, I nearly fell onto my ass. I turned to find Helena watching us both with a look of both fear and curiosity on her face.

"Am I interrupting?" She chuckled softly as she placed another handful of dirty plates and glasses into the sink. "Kill, I don't think this is a good idea," she continued, turning to face us and folding her arms across her chest.

"I couldn't agree more," Matthias replied before shoving me away. "He was just leaving anyway," he added.

I was? My brows dipped at the comment, but I didn't say anything. I wasn't going to fight with Matthias now. Not while he had too much to drink, a house full of guests or in front of my sister. I had no plans on leaving unless I was forced to so Matthias would either have to deal with me or move out. Without another word, I stood up and slipped out of the kitchen, venturing back into the crowded living room. I moved down the hallway toward my room, only to turn to the left to go into Matthias's instead.

Memories hit me like a brick the moment I stepped inside. Our second kiss happened right there on that bed, right after I had chased Matthias down to finish what we had started. The first time I saw him naked was in this room, too. Oh fuck, this was too much. I had broken him. He had been so innocent, so perfect, and I had let him believe that I'd used him. I had to get out of here. I couldn't breathe, and as I hurried out of the house, I hardly felt the way the frigid air hit me when I stepped outside.

I sucked in a couple of gulps of the cold air as I looked around the neighborhood. It was quiet, considering all the cars parked up and down the street. My high school friends were no longer standing outside drinking, which flooded me with relief. I remembered how much I had loved living here growing up. Everything had seemed so normal, so easy, and now...wait a second. I noticed movement and watched as a figure tried to sneak across the front yard before me. I knew instantly that it was Matthias. His body had changed some since the last time I was here, like he had filled out more, but it still did things to me that I couldn't explain.

Just what the hell was he up to? He must have gone out the back, because if he had snuck out the front, he would have run right into me. I was happy to see he had a coat on now, but without gloves on his hands or a hat covering his pretty little head, Matthias was letting out all the warmth.

He looked around to make sure he wasn't being watched—was Matthias being serious right now?—before he hit the button to open the garage and headed inside. He either had sobered up remarkably quickly, or was drunk off his ass right now. I knew it had to be the latter. To my surprise, when Matthias came walking out of the garage moments later, he was dragging an axe behind him. Just what the hell did he intend to do with that?

Chapter Four

Matthias

I dragged the heavy axe behind me as I walked through the snow. *I'll show him,* I thought to myself. That prick thought he could just show up here and I'd what? Drop at his feet like I used to? Suck his cock for old times' sake? No, I didn't think so. I wasn't one of his groupies, and I certainly wasn't the wallflower he thought I was. Not anymore. The interaction with him earlier had dug into my skin, and I needed a way to get rid of this pent-up aggravation that was building inside of me.

"What the hell do you think you're doing?"

I nearly dropped the axe, but gripped it in my hand as I glanced over my shoulder. "Are you stalking me now?" I grunted. "Go away, Killian. I thought I made it clear how I feel about you." I turned back, gripping the handle tighter. Shit, why did this thing weigh so much? It wasn't like I was some ninety-pound weakling.

Without waiting for his reply, I started walking again. I knew Killian would follow me, but he was unusually quiet as he did. I trudged through the now knee-deep snow, wishing I chose a better pair of shoes. It was too late to change now, though, so I just hoped that my toes didn't freeze and fall off. I was glad that the walk wasn't too far, and when I finally reached my destination, I had to stop to catch my breath. The hours I'd spent in the gym didn't prepare me for this.

Killian let out a forced laugh. "You must be joking," he snorted. "You're going to what, cut down the damn tree all by yourself? Babe, please." His condescending voice made me remember all the times he'd brushed me off, knocked into my shoulder, or ignored me altogether. Or how he and his friends would tease me and make fun of me, yet all the while he was jerking me off and letting me take his load in the dark. *Asshole.*

I didn't say anything as I picked up the axe and gripped it tightly between my hands. I had no idea what I was doing, or even how long it would take. The whole point of this was to destroy those fucking initials that Killian had carved. They meant nothing now—they never had—and I wanted him to know that. After all, he was the one that had made sure of it.

"God damn it, Matthias." Killian grabbed at the axe in my hands. "Stop it! You're going to end up hurting yourself before you even fucking hit the damn tree. You know the only tool you were ever good with is mine."

I tried to push him back, but Kill was still made of bricks. "Fuck off, asshole, because I'm doing this," I told him. "Those initials mean nothing, and they never did. You were only using them to get what you wanted."

Killian took a step back but stood there watching me with surprise in his blue eyes. "Can you at least talk to me first?" I then noticed he didn't have a jacket on, but I tried to resist caring. Maybe he would freeze to death, right here, where he'd broken my fucking heart.

"Do you have any idea? Any idea at all what you did to me?" I narrowed my eyes at him. "I hate you. I hate you with every fiber of my being, and I can't go back to that place. The person I was with you..." I swallowed my nerves. "You treated me like a dog; like a piece of trash that you could throw away. I won't let you do that again."

Killian dropped the axe before his lips slammed against mine before I could stop him. The low moan that escaped my throat caught me off guard, and I clawed at his shirt, trying to stay on my feet. God, he always knew how to kiss me; how to twist my mind into knots and make me want more. I bit at his lips as our tongues fought for control, and I felt my cock surge to attention.

"Your perfect lips still taste just as sweet," he murmured. "But nothing ever tasted as good as your cum—"

I yanked myself away from Killian before he could finish the sentence before I could lose myself in him completely. "No, fuck off! Don't touch me again," I warned as he stared at me with surprise on his face. "This tree will come down whether you like it or not," I added, getting back in his face. It was a huge mistake. He grabbed my arm and spun me around, knocking me into the snowing ground.

"You want to make this fucking tougher than it has to be?" Killian pressed himself against me, making sure I felt how hard he was. "You always did like it when I got rough." He dragged his nose down my neck before he bit into my skin. "You would moan and cry with pleasure. You begged me for more, begged me to stop, but you fucking loved it." Killian dragged his teeth over my neck. His hand dug into my pants and found me to be just as hard as he was.

"Yes, I loved it," I agreed as my fingers ripped his beanie from his head, just as I remembered his beautiful chocolate curls were gone. Killian's hand gripped my length, and my eyes rolled back in my head. "Don't." I wanted this but would hate myself in the morning. I needed him to stop before it went any further.

Killian's grip tightened around me. "So, fucking hard for me, so ready," he growled against my neck. "Fuck, I missed you." He dragged his tongue up my skin before he swiped it against my mouth and shoved it between my lips. When his blue eyes met my hazels, he suddenly pulled back and released my dick. "Holy shit, you really don't want this." Kill's breath was hot against my face in the cold night air.

"I do...but I don't. You broke my heart, Killian."

He jumped to his feet and dragged both hands over his shaved head, turning his back to me. "Fuck!" He screamed into the night. "Fuck!" Killian cried again. "What a fucking idiot. I can't believe I thought..." he spun back around to look at me. "You know what? I don't know what I thought." He barked out a bitter laugh.

That's when I noticed the exhaustion that was written all over his beautiful face. His sky-blue eyes, that used to dance with devious happiness, looked anything but happy. When I took a step forward—to do what I wasn't sure—he took two back. "Are you...okay?" I asked softly.

"Of course, I'm okay, Matthias. What kind of a question is that?" he spat, but this time when he looked at me, he kept his eyes away from mine. "Don't do it," he added.

"Don't...what? You mean don't cut down the tree?" I watched Killian's brows dip as he nodded. "You know if I don't do it now, I'll just find a way to do it later. Even if I have to wait until you're gone. I'm surprised it took me this long to do it." I hated the memories I had of this place.

Killian was suddenly next to me, his hand gripping my jaw between his fingers. "Because you told me the truth about how you felt?" His blue eyes looked sad for a split second before his entire face changed. He looked angry, evil even, and he ducked down to grab the axe from the snow before I had a chance to stop him.

"Killian, wait!"

He didn't stop, didn't even look back at me, before he took a swing at the tree. "You want it gone?" The axe landed with a thud into the oak. "Fine, I'll do it for you."

I grabbed his elbow. "Stop it!" Killian shrugged me off as if I weighed nothing. "I was angry. Not only with what you did and what you said, but also how you broke my heart. I wasn't really going to do it." But the truth was, I wanted to. I wouldn't have gotten very far, though, because I didn't have half the strength he did.

Smack! Killian hit the tree again. "You brought the axe here, didn't you, Matty?" He glanced over his shoulder at me, a sheen of sweat breaking out on his forehead despite the cold. "You wanted to get rid of the memories." He brought the axe back up. "What's next, huh? Want to burn down the movie theater? My grandmother's house?" He started to swing again. "Want to watch all of our memories go up in smoke?" He made contact with the tree for a third time before he dropped down into the snow with a loud sob and buried his face in his hands.

I hated to see Killian like this.

I climbed down onto my knees. "Killian." I pried his hands away from his face, but he slapped my hands away. I lifted my hand back up and caressed the back of it over his cheek to wipe away his tears. "What happened to you?" His blue eyes darted to my face.

"Fuck you," he growled. "Go back to your perfect life, Matthias, and leave me here." Killian's eyes were angry. "I'm fucking fine." He was most certainly anything but fine.

"Why don't I believe you?"

"Because you always wanted to fix me."

He wasn't wrong about that. "You used to talk to me," I reminded him. "You used to tell me your dreams, let me see the songs you had written and ask me if I thought they were good enough." I wanted to get Killian up and out of the snow. He had to be freezing. "Do you remember?"

"I'm not that person anymore." Killian climbed to his feet. "Leave the tree alone," he warned as he grabbed the axe.

I stared up at him, his blue eyes meeting mine as memories of that night ran through my mind. "Why?" I whispered. "Why did you do it?" I couldn't help the question as it tumbled from my mouth. "You knew...you knew how much I loved you, yet you did it anyway." Tears stung my eyes, and I had to duck my head before Killian saw them slip down my cheeks.

"I don't know." His words felt like a knife to my heart. "I guess I thought it would be funny."

Rage burned through me. "Funny? You thought recording me confessing my love for you would be funny? That letting all your friends, and everyone we went to school with, hear it would be fucking funny?" I suddenly want to rip Killian's body apart. "It was cruel." My voice shook. "Do they know what we did before that? Did you tell them how you fucked me? Or how you put your mouth around my dick until I came down your throat. No, I'm betting you left those parts out. But, by all means, share the part where I tell you that I love you. Oh, and the part where I asked you if there's a chance you could ever love me back." I had to get away from him. I started to walk back toward the house I felt a hand grip my elbow. "Let go." I tried to shake him off.

"I'm sorry."

I laughed. I couldn't help myself, because it sounded so ridiculous. "Sorry?" I spun around while making a fist ready to draw blood, but Killian caught it before I made contact. "You think that changes things? You humiliated me! You fucking left, but I had to deal with that for years! I still deal with it with some of your jock friends that are here. You ruined my life, Killian, and there is no amount of sorry that can change that. I hate you!" I managed to pry his hand off me, and this time, he let me go.

By the time I made it back to the house, I was full-on sobbing. I wasn't sure how long I sat outside on the porch before I gathered myself together, went into the house, and hoped Killian would leave me alone until he left to return to his perfect life in California

Chapter Five

Killian

I walked around town for a while after my fight with Matthias before I finally went back to my grandmother's house; not before stopping at the bar to have a drink or six, though. When I got home, the house was quiet—everyone had left following the small reception after Grandma's funeral—and the room to Helena's door was shut. I thought about going in to talk to my sister, but decided against it. Instead, I walked straight down the hall to my room, which just happened to be directly across from Matthias's. I expected his door to be locked, but when I saw it was wide open and looked in to see his body curled up under the covers, my stomach clenched.

I knew I shouldn't—he'd made it perfectly clear how he felt about me—but I stepped inside his room despite knowing it might not have been welcome. He hadn't come back the night before, and the only thing Helena would tell me was that he was at a friend's. Did she mean a boyfriend, or was Matthias single? Was it possible he had someone who loved him the way I never could? Who kissed him the way he liked, and held him tightly at night while he slept? It made me sick just thinking of it.

"Killian?" His sleepy voice caused my breath to get caught in my throat. "What are you doing?" He sat up. "Are you okay?" Was he really concerned, or just worried for himself?

I closed the door behind me, then made my way toward him and dropped to my knees next to the bed. "I fucked up," I confessed.

"Are you drunk?" Matthias reached for the light next to the bed, and I was temporarily blinded when it flashed in my eyes.

"I'm sorry, I didn't mean to wake you." I started to climb back to my feet so I could leave, but I felt a hand on my elbow. Matthias's fingers tightened around my arm as I stared down at him. "Can I stay just for a second?" I asked when he showed no signs of letting go. When he nodded, I pulled the blanket back before I eased myself down onto the mattress, feeling it dip under my weight.

Matthias covered his nose with his arm after I was fully settled beside him. "Jesus, you stink like a distillery." He narrowed his eyes. "Did you drink the entire bar tonight, or just half? With your great friends, catching up and gossiping, I'd imagine," he snapped.

"No, it was just me." I looked down at my hands. "I need you, babe. I can't sleep, and I just...can I lie here? With you? I promise I won't touch you," I whispered.

"No."

I stiffened at his refusal, but what did I expect? He hated my guts. My Matthias would never tell me no; would never push me away when I needed him. Wait...there was no *my Matthias* anymore, swas there? Tears stung my eyes as I watched him, and noticed the way his eyes had a hardness to them that they never had before. I reached my hand up to touch his face, only to have Matthias push me away. "I'm sorry," I whispered. "I know that I can't fix this, and saying sorry will never change what I did, but I just..."

"I'm tired, Killian," Matthias cut me off before he plunged the room into darkness again. "You can stay." Desire curled through my body as I kicked off my shoes and moved onto my back. I sucked in my breath when I felt Matthias's hand against mine, tracing his thumb over my palm, the back of my hand, and then over my wrist. *Oh shit.*

"Don't." I tried to pull away, but he held on tightly.

Matthias tugged my hand closer. "Kill, what did you do?" His voice cracked as he continued to trace the jagged scar that I could see even with my eyes closed.

I missed you. I hurt you. I loved you. "I just—" I couldn't even come up with an excuse. "I'm so fucked up in the head sometimes, and that day, I couldn't breathe. It was worse than before, you know? I hadn't cut in a while, and I just went too deep." Shame mingled with fear in my throat. "Everyone thinks I'm so great. I'm known as the life of the damn party because I'm Killian fucking Hampton, the rock star. Sometimes, though, I just can't be that person. They don't know the real me." I slapped a hand against my chest. "But you, you know me. Don't you, Matthias?"

"I thought I knew you once." His thumb dragged over the scar on my wrist again.

"I'm still that guy, babe."

It grew eerily quiet in the room. Matthias's spicy scent invaded my senses as he rolled onto his side. "Are you?" His voice was hardly a whisper, but I heard him.

I moved to face him and gripped his chin with my free hand. "Tell me something," In the moonlight I could see his eyes as they searched my face. "Who patched up the bruises on your face when he found you hiding from your piece-of-shit old man?" I let my thumb stroke his jaw. "Who punched Alex Sherman when he tripped you while you were getting off the bus?" I pulled my hand away from his so I could stroke his hair. "That was me, wasn't it, Matthias?" I asked.

"Yes." His voice sent shivers up my spine and my cock grew hard as stone despite the booze buzzing through my system.

I wanted to believe that somewhere inside of his beautiful brain, Matthias still cared for me despite what had happened between us. "I missed you, Matthias," I croaked before pressing my face into his neck. When his hand combed over my hair, I felt a sense of relief wash over me.

"Me too," Matthias admitted. "I missed this. I missed the real Killian that no one else ever had the chance to see." I wrapped my arms around him as he spoke, the way I used to when he would find me huddled up during a thunderstorm.

I let out a low sigh. This felt like coming home. "My Mathias." My lips brushed his skin, right in the crook of his neck. I felt his hand tighten in my hair in response. "Forgive me," I whispered before I closed my eyes and fell asleep.

***

The pain behind my eyes was atrocious when I woke. It felt like someone was inside my head hitting my brain with a hammer, and I was afraid of what might happen when I opened my eyes. I listened to the sound of a closet door opening and then shutting before I dared pop a lid open. Shit, did I spend the entire night with Matthias? He let me stay in his room. I noticed him standing at the foot of the bed with his back to me, wearing nothing but a pair of blue jeans. I sat up, admiring the contours of his muscles.

"You let me sleep here." It wasn't really a question. "You didn't wake me. Shit, what time is it?" I dropped back onto the bed.

Matthias turned around as he pulled a gray Henley over his head. "It's almost eight o'clock." He dragged one of his hands through his hair. "I left some water and a bottle of Advil next to the bed," he told me.

"Where are you going?" I didn't want him to leave. I needed more time with him.

A smile tugged at Matthias's mouth. "I have to work," he answered. "It snowed last night, so people want their driveways cleaned." He sat down on the bed to pull on his socks. "You're more than welcome to stay here until you feel better." His eyes were so distracting. "I'll be back later."

"Can I come with you?" I wanted to be wherever Matthias was. What if he changed his mind again while he was gone? I watched as he shook his head, the smile spreading further across his handsome face. "What, you don't want me there?" I sat back up and ignored the scream of protest from my head.

Matthias let out a low chuckle, which did absolutely nothing for the morning wood I was sporting. "You don't want to shovel driveways, Kill. Trust me. It's hard work, and you should rest." He moved closer. "I'll be back later." He reached for my hand to thread our fingers together.

I yanked him onto the bed using our clasped hands. "You think I can't do manual labor? What do you think getting on stage six days a week for three hours a night feels like?" I released his hand and moved so I was straddling his waist. "I can handle it, babe, trust me." I watched the way Matthias's mouth opened slightly, his eyes growing wide before he reached up to cup my head between his hands. God, I was so hard right now, all I could think about was him sticking his hand into my jeans and getting me off.

"Did I say that? I wanted you to stay here. In my bed so that I had something to look forward to when I got home. A warm man waiting for me." He nipped at my chin.

"Are you...don't you hate me?"

"Very much."

I stared down at Matthias as he watched me, taking in all the little details. The long lashes that framed his eyes. The dirty-blonde hair that lived in my dreams. His smile—damn did I miss seeing that smile. The way he was looking at me right now made me want to strip off all his clothes and do everything I could think of to him. "Will you ever not feel that way about me?"

"I don't know." Matthias dragged a finger down my neck. "All these tattoos, do you think you'll give me a chance to see them all? Count them, lick them, and make sure I know each and every one by heart?" He dipped his hands up my shirt. "Your entire body?"

"You still hate me." That's all I could think about as I jumped off the bed and away from Matthias. "You...why would you let me stay here, or want me to be here when you come home, if you hate me? To make me pay for what I did? Believe me, I pay for that every single day," I exclaimed. "I shouldn't...I shouldn't have stayed with you last night," I muttered.

Matthias was on his feet in a flash. "You needed me." He reached for me again, but I pushed him away. "Killian, you were drunk and upset. You know what that does to me. It breaks my heart to see you that way. I still care about you despite my better judgment." His eyes were no longer laughing, but instead filled with pity.

"I don't need anyone," I growled. "Fuck, I'm an idiot," I shoved past Matthias to get to the door. "This can't happen again," I said over my shoulder. "Lock your door at night." I added before I left the room.

I couldn't get into the shower fast enough, stripping off my clothes and dumping them on the floor before I climbed into the tub. I turned the water on as high as it would go, needing to feel the scalding heat against my skin so I didn't rip holes in it instead.

"Killian." Matthias's voice carried through the bathroom. "I left my cell number for you in case you need it. Helena's at work, too, and can't really take calls in the emergency room." Ironic, don't you think?

I slammed my fist against the wall. "Fuck you," I muttered, knowing he couldn't hear me. I didn't need anything from Matthias anymore. I had everything I wanted, and all I had to do was ask. People wanted to be just like me, wanted to hang around me, and hell, most of them wanted to fuck me.

Once I was sure Matthias was gone, I dried off and wrapped the towel around my waist before I strode into my room, only to find a piece of paper stuck to the mirror with a phone number scribbled on it. "No, thank you," I hissed before crumpling it up and tossing it into the garbage. I had people I could count on here in town. Ones that didn't hate my guts. It was time I reminded them who I was.

Chapter Six

Matthias

Finding Killian in my room last night was something I didn't think would happen. He'd surprised me, but what had shocked me the most was the scar I'd felt on his wrist. I had gotten a better look at it this morning in the light, and it was bigger than I had first thought. White and ugly, it slid down from his wrist to his elbow in a jagged line. The tattoos he now had that covered his body did a decent job of hiding it, but if you got close enough and touched the skin as I had, you would know what it was.

I thought about him all day while I was shoveling snow, plowing driveways, and spreading down sand with salt. He had apologized more than once, and even though I hated him, I still loved him. When he had called me *his Matthias*, well, that was when my heart nearly thawed completely.

Until this morning.

Killian did a complete one-eighty on me, and it hurt. I had known he was drunk when he came to me, but I also knew he had been telling the truth. The way he'd spoken to me was how he used to act when we were together, with no one else around. I missed that, and honestly, I missed Killian more than I wanted to admit. He was always kinder to me than the other kids in school, funny yet shy, and smart as hell. Kill knew what he wanted in his life and he wasn't afraid to go after it. That was the man I fell in love with, not whoever he was pretending to be now.

What he'd done was wrong, and he knew that. Recording me and playing it for all his friends was a horrible thing to do, and I should hate him. I should push him right out of my life without thinking twice about it, but that wasn't who I was. I wasn't a mean person, and I generally cared for Killian. Deep down, I knew I still loved him.

Driving home from work, exhausted and drained, all I wanted to do was shower, change into some clean clothes, and try to fix things with Kill if I could. Helena had texted that she was picking up a second shift and I was on my own with dinner, so I grabbed a pizza. I figured we might be able to have a civil conversation, until I pulled down the street to find cars littering the driveway. Was he...was he having a fucking party right now? Helena was going to lose her damn mind. I parked my vehicle before I turned it off before I climbed from my truck and moved toward the house, only to be greeted by Evan Combs.

"Look who's home," he sneered, holding a solo cup in his hand.

"Fuck off." I flipped him the bird as I slammed the door open. "Killian!" The music was deafening when I stepped into the house, and I knew he couldn't hear me. "Motherfucker, I swear to God," I hissed, stalking through the house, only to find who I was looking for with some half-naked, blonde woman on his lap. "That's fucking great." I moved over so I was right next to his ear, not caring who saw me. "Killian!" I screamed his name loud enough to wake the dead.

He nearly pushed the poor girl off his lap. "Jesus Christ!" He turned to stare at me before he flashed me that smile. The one that always made me weak in the knees. "Can't you see I'm busy, Matty?" He hooked his arm around the blonde to pull her back against his chest.

"You don't live here," I reminded him. "What do you think is going to happen when Helena comes home and finds her house a mess because of your asshole friends? Not to mention you making out with some bimbo. Don't any of these idiots have jobs?" I tried to ignore the way Killian tugged on blondie's hair to bring her face back to his.

He murmured something to her I couldn't understand before she stood up, rolled her eyes, and took a couple of steps back, just as someone turned the music down. "I was bored. This town has nothing for me, and I'm counting down the days until I get back on the plane to Los Angeles." Killian's blue eyes finally seemed to notice I was holding a pizza in my hand. "Did you bring home dinner, babe? That's so sweet." He chuckled as he looked around the room. "I'm not hungry, but I'm glad you thought of me." His so-called friends laughed as if he were the funniest man on the planet.

"You're an asshole." I gritted my teeth before I spun on my heel and headed to my room, making sure to lock the door behind me. Maybe everything he'd said to me last night had been nothing but a lie; nothing but the booze talking. I needed to realize that Killian would never feel the same way about me that I did about him.

***

I took a shower, changed into a clean shirt and pajama pants, and then ate a couple pieces of pizza. Around eleven o'clock, the party was ending because I heard Killian telling everyone to leave, and then I heard all their cars starting. At least I would be able to get a decent amount of sleep before tomorrow. There was more snow in the forecast, so I would have to be up early for work again. Once I was comfortable in bed, I turned off the light and was nearly asleep when I heard it.

The obvious sounds of people having sex.

Dread spread over my body, just like it did the first time I'd had to hide from my father. Helena was still at work, and I clearly wasn't getting any, which left the only other person in the house.

"Yes!" the female voice cried out, and I wanted to throw up. Would Killian actually do that to me? Sleep with a girl, knowing I could hear everything, and not care how it made me feel? The low growl I heard next was more than enough evidence for me to know that yes, he would.

I yanked the blanket back from my legs before I stormed out of my room. "I can fucking hear you!" I slammed the palm of my hand against Killian's door repeatedly, but when I didn't get a response, I saw red. "You're a real asshole, Killian, doing that with me here. You may be able to get away with that shit on tour with your bandmates, but the rest of the house doesn't need to hear you fucking the entire female population of Canfield." When the door to his bedroom suddenly opened, I took a step back.

He was shirtless, and I could see that colorful ink was splattered over his massive chest. My eyes traveled down his torso, and when I saw he was just in a pair of boxer briefs, I felt my throat grow dry with want. "What's wrong, babe?

Jealous?" The lazy smile on his face made my heart race. "Because I'm sticking it to someone else instead of you?" Killian glanced behind him before he met my eyes again.

"You're a real piece of work," I growled. I turned to go back to my room, but not before Killian's hand wrapped around mine and he yanked me back against his chest. "Let go." My voice was stronger than I felt.

Killian used his free hand to grip the back of my neck. "Or what, Matthias?" He walked me backward, nearly pushing me into my room. "You honestly thought I was fucking someone with you in the next room?" His blue eyes danced with laughter, the stench of whiskey on his breath.

"Aren't you?" I felt the edge of my bed at the backs of my knees just before he shoved me down. "Killian, what are you doing?" I whispered as his body flattened over mine. His lips were so close to mine. All I would have to do...

Killian's lips slammed against mine, catching me off guard. The moan that escaped my throat sounded like an explosion in my ears. He tasted like nicotine and booze, his tongue curling against mine. I could feel his hard length digging into mine, and when he ground down against me, I reached up to drag my hands through his hair.

"What are you doing?" I asked again in between punishing kisses. "Is this...are you fucking with me again? Are you going to use this against me somehow?" I couldn't think straight with Killian's muscled body on mine.

He pulled back to stare down at me with desire in his eyes. "Do you think so little of me, Matthias?" he asked softly.

"No, but you were kissing that girl earlier."

"Now I'm kissing you instead," Killian finished for me, and then his mouth was on mine again, his hands up my shirt and his fingers all over my skin. I dug my nails into his back as my hips arched up against him. "You're so eager, so ready for me," he whispered before his hand dove into my pajama pants.

My eyes rolled back into my head. Hadn't I been dreaming about him returning to do just this? I'd jerked off to thoughts of Killian touching me in this exact way like he used to do. He fisted my cock and began to pump me slowly.

"You like that, don't you? Having my hand wrapped around your thick, hard cock?" he teased into my ear. "You want to come all over me? Huh, Matthias?" His tongue flicked at my skin, and I groaned. "Say it." Killian squeezed tighter. "Say you want me, say you want only me to make you come or I'll stop right now," he growled.

I groaned in pleasure. "Yes, fuck, I want you to make me come," I admitted.

Killian nipped at my ear. "Touch me." His finger grazed my tip and over the pre-cum that had begun to ooze from my cock, running it over my shaft. "Touch my dick like you've been dreaming about, babe." He moved his mouth to my neck, sucking and biting hard, but I didn't care. All I cared about was him.

I had to be dreaming. There was no way I wasn't. I slid my hand down Killian's chest, over his hard, muscled pecs and abs, and wished I could stop to count the six pack he worked so hard on. I realized that once we did this—if we went back to where we had been—this would change everything.

"Hurry up." Killian rolled his hips, and I shut out the voices in my head.

Killian's dick was rock hard as I shoved my hand into his briefs. Warm to my touch, soft against my palm and just the way I remembered. I made a fist around his length, pulled him free from his underwear, and began to slowly jerk him.

He groaned low and deep in his chest. "That's good, Matthias, just like that." We began to move together in rhythm. "Squeeze it like you would your own cock. Fuck, yes, that's it. So good. God, I missed you." Killian's head fell back as he moved his hand faster in my pants.

I'd always loved that Killian was a dirty talker. I admired how he wasn't afraid to tell me what he was thinking or wanted. The guys I tried to be with after him, with the sloppy blowjobs and messy kisses, were nothing compared to him. This, however,? This was fucking sexy, and hot as hell.

"Did you miss me touching you?" Killian was watching me again. His blues darkened to shade of denim. "Did you miss getting me off?" He moved to grip my throat with his free hand.

I grunted. "Yes, I told him. "It's..." I felt pleasure roll through my body and warmth on my skin. "It's exactly the way I remembered," I confessed.

"That's right, it is." He tightened his grip on my throat. Not enough that I couldn't breathe, but enough that my balls tightened and I knew I was going to come.

Every muscle in my body tightened as my release hit, and I barked out Killian's name as my hot cum spilled down his fingers, his hand still gripping me as I thrust up into him. I arched my hips harder, one hand pumping his cock, and the other fisting the sheet as I rode out the wave of pleasure.

"Fuck, yes, you're so good, don't stop," Killian groaned, and then I felt it. His own release was violent and savage, like him. He ground his hips down against mine, growling and grunting as he smeared his cum against my pajamas until he collapsed next to me on the bed.

I stared up at the ceiling as I tried to catch my breath. That was not on my list of things I thought would happen tonight. I started to sit up, to get something to clean up with, when Killian wrapped his arms around me. I turned my head to see that his eyes were closed, his lashes brushing the tips of his cheeks. My heart jumped in my chest at the sight of him. *My Killian.*

"It was porn," he whispered before his eyes flew open. "I was watching porn." He grinned, and I reached up to touch the dimples on his face without hesitation. "Hey." Killian gripped my fingers in his hand. "I wouldn't hurt you like that again, Matthias," he whispered before pressing my palm to his lips. Then, he released my hand to pull me closer.

He wouldn't hurt me again? I wanted to demand he tell me why he had that girl on his lap when I walked in; why was he kissing her if he didn't want me to feel useless. Instead, I found myself lost in his arms, and falling asleep covered in our cum.

Chapter Seven

Killian

I woke up in Matthias's bed the next morning with another hangover raging heavy in my head. I reached for him, only to find the spot he had been sleeping in empty and cold. *Of course, he had to work again. Why would he stay here with you, idiot. He has a life now. One you're not a part of anymore.* My inner voice laughed at me as I dragged myself off the bed and shuffled back to my room.

I hated myself for the way I was treating Matthias—pushing him away and pulling him back. He deserved someone good, someone who wouldn't ruin him the way I did, and probably would again.

I managed to shower, make coffee for when Helena woke up after her double shift yesterday, and then thought maybe I could clear my head by taking a walk. I was suffocating in the house. There were too many good memories, followed by too many bad ones, and I felt like I would drown if I didn't break free.

The cold smacked me in the face as I stepped onto the front porch, but I hardly noticed. I felt run-down, sleep deprived, and like a monster with everything running through my brain. I shoved my hands into the pockets of my coat as I moved along until I found myself at the church where we had my grandmother's service. I slowly opened the heavy door and stepped inside to find that the church was empty. I sat down in a middle pew before I slipped my phone from my pocket. I had added Matthias's number as a contact after he left it for me, and I suddenly felt the urge to talk to him.

Killian: *I'm sorry, Matthias.*

Matthias: *Killian?*

Killian: *You deserve so much better, babe.*

Matthias: *What's going on?*

I silenced the ringing phone instead of picking up the call.

Matthias: *Answer the fucking phone, Killian! You're scaring me.*

Placing the cell next to me on the pew, I bowed my head, clasped my hands together, and prayed that God didn't hate me too much for everything I had done in my twenty-four years on this earth. I'd wanted nothing more than to be a musician when I was growing up. I had wished for it every night, wrote my own songs, and took voice lessons when I was younger until I knew exactly what range was the best. I sang all the time, then I picked up the guitar and sang some more. I left here for California with my band, Mulligan Downtown, knowing I could make everything come true; but I left behind the one thing I needed the most in my life.

I wanted to love Matthias the way he loved me, only I was too scared to admit it aloud. I could never be the man he needed in his life. I wouldn't be able to make him happy; I wasn't comfortable enough with myself to hold his hand in public, but I loved kissing him in the dark.

"Make it stop. Please God, make it stop," I begged softly. "It hurts too much, make it stop. I'll do anything you want me to do. I'll stop sleeping with strange women. I won't drink anymore, and I'll stay away from the drugs backstage.

Fuck, I'll stop swearing, too, if I have to. Just make it stop." I choked back the sob that threatened to escape my mouth. "My brain, it doesn't seem to work right...the medication makes me feel like a useless sack of shit." Tears burned my eyes, clung to my lashes, and then slipped down my cheeks. "I want to die," I whispered. "I don't want to be this burden anymore. I can't be...I can't love him like he deserves to be loved, but I can't let him go."

I spun around as the door to the church slammed open loudly. "How did you know where I was?" My fingers tightened together as Matthias walked toward me.

"I needed to make sure you were alright, Killian. Your texts scared me, and then you didn't answer the phone." His eyes were angry as he moved to sit next to me. "Talk to me." He reached for my hand, but I pushed him away.

"Leave," I sneered. "I don't need your damn help, Matty, and I don't fucking want you here." My lip curled up over my teeth. "What happened last night was a mistake, and I can fucking promise you it won't ever happen again. I'm not like you. I'm not gay." The words on my lips were not the words I wanted to say. The shock on Matthias's face made me realize what a complete fuck up I really had become.

Matthias stood up. "That's uncalled for Killian," he hissed. "You wanted it as much as I did, if not more," he reminded me.

"I wanted to come. You were just another hole; another useless groupie willing to give it up. That's all it was."

The punch Matthias threw caught me off guard. It hit me in the jaw, and my head flew back. When I pinned my eyes back on him, feeling the warm blood seeping from my lip, I saw the shock on his face, too. He turned to flee from me, but I jumped up to grab him by the hood and yanked him back, directly into my chest.

"I don't fucking thing so, babe." I spun him back around to face me, my forehead slamming against his. Stars flashed behind my eyes as my mouth found his, our teeth biting and tearing at one another. I wasn't sure if the blood I tasted was mine, his, or a combination of both.

Matthias tried to push me away, but when he felt my hard cock pressed against his stomach, he realized how much I was enjoying this. "What the fuck, Kill," he growled. "You're getting off on this?" He stared into my eyes as the smile spread across my lips.

"Babe, you have no idea what this is doing to me," I growled. "Lie down." I pointed to the floor.

His brows shot up. "In the church? Are you fucking crazy?"

"Pretty sure you already know the answer to that."

"Killian, anyone could walk in. I'm not doing this here." However, when my hand shot out to wrap around Matthias's throat, I saw the way his eyes rolled, and it caused fire to blaze through my stomach.

My free hand started to unzip his pants before I yanked them down to his thighs. "Think you're enjoying this, too." My heated gaze met Matthias's as I wrapped a fist around his hard dick.

He opened his mouth, to either protest or tell me no again, but I pressed my lips against his before he had the chance. "Fuck, you feel good," I grunted, dragging him down onto the dirty, cold, and damp floor so I could climb on top of him. "You always did, too, babe." My tongue fought with his as I dry humped him. "I need to get my pants off. I want to feel your cock against mine. Skin on skin." I lifted my hips so I could unbuckle my jeans.

Matthias dragged his hand over my hair. "I miss your curls," he whispered.

"I know." I stopped to stare at him, searching for what. I wasn't sure. Then my pants were gone and I pressed against his thigh. "I missed this," I confessed. "I missed…" Matthias didn't let me finish the sentence. Instead, he gripped the back of my neck and pulled my face back to his.

When this was done, when we had both come together and felt good, I would stop hurting Matthias. I would tell him how I felt, and promise that I would change to become the man he deserved. He just needed to be patient with me.

"Killian," Matthias murmured my name against his lips before sucking hard on the bottom one the way he knew I liked. I shifted my body so I could wrap my hand around both of us, and I groaned as I felt the heat of his shaft against mine. "Killian," he said my name again, and I dug my free hand into his hip.

I dragged my tongue around his jaw. "You like that, don't you, Matthias?" I bit his jaw before burying my face in his neck. "I thought about you all the time when I was gone." My teeth grazed his skin as I pumped us up and down in my fist. "Didn't matter if I had a chick with me or if I was alone." My grip grew tighter. "Your face was the only one I ever saw. You were the only one I wanted wrapped around me." I bit down hard enough on his skin to hear Matthias cry out.

"I don't believe you." Matthias's hips bucked like they had a mind of their own. "You've always treated me like a dirty secret," he hissed.

I kissed the spot I had just bitten. "You're right, babe, and I'm sorry," I whispered before taking his leg between both of mine. "You deserve someone better, someone who can love you out loud and in the open." I heard the catch in my voice and started to slow my hand just as Matthias gripped my wrist.

"Don't stop, Kill, don't you ever stop. I might hate the way you treat me, but I love the way you make me feel."

I groaned into Matthias's ear, "Fuck." Hot cum spattered from my cock, running down my fingers and onto both of us, but I didn't care. *I love you, I love you, I love you.* I repeated in my mind. *Please don't hate me, Matthias, I fucking love you.*

His eyes met mine, and I felt his muscles tighten as his mouth opened. I saw the pleasure roll over his face before I felt the warmth on my hand. We were both silent for a few seconds as we recovered from the orgasmic high before Matthias started laughing. "I can't believe we just did that here," Matthias snorted. "You're a terrible influence." He pressed his face against my chest.

"You liked that?" I dragged my finger through the mess between us, over his thigh, and then over mine before I brought it up to his mouth. "Tell me you liked it." I groaned as licked the cum off without hesitation.

I watched as Matthias's cheeks turned red as he gripped my wrist. "I liked it," he admitted. "We should probably, uh, go, though. Before someone walks in on us, dicks out and cum everywhere." His face grew redder.

"You're cute." I slid my mouth over his before I helped Matthias get to his feet. I tugged my jeans back up and buttoned them before I realized just what we did. "I'm going to hell." I grabbed my phone from the pew to slip it into my pocket. "I just made you a sinner, babe, and you're going to hell with me." I reached for his hand. "Have lunch with me. I haven't been to Holiday in a while and I've been missing their sandwiches."

Matthias's eyes went wide. "You want to be seen in public with me?" he asked as we started toward the door.

"I really treated you horribly, didn't I?"

"Horribly is not the word, Killian."

I stopped and dropped Matthias's hand so I could cup his head instead. "I'm sorry. I am an asshole. I fucked everything up. I ruined your life, and I can never change that." I saw the pain that flashed through his eyes. "You deserve someone so much better than me, Matthias, but for some reason, you care about me. I will never understand what you see in me. If you're willing to give me a chance, though, let me try to prove to you that I'm worth it. I'll try to make everything up to you." I searched his hazel eyes and silently begged Matthias to tell me yes.

"I want to," he whispered. "You know how I feel about you"—he dropped his gaze—"but what you did may not be forgivable."

"Don't give me an answer yet." I tipped Matthias's face back up. "Think about it and let me know." I slid my lips over his. "Now let's go get something to eat. I'm starving." I said, pulling him outside into the cool afternoon.

Chapter Eight

Matthias

I was worried about Killian. The text messages he'd sent me scared me to death, and then when he wouldn't answer my calls, I nearly lost my mind. I was lucky that someone said they'd seen him walking into the church when I came back to the house, but finding him in that state had been heartbreaking.

After we cleaned up with the napkins and water I had in my truck—neither one of us knew whose fluid was whose—I drove us to lunch. Killian didn't say much on the drive over to Holiday Restaurant. He held my hand with his head pressed against the window while I kept glancing over at him. I was surprised that he was touching me, even though no one could see, because the Kill that I knew never liked to touch me in public. He seemed so different, so sad, and I was scared for him.

"Are you alright?" I asked softly as I turned down Main Street. When he glanced over at me, my heart raced in my chest. Those blue eyes, damn if they didn't do me in every time. "The Killian I knew would never be caught dead holding my hand like this. Don't get me wrong, I'm all for it, but it's just something I'm going to have to get used to." I gave him a smile, hoping he would return it.

Killian's lips twitched slightly. "I like touching you, babe." That was all he said before he turned back to the window. This was not my Killian.

I parked my truck and pulled the keys from the ignition. "Are you going to talk to me about what happened? About the texts, and about not answering the phone." I tugged on Killian's hand so he would look at me again. "You're scaring me," I whispered.

"Nothing to be scared about."

"Talk to me, Kill, please."

He smiled at me with exhaustion written all over his face. "I will, babe, I will. Can we get something to eat first? I'm starving." He released my hand to remove his seatbelt before he opened the truck door and climbed out. "Come on," Killian called before he headed inside.

I hurried after him only to find the entire restaurant already on their feet greeting him, telling Killian how wonderful it was to have him home, and how sorry they were to hear about his grandmother. I caught the looks some of the people gave me, questioning why were we together after what happened, and wasn't he too good for me now? I found us a booth, sat down, and waited for Killian to finish taking pictures, signing autographs, and catching up before he joined me.

"Does that ever bother you?" I asked as he slipped in across from me. "The fame, and everyone wanting your attention like that?" I kept my voice low in hopes that no one would hear me.

Killian shook his head. "No, because if it weren't for the fans, I wouldn't be where I am today." He flashed a smile as the waitress came over to our table.

"I'm a huge fan," she gushed. "I don't want to be rude, because I know you're technically eating, but would it be too much to ask for a picture?" Her hand shook as she filled our glasses with water.

Killian stood up. "Of course not, Ciara." He'd noted what was written on her nametag. He took her cell phone and casually slipped his arm over her shoulder to take a selfie. "I always have time for a fan." He winked, causing her to turn three shades of red.

"My friends are going to be so jealous," she giggled. "Do you both know what you want to eat, or should I come back?" she asked. Her eyes hadn't strayed from Killian, but I couldn't blame her. Watching him pull off his jacket was like a strip tease, and the way his biceps filled out his sweater was enough to make my dick start to perk up again.

"Matthias?" Killian raised his brows at me. "Do you need a minute? Because I know I'm ready." His whole demeanor changed when it wasn't just us. It was as if he was putting on the Killian Hampton they all wanted to see.

I nodded. "I'll get whatever you're having." We used to get takeout from Holiday all the time. One of us would pick it up and bring it back to the house to eat.

"Two grilled chicken sandwiches on rye, with American cheese and fries, please," Killian told Ciara. "I'm good with the water, you?" He dropped his chin as he waited for my reply.

I nodded. "Yep, water is good for me, too, thanks." I smiled.

"Fantastic, I'll go put these in for you." Ciara hurried off, and I couldn't help but chuckle.

"What?" Killian nudged my foot with his. "Why are you laughing?" He removed the paper from his straw so he could take a drink.

Just him touching me out in the open was enough to make my dick hard. "You made her day," I teased. "She's going to remember this for the rest of her life." I grinned, and when Kill tapped my foot again I couldn't help the way my heart sped up.

"She's a kid," he noted. "Probably the same age as you when…" His voice faded off when I dropped my gaze. "Hey." Killian tapped the table with his knuckles. "Matthias, look at me," he ordered. "I didn't mean that. I meant the first time we, you know." He flashed his dimples and flattened his palm on the table. "Touch me," he begged. "Please, just to let me know you're not thinking of bailing and leaving me here alone."

I looked down at Killian's hand, at the colorful tattoos spread out over his skin, before I splayed mine over it. "I wouldn't do that." I glanced around the restaurant to make sure no one was watching, because I remembered how he hated that. That's when his hand gripped mine.

"I'm working on it, Matthias." Killian's brows furrowed together as he squeezed my hand and then pulled away. "Thank you," he added.

"For?"

"Everything today."

I took a sip of my water as I watched him. "You scared me." I chewed on my bottom lip. "After you told me about the scar, I thought—"

"You thought I was what, going to off myself?" Killian nudged my foot again. "I didn't mean to upset you like that." I noticed how he didn't answer the question.

I opened my mouth to ask him more, but Ciara returned with our food. As she made goo-goo eyes at Killian, I wondered just what was going on inside his mind. I knew he struggled with depression. I knew he needed medication, but hated how it made him feel. I couldn't help but wonder if the touring, the fame, and everything that came with being who he was now, were taking a toll on him.

"I'm leaving tomorrow," he blurted out when Ciara was gone.

I stared at him. "So soon?" I wasn't ready to say goodbye already, and as I watched Killian take a bite of his sandwich, I realized this might be the last time I saw him for a very long time. He hadn't been back to Canfield since he left four years ago, and I had a feeling he hated it here.

"The band has a tour to finish." Killian wiped his mouth with his napkin. "You could, uh, come see me." I must have looked as shocked as I felt, because he laughed softly. "Or not, that's fine." But I could tell he actually meant it.

I reached for the bottle of ketchup. "You want that? Me to come see you?" I chewed my food and waited for his answer. Would that be weird? Would there be girls throwing themselves at Kill backstage? Would he want me backstage? Did I even want to see him in concert?

"I wouldn't suggest it if I didn't, babe." The blush that began to creep up Kill's neck and over his face made my mouth drop open. "What?" He wiped at his face again with the napkin.

This time, I nudged his foot. "You fucking like me," I teased.

"I do."

***

"Where were you two?" Helena exclaimed as we walked into the kitchen. "You know, I tried texting both of you and...wait a second." She arched a brow. "You were together?" A smile began to spread across her face.

"Relax." Killian rolled his eyes. "We had lunch." He hadn't tried to touch me since we left Holiday, and even though he had invited me to come visit him on tour, he seemed different than earlier.

Helena nodded. "Right, but you were together. Not fighting or yelling at one another, but together." She moved to hug her brother. "That's a step in the right direction." She winked at me when we made eye contact.

"Sure," he said. "I need to shower." Killian started to head to the doorway. "I'm leaving tomorrow, Hel. I wish it wasn't so soon, but my tour manager texted me last night. I have no other choice." He disappeared from the room.

Helena swatted at my arm. "So?" She wiggled her brows at me.

"No way." I shook my head. "Things are...I don't know." Which was the truth. I wasn't sure what was going on with Killian right now, and I was honestly a little scared.

"But, lunch?" She sat back down at the kitchen table. "How is he?"

Shit, how did I tell my best friend, Killian's sister, that he wasn't good; that he was fucked up, he ended up in the hospital after slitting his wrist, and that I was worried about him. "He seems tired." Not exactly a lie.

"That's all you're going to give me?" Helena sighed. "He seems different though, right? I don't think he's taking his meds, and good God, what is going on right here?" She flicked her fingers at her neck. "You have some serious hickeys, Matty." She snickered as I hurried to my room.

They were more than obvious. I'd gone out in public like that. How was I going to explain this? Bright, red-and-purple hickeys in the shape of lip prints on my neck, left by the tortured man I'd been in love with for as long as I could remember. I ran my fingers over them remembering just how they got there.

"You like how I marked you?" My head whipped around to find Killian leaning against the doorframe with a smile on his beautiful face.

"I thought you were taking a shower?"

Killian stepped into my room. "I needed everyone to know you were taken, babe." He moved to pin me against the dresser with his body. "You liked it, right?" His mouth hovered over my lips. "How I made you come so hard you nearly blacked out? How fucking wrong it was being in a church?" His tongue snaked out over my lips.

"God, yes." I gasped.

Killian smirked at me before he took a step back. His sky-blue eyes had darkened, and he let his gaze drop down my body to where my cock had thickened between my legs. "Yeah, I liked it, too." His husked voice sent shivers up my spine. "Take a shower with me, Matthias." He wasn't asking, and I wanted that. I wanted to spend as much time with him as possible before he left tomorrow. I wanted to hold him, touch him, and be close to Killian. Just in case I never had the chance again.

"Yes," I croaked. "I'll do whatever you want." God, that sounded so pathetic.

Killian touched my face with the pads of his fingers. "You don't have to say that," he assured me. "But I like that you did." He reached down to cup my crotch with his other hand. "You don't have a boyfriend, do you? Someone you're seeing that's going to be pissed that I took you away from him?" he asked.

"Of course not." I hadn't been with anyone in months, and never like I had been with him.

"Who was it?"

"Who was who?"

Killian nipped at my jaw. "The last guy you were with," he murmured. "Do I have to worry he's going to get jealous that you're with me? Kissing me while I'm sleeping in your bed?" He dragged his tongue over my skin.

I shook my head. "No, no way. We're over," I assured him.

"Good. Bathroom, babe, now." Killian pulled back. "I need to spend as much time with you as possible before I leave tomorrow," he whispered.

Chapter Nine

Killian

Matthias's naked body was a pure work of art, but Matthias naked in the shower? Nothing compared. I could get used to this. I watched as he squeezed the shampoo into his hands, lathered it into his hair, and then rinsed the soap out, all with a raging hard-on. I wanted to touch him. I wanted to help him. I felt like if I touched him, though, the magic would be broken. I admired the scattering of beauty marks on his face and chest and recognized the scar on his forearm from when his father had beat him for the last time. I damn well made sure of that.

"Hey, do you want...Killian, what's wrong?" Matthias pushed his wet hair back from his face.

I blinked in surprise. "Nothing's wrong," I assured him. "When did you get so built?" I teased, finally reaching out to touch his thick, muscled arms and shoulders. "You look amazing." I watched the way his pupils dilated, and I moved closer. "You're so sexy." I cupped his jaw with one hand.

"Killian." Matthias gasped.

"It's okay, babe, I know." It would have been strange to fool around with my sister awake in the other room, and honestly, I just wanted to hold him before I had to leave again.

Matthias's fingers dragged over my chest. "The tattoos, will you tell me about them?" He had asked me before if I would let him touch them, lick them, and trace them all over—I wanted nothing more.

I nodded. "Of course," I assured him. "This one, well"—I pointed to the cardinal Matthias was currently staring at—"you know what this one means." I watched his face as he realized what I meant. "It was the second tattoo I ever received." I gave him a lazy smile before I pressed my lips over his. "Reminds me of you every day, babe."

The tattoo was a memory from when the damn bird slammed into the sliding glass door, and we helped it heal so we could release it a few days later. It was the first time I realized how special Matthias was. I'd noticed how he'd looked at me with those hazel eyes full of desire, and something more. I had never felt that way with any of the girls I had been with before, and no other guy made me feel the things that he did.

"I can't do this." Matthias turned like he might yank the curtain open. "Do you have any idea—other than what I'm sure Helena told you—what I went through every day after you left? You gave that recording to your fucking friends, who then sent it to every single kid at our school. I had to deal with that. The names, the teasing, the bullying I went through. Like I was just a stupid kid with a crush." His shoulders slumped forward. "I hated you. I hated what you did to me, and that you just waltzed off into the sunset like it didn't matter. Why would you get a tattoo that's a reminder of me when you ruined my fucking life, Killian? I thought about hurting myself, but I couldn't do that to your grandmother or Helena. But most of all, I didn't want you to think you had won." Matthias spun around, his face twisted angrily.

I went to reach for him, but he slapped me away. "Do it, babe." I felt tears prick my eyes, but I didn't care. "Hurt me, hit me, scream and yell, because I deserve that. What I don't deserve is you, Matthias. You were the light in my life, and I blacked it out without a second thought. I didn't mean to...I wanted to die," I choked out. "Every day, every night, when Helena told me what you were going through, I put that blade to my skin. One day, I finally dragged it over my wrist, up my arm, and straight to my elbow. I was so drunk, so high, that I didn't even feel it. Dean found me." That was the guitar player in my band, and one of my best friends from Canfield. "When I came to, I was in the hospital. I wouldn't tell anyone a single thing about what I did, and because of who I was, my publicist was able to keep it under the radar. Money can do that." I barked out a bitter laugh. "I'm fucking useless, Matthias. I don't—" His lips landed on mine, and I tasted the salt from my own tears.

"Don't cry, baby. It hurts me to see you like this," Matthias whispered against my mouth. *Baby.* In all the years I'd known him, and that we'd been doing whatever the hell this was, he had never called me anything but my name. "Here." He reached for the bottle of shampoo and began to rub it into my hair. "Relax, okay?" He began to massage my scalp with his fingers, and I couldn't stop the groan from escaping my throat. "Step back into the water," Matthias instructed.

I did as he told me and let the warm water rinse the suds from my hair. When I felt his hands washing over my body with the washcloth, I grew stiff as a board. "Matthias, babe, you're killing me." I heard him chuckle softly as he made sure to soap up my cock and balls more than was necessary.

"I love you, Killian," Matthias whispered. "Please don't leave me." He gripped me tightly. "Tell me you won't do that again." He stroked my length, but the cloth wrapped around my cock deprived me of the touch of his hand that I craved.

My legs shook as pleasure rolled through my body. "I won't...Matthias, fuck. If you don't stop, I'm going to come." I opened my eyes to find him staring at me with hooded eyes. *I love you.* Fuck, why couldn't I tell him that? Why was it so hard?

"Promise me."

"I promise you."

Matthias smiled as he dropped his hand. "Thank you," he said.

"Wait, I wasn't..." I grabbed the back of his head to pull him closer. "You're playing dirty, babe," I murmured as our lips collided, teeth clashing together.

Matthias chuckled softly as our kiss deepened. "We're not done," he promised. "But I want to put on clean clothes, cuddle up in my bed while watching shitty movies, and just hold you. Before I have to say goodbye." He turned off the water and reached over to grab a towel, which he handed to me before doing the same for himself. "Maybe you can tell me about some of your other tattoos, too." He winked.

***

I never wanted to move from this spot. Matthias was wrapped around me while I was on my back, and his head rested on my chest. Every now and then, I would run my hand through his hair and curl pieces around my fingers. He would sigh happily into my shirt, his fingers tightening their hold on the fabric.

Like I said, I never wanted to leave this spot.

"Can I ask you a question?" Matthias turned his head to look at me with a smile on his face.

I arched one brow. "Is it a sex question? Because my publicist doesn't like those." I dragged my thumb over his bottom lip, but started laughing when he slapped at my chest before he started to tickle my ribs. "Uncle!" I cried as he jumped onto my lap to straddle me. "Wait, I like this position better, babe." I smirked as he looked down at my cock to find it straining against my pajama pants.

"I just wanted to know what it's like to be famous. Do you get into places for free? Do you pay for things? What's it like to go to the Grammy Awards? How many pairs of shoes do you have?" Matthias splayed his body over mine.

I touched his cheek. "It's not as great as everyone thinks, the famous thing. Being here is different because it's where I grew up, but I have to take bodyguards with me sometimes when we're on tour. I miss being just Killian." I kissed the tip of Matthias's nose. "When people give me things for free, it's because they want me to promote their items, and I don't like to do that. If you need shoes, babe, just ask, and I'll get you some. I have more than enough to share. The Grammy's are fun. You should come with me next time." I watched the way his face lit up at my words. "I mean it, Matthias. I would love for you to come with me."

"What would everyone think? You wouldn't want the gossip," he whispered, and I flipped him over onto his back. "Killian, you're not gay. You said so yourself."

"Fuck what everyone thinks." I pressed my lips over his, sucking his tongue into my mouth before I spoke again. "You're who I want. I'm gay for you, babe, and that's the fucking truth." It felt good to admit that to him.

Matthias's fingers came up to touch the bruise on my chin: The one he gave me at the church. "I wish you didn't have to leave." He slid his hands up around my neck. "I wish...I wish that..."

"Ssshhh." I slid my mouth over his again. "You'll come visit me. I'll come visit you. We can make this work. You'll see," I assured him, but my stomach clenched at leaving him. "Here." I slipped off Matthias to grab my phone from the table next to the bed and unlocked it. "I'm flying back to California tomorrow, and then we leave for Houston the next day. We're there for two nights." I looked over at Matthias, who was watching me with tears in his eyes. "Hey, hey." I caught one with my thumb before it made contact with his cheek. "What's this about?" I dropped my phone on the table next to the bed to pull him against my chest.

Matthias shook his head. "It's stupid."

"Not stupid, babe, tell me."

"This feels like a dream. Something I've wanted since you first kissed me is for you to want to take me out and not care what people think. I don't expect you to hold my hand or kiss me or do anything like that, but just you saying you want me with you means so much to me."

I love you. I love you, Matthias. Fuck, I wanted to be able to tell him that. Had I ever told anyone but my grandmother and Helena that? I never dated girls in high school long enough to get attached, and the women I saw these days were nothing but marketing tools to make everyone happy. I never touched them; I didn't want them. Who I wanted was staring up at me with the most beautiful hazel eyes without asking me for anything, and I couldn't even tell him how I felt.

"I want people to know we're together," I whispered. "I want them to know you're the one who has my heart. You're the one I want to be with, and the one I'm going to spend the rest of my life with."

Matthias moved onto his back. "What will your publicist say? Aren't you worried about your fans?" he asked.

"No." I wasn't, because if they were really my fans? They would be happy for me no matter who I was. "Are you having second thoughts, Matthias?" He shook his head. "Babe, look at me." He turned his gaze on me. "Are you?"

Again, he shook his head. "I'm not, but I'm afraid you will, Kill." It broke my heart to hear him say that.

"I won't."

"Right now." Matthias sighed and sat up. "What happens when you tell your bandmates? They all know me. Everyone is going to hate me. I can't...no, I can't." He jumped up from the bed. "I think we should go back to the way things were. Forget about me, and just live your life, Killian. Find some pretty blond to settle down with, have a couple of kids." He turned his back to me.

What the hell was happening?

"Fuck that." I climbed back onto the bed. "I tried that already, and look where that got me, babe. I tried to kill myself. I'm miserable, and I miss you." I touched his shoulder. "Matthias, look at me. Don't shut me out." When he turned around, I wrapped my arms around him to pull him tightly against my chest. "I'm leaving tomorrow, and I don't want to fight with you. I want to spend the time I have left in Canfield with you." I kissed the top of his hair.

Matthias squeezed me closer. "I'm scared, baby," he admitted. "I'm scared you'll forget about me again." He leaned his chin on my chest.

"I never forgot about you the first time, so that isn't going to happen," I whispered.

Matthias nodded, giving me a shy smile. "Okay."

Chapter Ten

Killian

I stared up at the ceiling as Matthias slept soundly next to me, wishing I could stay with him. I was scared to leave him. Scared to go back to the life I was living before he came back into my life. What if, in a couple of days, he changed his mind? What if Matthias decided he hated me enough to not want to see me again? Fuck.

I reached over to wrap myself around him, needing to feel his warmth against mine. *I love you*, I shouted in my head, combing my hands through his hair. "Matthias, you're everything," I murmured, and pressed a kiss against his head before I climbed from the bed. An idea had just hit me, one that I couldn't let slip through my fingers; if I didn't write it down now, I would forget it. I dug around for a notebook, grabbed my phone for a flashlight, and sat down on the floor so I wouldn't wake him. After taking a moment to get settled, I began working.

My fingers flew across the page, my mind going a million miles a minute. I glanced up a couple of times to make sure Matthias was still sleeping, but quickly went back to what I was doing. I couldn't get the words out fast enough before more would come to me.

Forgive me Father for I have sinned
I ruined the only good thing in my life
He gave me his heart and I took it
Broke it, choked on it, and wanted to die
Forgive me Father for I have sinned

He loved me when I couldn't love him back
Why can't he see I'm no good for him?
I ruin all the pretty things

"What are you doing?" I jumped at the sound of Matthias's voice.

"Did I wake you?" I closed the notebook and turned off the light on my phone. The glare from the silent television danced across the room.

Matthias held his hand out. "You didn't answer my question." He gripped my fingers when I took it.

I climbed up into the bed with him. "Writing." I brushed the hair from his face.

"A song? That's right, you would get the urge and sometimes jot it down on napkins, receipts, anything you could get your hands on." Matthias gave me a sleepy smile.

I nuzzled his neck. "It's about you, babe," I confessed.

"You're writing a song about me?" He sounded surprised, like every single one I had written in the past hadn't been about him in one way or another. One of our most successful songs was about the night we first kissed. Simply titled "Goodbye," I wrote it on the car ride from Canfield to Los Angeles. I had tweaked it of course, but I poured my entire soul into that song.

"Why do you sound so shocked?"

"Is it really about me? Can I see it?"

I chuckled. "You know the rules, babe. When it's done," I told him. I heard Matthias sigh softly and I pulled back to look at him. "I know." I slid my lips over his. "I wish I could stay, but it's only for a little while, and then you're going to come see me. It won't be long." We had decided Matthias would meet up with me in New York and stay as long as he wanted. I had invited my sister, too. She said she would come for the show but didn't want to get in our way. I wasn't sure if Helena was happy for us, or worried I would hurt Matthias again. I couldn't say I blamed her if it was the latter.

"Don't change your mind," he whispered into the dark.

I turned onto my side. "I won't change my mind," I promised again, and then took his hand to drag his finger over my heart. "Cross my heart, babe." I pressed my lips to his as I felt him start to fall asleep again.

***

"You'll text me?" I pleaded with Matthias as we stood inside the airport waiting for my flight to board. Matthias had driven me to the airport after I'd said goodbye to a tearful Helena. She'd had to go to work, or she would have come, too. I knew that the hospital kept her busy, though, and they relied on her.

He nodded. "Yes, of course, all the time." He smiled up at me. "You're sure, I mean it's okay if you change your mind."

"Stop saying that. I'm sure as fuck about you." I yanked him against me, wrapping my arms around him in a tight hug. "What? Why are you looking at me like that?"

His eyes were wide with fright. "Everyone can see us right now."

I hadn't even thought about that; I'd just wanted him in my arms. "Don't care," I assured him, and for the first time, I meant it.

"What about—"

"Matthias, I swear to God. If you don't stop, I'm going to take you into the bathroom and spank you," I growled. He pulled back to stare at me with fire in his eyes. "You like that idea?" I whispered.

He nodded. "If we had time," Matthias whispered. "I'll miss your touch." He gripped my shirt in his hands.

"Not half as much as me, babe." We had fooled around last night after our shower, and quickly this morning before we left for the airport. In the short time I was here, though, I hadn't put my mouth on Matthias's dick, nor had he on mine. I already missed him, and he was standing in front of me.

"If you had told me a week ago, this was what I would be doing I would never believe it." He chuckled softly.

I swallowed the lump in my throat. "You have no idea." I reached up to touch Matthias's face to burn it into my memory until the next time. Not that I hadn't taken pictures—because fuck, of course I did—but this, this was what I would miss: The way he was looking at me right now. "I'll text you from the plane. I'll get Wi-Fi," I promised. "I have to go." I hated this part.

"I love you, Killian," Matthias reminded me. I opened my mouth to say it back, but he just pressed his mouth over mine, and then dragged his finger over my heart over my shirt. "Cross my heart," he whispered before taking a step back.

I turned to walk away, afraid if I didn't that I would stay, miss my flight, and never think twice about it. I made it about ten feet before I went running back to where Matthias stood watching me. I wrapped my arms around him, slammed my mouth against his, and heard the groan that escaped from both of us. "Now I really need to go, babe."

This time when I left, I didn't turn back around because I knew if I did, I would never leave.

***

Killian: *I hate flying.*

Matthias: *I can't relate.*

Killian: *Wait, you still haven't been on a plane?*

Matthias: *Just once.*

Killian: *You let me pop me pop your actual cherry, but your flight virginity? I'm heartbroken.*

Matthias: *OMG.*

Killian: *You know I wanted to be all your firsts.*

I stared down at the phone, waiting for his response. I knew Matthias was a virgin before me: He had never been kissed or touched in any way sexual until me. That didn't mean I didn't need him to tell me, though.

Matthias: *Only the one that mattered, Kill.*

Killian: *Miss me?*

Matthias: *It's been an hour.*

Killian: *Answer the question.*

Matthias: *Do you miss me?*

Killian: *Fuck yeah, I do.*

Matthias: *Me too. If I were there with you, I'd keep you from worrying about flying.*

Fuck, was he kidding? Was he going to start sexting me now?

Killian*: Are you trying to make me hard? Because it's working.*
Matthias: *Is that what you thought I was doing?*
Killian*: Babe.*
Matthias: *Okay, maybe a little.*
Killian: *I gotta go, but I'll call you later.*
Matthias*: Miss your face.*

Two Days Later

Killian: *I'm sorry I couldn't call you last night, babe. As soon as I stepped off the plane, everything exploded in my face.*
Matthias: *It's fine.*
Killian: *You're mad.*
Matthias: *I'm really not.*

I hit the FaceTime button on my phone, and Matthias's face suddenly stared back at me. "You're really mad." I could see the pinched look of his lips, and the way his brows were dipped down. Totally pissed.

Matthias rolled his eyes. "It's late, Killian, what do you want?" He was lying in his bed and the lights were off, but I could see the glow of the television in front of him. A sudden feeling of homesickness fell over me as I stared at his beautiful face.

"I'm sorry, Matthias." I had wanted to call. I'd pulled out my phone multiple times to text him and tell him I was running late, and that I was thinking of him. Someone always needed me, though, and pulled me in another direction. By the time I made it home to my apartment, it was nearly two o'clock in the morning, my time.

Matthias shrugged. "It's fine, okay? How's California?" He glanced behind the phone.

"Don't do that," I growled. "Look at me, and turn that shit off." Relief flooded me when the light from the television disappeared. "Matthias, babe, I'm fucking sorry. I miss you. I hate being so far away from you. Now you're pissed at me because once again, I screwed up."

He rolled his eyes. "You don't have time for me." He kept his eyes cast down. "It's fine, Killian. I get it, okay? I'm used to that." He looked back up at me and my heart stopped.

"Talk to me. Tell me what you're thinking."

It was the tears in his eyes that broke me. "I just thought...I thought—"

"You thought I forgot about you."

Matthias nodded. "It's stupid."

"It's not, babe, and I'm sorry. I don't want you to think that every time I don't call or text, or you don't hear from me for a little bit, that I'm leaving. That's not happening again. I promise." God, I hated how terrified he looked. Had Matthias gone the past two days thinking I forgot about him because I promised to call, and I broke that promise?

He shrugged. "Your Instagram."

"I don't even run that." I stopped him off before he could say anything else. My publicist ran my Instagram account—hell, most of my socials—although I could post if I wanted. I rarely did, other than to maybe comment on a friend's picture or tweet. "She just likes to keep the fans happy. She posted that rehearsal photo of the band, not me, Matthias." I dragged my hand through my hair. "Don't believe shit you read or hear about me. I'm yours."

"Are you?"

"Jesus fuck, Matthias." I wanted to reach through the phone to shake him, but this was all my damn fault. I really fucked him up. "Hold on." I quickly opened the Instagram app on my phone, added a photo with a caption, and then posted it. "Look at my Instagram now, babe."

He sighed, and then his face disappeared as he did what I asked. I had uploaded the last photo we took together the morning before I left: Us sitting on the couch with my arm around Matthias's shoulder, and his head nestled into my neck. I captioned it with one word: *Mine.*

"Killian, you have to take that down." Matthias's face appeared back on my screen. "Your fans, your manager. Fuck, your publicist. Everyone is going to see it. They are all going to hate me." His eyes were wild with concern.

"Too late." Already my phone was blowing up with notifications, text messages, and the shit show I had just unleashed on the world. "Should I have tagged you?" I grinned.

Matthias shook his head. "Don't you dare!" he hissed, but then I saw it. A smile began to spread over his face, and his eyes lit up. "I can't believe you did that." He looked stunned, surprised, and fucking happy. That's why I did it: To put the light back in his eyes.

"It's true," I admitted.

Matthias smirked. "You just admitted to everyone that you're with me."

"That I'm yours." My phone began ringing, and *Lou PR* flashed on my screen. "Fuck, babe, I have to take this call. I swear I will call you tomorrow. Miss you."

"Love you," Matthias told me before I hung up.

"Hey, Lou." I grimaced out how corny I sounded.

"Don't you fucking 'hey Lou' me, Killian. Who the fuck is that? You can't just go posting pictures of strangers with captions like that. The internet is losing their ever-loving minds right now!" Lou was loud enough to wake the dead.

I chuckled. "My boyfriend."

"Your boy...Kill, you're not gay. You've always dated girls; had plenty of women on your arm. What happened when you went home for that funeral?" Lou asked.

"I'm not gay for just anyone, Lou. Only him. My boyfriend. I'm not telling you his name because everyone will be all over him. You'll meet him next month when he comes to New York." God, she was going to castrate me for this tomorrow.

Lou sighed loudly on the other end. "You met him when you went home? He's some guy that knows you're in a band, he's just interested in the fame thing, and—"

"Matthias isn't fucking like that, okay?" I stopped her before she could go any further. "We've known one another since we were kids. He's not some groupie or money-hungry asshole. He fucking loves me." And I just realized I gave Lou what she wanted. She would be on the phone with Matthias first thing tomorrow morning, getting him to sign an NDA. Which he had better not even think about doing.

"Matthias, okay. From your hometown?"

"Fuck off, Lou." I hit the button to end the call.

Killian: *Babe, the world is going to know who you are.*

Matthias: *What? How?*

I smiled as I went back to Instagram and started following Matthias, thanks to my sister. I then added another photo. This one was of him sleeping, the blanket pulled up around his chest and the hickeys I decorated him with on full display. I captioned it, "Watching babe sleep." Then I tagged him.

Matthias: *Killian stop!*

Killian: *Talk to you tomorrow.*

I smiled to myself as I scrolled through Instagram until I received the notification that I had been tagged by FullerMatthias. It was a throwback that took my breath away: It was of us back in the treehouse from that night together, my arm slung over his shoulders, and both of us with bedhead and sleepy smiles. I broke into a full-on smile. "Us," he'd titled it.

Damn right, I commented.

Chapter Eleven

Matthias

Four years ago

I wrapped my arms around my legs and pressed my forehead to my knees as I held back a sob. No one would think to look for me here, especially him. My old man had used me as a punching bag for the last time tonight, because I wasn't ever going to step foot back in that house again. Not ever. The pain in my head was getting worse, but it wasn't anything I hadn't felt before. I could wait until I knew my best friend's grandmother was asleep and then sneak into Helena's room. Helena would help me; she was the only person who cared about me anyway.

Dad had hit me plenty of times over the past few years, but tonight felt different. He was angrier than ever, spouting off the same nonsense about how it was my fault that mom left. I could see in his eyes that he believed it. He hated me for her leaving and wanted to hurt me for it; make me feel just as miserable as he was. Never again.

Tears pricked my eyes as I hugged myself tighter. I couldn't wait to get out of this town without looking back. Getting out of Canfield was the first step of my escape plan, even if I died trying. My head was pounding so hard that I wondered if my father gave me a concussion. Was that even possible? I couldn't go to the hospital because that would lead to questions, which would lead to the police, and that would only make this worse.

"No, just give me a second. I have to grab something before I head over to your place."

I froze at the sound of the voice below. I had chosen the old treehouse that was in my best friend's backyard only because I didn't think anyone used it anymore. I always came here when I needed to get away from my father, and up until now, no one had ever bothered me. We used to play here all the time when we were kids, but that was years ago.

"I can't stash it in the house, man. What if my grandmother found it?" The deep chuckling caused sweat to break out over my skin. The voice was closer now, and I knew exactly who it belonged to: Killian Hampton, Helena's older brother. This was technically his treehouse, built for him by his father before his sudden death, and if he found me here, I had a feeling he might lose his mind.

Killian and I weren't exactly close. He tolerated me because I was Helena's friend but ignored me the rest of the time. He was much too cool and popular when he had been at our school to be bothered with the likes of me. He had been captain of the soccer team and lead singer of a rock band. Killian was going places, and he was only biding his time before he split for California. At least, according to his sister.

The door in the floor suddenly flew open, and I watched from the cover of darkness in horror as Killian heaved himself up inside the treehouse. He had his phone in one hand, with the flashlight on, as he looked around. When he saw me, he blinked, as if I might be a mirage. "Hey." He was talking into his phone now. "I gotta call you back. I might be later than I thought." Killian hit the end button on his phone before he took a step closer to me. "Matthias."

Everyone called me Matt or Matty, but not Killian. He stared down at me, waiting for me to respond or move, and he sighed when I did neither. "Jesus Christ." He started toward the light switch on the wall as fear scorched through me.

"Don't." I didn't want Killian to see me like this—like I went two rounds with Chuck Liddell, even though I had absolutely no business doing so. "I'll go." I didn't want to explain this to him. The only person who knew about my father was Helena, and I trusted her. I didn't know Killian well enough to be sure he wouldn't blab this to the entire town. I slowly climbed to my feet, ignoring my screaming muscles.

"Who did that to you?"

I stopped halfway to the door and let my shoulders slump forward. "It doesn't matter," I whispered.

"You're hiding up here so yeah, it does. Sit back down." Killian wasn't asking. "Now, Matthias," he demanded.

I turned back around to face him. "I think I should probably just go." His hand shot out to grip my chin, and I felt all the air leave my lungs.

"I said sit the fuck back down," Killian hissed before releasing me. "Right where you were." He folded his arms over his massive chest as he waited for me before moving to flip on the light. "What in the actual fuck?" He grunted as I raised my hand against the glare that flashed in my eyes.

The way Killian's eyes blazed angrily made me drop my gaze to my hands. So perfect, those blue eyes, and everything about him made me feel like I was suddenly suffocating. Was it wrong that this might be turning me on right now? All I could smell was the soap from his shower, the scent clinging to him like a second skin, and his chestnut curls were a casual mess on his head. People at school and around town talked about how beautiful Killian was—perfection of the male species—and right now I couldn't agree more. The sound of his sneakers on the floorboards brought my attention back to the here and now. Why did he look so pissed? Okay, sure, I technically broke into his treehouse, but I wasn't destroying the place. I was just waiting for the storm to pass in my life.

Killian squatted down before me; his jaw set in a tight line. "I'm going to ask you again, Matthias. *Who* did this to you?" His blue eyes moved over the cuts and bruises on my face, taking in my father's handy work. When I just stared up at him, he rolled his eyes. "You're worse than Helena." He stood up. "Come with me. I'll take you home," he said.

"No!" I exclaimed, and I watched as realization appeared Killian's face. His gaze became angrier, eyes narrowing even further into furious slits while his lip curled over his teeth.

"Your father did this to you?"

I licked my lips nervously, only to have the taste of copper invade my mouth. "I don't...it's not important." I climbed to my feet again. I had to get out of here.

"What kind of man does this to his own son?" He asked as he dragged his hand through his curls. "I take it this isn't the first time?" When I didn't answer, Killian sighed before he dropped down onto one of the chairs in the treehouse. "Sit." He kicked out the chair next to him. "He do this a lot. I need you to actually answer me, Matthias," he paused.

"Because I'm not a patient person." He leaned back to watch me as I sat down.

I shrugged. "No." *Lie.* "As long as I stay out of his way, he usually leaves me alone." More like I tried to stay away from the house when I knew he was home so this wouldn't happen.

Killian stood up. "Jesus Christ." He dragged his hands through his hair again, but I could feel the anger as it radiated from his body. "I'll be right back." He started toward the door before he pointed a finger at me. "When I return, you're going to tell me exactly what happened. Do you understand?" He didn't wait for my answer, but instead flipped the door open so he could climb down the ladder. I could hear him grumbling as he walked away, and I wondered where he was going.

I took a shaky breath as I glanced around the treehouse. A few posters of soccer players I didn't recognize hung on the walls, and empty bottles of booze littered the floor. That's when I realized that Killian must use this place for himself from time to time. He needed space away from his family—his sister and his grandmother—so he could be by himself, and I was ruining that. Was that why he had been coming here in the first place? Maybe if I just snuck out now, he could go back to whatever had planned. We could sweep this under the rug like it never happened. I had nowhere else to go though. I couldn't go home, and I couldn't go to his place. I had no other friends besides Helena.

"Matthias." Killian's deep voice caused me to jump. He wasn't gone that long. "Come here, please," he instructed. Getting up from my seat, I looked down through the still-open door and found him halfway up the ladder, holding on with one hand while gripping what looked like a first aid kit in the other. "Can you take this for me?" He held out the red box, which I bent down to take. Our fingers brushed for just a second, causing me to nearly drop the container, but I managed to gain control before that happened. My entire hand and arm felt like I was just hit by lightning as the hair on the back of my neck stood straight up. Did Killian feel that, too?

He climbed up onto his feet before pointing at the chair I had been in. "Sit," he growled, and I felt myself shrink away. Was he mad at me now, too? I hadn't asked for his help, nor did I want it. Killian's face softened as he watched me. "I didn't mean...please sit." He held out his hand.

I eased myself down as he moved closer. "Sorry," I heard myself whisper, and I averted my eyes from his gaze. It was too much for me. The crush I had on my best friend's older brother was just that. *A crush.* Killian was straight, I was not, and this was just him being nice. Or at least as nice as he got.

"Sorry?" Killian took the first aid kit from hand and pried it open before placing it on the empty chair. He kneeled before me. "You didn't do anything wrong." He began to remove items that he placed neatly on the floor before he reached up to force me to look at him again. "I'm the one who is going to need to apologize." He chuckled just before his free hand moved to swipe at the blood around my nose.

"Crap!" I exclaimed, starting to climb to my feet, but Killian forced me to stay seated. My head began to pound where he had touched it, and I felt sick to my stomach.

A smirk tugged at Killian's pink lips. The bottom one was slightly fatter than the top, and I wondered just how many girls had tasted his mouth. How did he taste? Was he a good kisser? Or maybe he was the type of guy who didn't kiss and just enjoyed sex. "Tell me what happened." His hand was gentler as he glided it over my skin. "If you don't, I'm going to have to tell my grandmother about this." When he tilted my face up with his finger, I saw the humor in his blues, and I felt all the blood in my body drop between my legs.

"He was drunk." I was mesmerized by my best friend's older brother. The curls, the eyes, the chiseled jaw: There was nothing about Killian Hampton that I didn't like. As he leaned closer, I caught the faint whiff of nicotine. It wasn't as strong as the soapy smell he usually carried, but enough for me to realize he must have caught a quick smoke between here and his house.

Killian's hand stopped. "So, he does this a lot, right? Drink and then knock you around?" He reached for another antiseptic cloth. This time when he leaned down to grip my wrist between his fingers, I sucked in my breath. He stopped to look at me for just a second before he cleaned up the deep cut on my arm. "This one could use some stitches, Matthias," he commented. "Go on, answer my question."

"Yes." I wondered how Killian knew how to do this. Just clean me up as if it was something he did every day. "He hates me." The words tumbled from my mouth before I could stop them. "He blames me for my mother leaving; thinks it's all my fault. He's not a nice guy when sober, but when he drinks? He's downright evil."

Killian ripped open a Band-Aid. "You should go to the hospital." He sat back on his feet. "Your nose looks broken." His fingers glazed over the cartilage between my eyes, causing me to gasp. I wasn't sure if it was his touch again or the pain in my nose.

"I can't do that. Hospitals ask questions. My father would get arrested, and things would get even worse for me."

Killian let out a slow breath. "You need somewhere to stay tonight?" He grabbed the rubbish and shoved it back in the first aid kit. "My grandmothers at work, but she'll see you in the morning. I can have her take a look at your nose and the cut. You know she's a nurse," he reminded me.

"Th-thanks." In the ten years I had been friends with Helena, this was the most her brother had spoken to me, let alone acknowledged I was alive.

I watched as Killian stood up, opened up the cooler sitting on the floor, and then produced two beers. "Here." He tossed one in my direction, which I barely managed to catch. He cracked his open and took a long swig, just his phone buzzed in his pocket. He yanked it out, sent off a text, and then sat down on the floor next to me. "Let me guess, you don't drink much?"

"This would be my first," I answered.

"Maybe it will help you relax, Matthias, because man you're uptight."

I stared as he watched me, his blue eyes intense with something I couldn't read. "Why are you doing this?" I asked before I pulled the tab back on the beer. When I took a sip, I cringed at the bitter taste that invaded my mouth.

Killian chuckled. "I'm not doing anything." He leaned against the wall before he slipped down to the floor, where he crossed his legs and then took another drink. His phone buzzed again, but he ignored it. Just stared at me with those eyes. "When did your mom leave?" he asked. When I didn't answer, he finished off his beer, crushed the can in his hand, and tossed it across the room. "My parents died when I was six in a car accident." Killian dragged a hand through his curls. "I'm sure you knew that," he added. I knew about as much as Helena told me.

"I did."

"You don't talk much, do you, Matthias?" Killian moved to lie down flat on the floor, his thick, muscled body now sprawled before me. "Join me." He patted the spot next to him. "Grab me another beer, too, if you wouldn't mind."

I swallowed nervously as I stood up on shaky legs. "You don't—" My mouth was so dry right now. "You don't have to stay. I'm sure you have plans." I dug around in the cooler to pull out another beer.

"You date much?" Killian took the beer I handed him without sitting up, only to place it on the floor next to him. When I shook my head, he gave me a half smile. "My advice is don't. You saved me from having to deal with my ex tonight. She's a stage five clinger and doesn't seem to understand the phrase 'we're over.'" He tucked his arms behind his head, and I couldn't help but notice the way his shirt moved enough to show off a bit of his flat, toned abs.

I carefully sat down on the floor, but didn't lie down. Even being this close was too much. I needed to encourage Killian to leave, go off to whatever it was he had planned, and convince him I would be fine. As long as I stayed away from my father. I felt a hand on my knee and nearly jumped out of my skin.

"So shy." Killian gave me a sleepy smile. "Are you afraid of me?" He gripped my leg tighter as he watched me before he slipped it up my thigh.

What was going on? "I'm not..." But I couldn't think straight. I couldn't do anything as I watched Killian move into a sitting position. His other hand came up to push a piece of hair behind my ear, and I closed my eyes at his touch. His body heat radiated from him, his scent was intoxicating, and I'd have thought that I might be dreaming if the pain my father inflicted on me wasn't making my head throb so much.

"You know what I think, Matthias?" Killian's breath was hot against my face as his fingers danced over my neck, the other one still on my thigh. "I think that you want me to kiss you."

My eyes flew open just as Killian's mouth brushed mine, his hand gripping my neck. His lips were warm, and softer than I had expected. When he caught me watching, he grinned at me. Was this actually happening to me? I had been crushing on Killian Hampton for years, but he wasn't gay. Was he?

"Say something," he whispered, dragging his thumb over my bottom lip before nipping my jaw. "But don't tell me you're not into me, because I've seen the way you watch me, Matthias." He growled.

Even the way he said my name was sexy. "Can you do that again?" I asked.

Chapter Twelve

Killian

I glanced at my phone for what felt like the millionth time. Fuck, where were they? Lou promised someone would pick Matthias and Helena up from the airport, but that was supposed to be hours ago. Why hadn't I heard from either of them yet? Did something happen? Did Matthias change his mind? That wouldn't surprise me. Over the past couple of weeks, we'd hardly had any time to talk, never mind text. When I did manage to do either, I was so exhausted I usually fell asleep halfway into the conversation. This tour was slowly draining my soul.

"Can I ask you a question?" Dean Frost, my guitar player, asked me as he stepped into the backstage area for the show in New York. Out of the three other guys in Mulligan Downtown, Dean was the closest thing to a friend I had. We had grown up together, were teammates on the high school soccer team and got into a hell of a lot of trouble when we were younger. He wasn't as much of a dick as the other guys, but when you put some booze in him. Dean turned into a real asshole.

I stared up at my friend, taking in his messy green mohawk, dark eyes, and tattooed arms as I did so. "Of course, man," I told him as I checked my phone again. *Damn it.*

"Are you and, uh, Fuller really a thing?" He dragged his hand through his hair before he gripped the back of his neck. "That whole thing back in Canfield was actually true, huh?

You know I don't care, right?" Dean sat down across from me. "That you're gay or bi or whatever, but..." He grimaced when he met my stare.

I tilted my head. "By all means, Frost, but *what*?" My lips curled over my teeth. "You have something against Matthias?" I leaned forward. "Or maybe Mav or Blake might? They have a problem?" Maverick Frost, our drummer, was Dean's older brother, and Blake Duncan was our bass player. Mav had never really liked Matthias and had gone out of his way to prove it. I would knock him into next week if one bad word came out of his mouth about my boyfriend.

Dean opened his mouth just as the door opened, and when I saw who it was I forgot all about him. Matthias stood before me, his dirty-blond hair covered beneath a backward baseball hat, and his hazel eyes as wide as saucers. I was on my feet and yanking him against me to taste his lips before I could even think twice about it.

Matthias grabbed at my shoulders as I attacked his mouth with a brutal force. I tightened my grip on him as I ran my tongue over the seam of his mouth. When it parted; I heard the soft whimper that escaped his throat as our tongues tangled together.

"Yeah, I'm here too, but okay," Helena muttered softly.

Matthias broke the kiss first, his hands moving to touch my face while his eyes searched mine. "Hi," he whispered before I wrapped my arms around him, afraid he might disappear.

"Hey, babe, I missed you," I told him as Matthias ducked his head under my chin. "You too, Helena." I chuckled as she flipped me the bird. "Sorry, love comes first," I teased, and felt Matthias grow tense against me.

Dean coughed softly. "It's nice to see you, Helena. How long has it been?" He climbed to his feet to make sure my sister knew he was in the room.

"Not long enough, Dean," she spat. I'd always had a strange feeling that something had gone on between the two of them, but neither one would tell me. It was better for Dean that way, because if he had touched my sister, I might have to break his face. "Where's Maverick?" I caught the way Dean bristled at his brother's name; there's no love lost between those two. The band had broken up more than enough fights over the past month that I was starting to worry about them.

Dean snorted. "Don't know, don't care." He folded his arms across his chest. "Matthias, how the fuck are you?" He grinned.

Matthias untangled himself from my arms. "Uh, good, thanks. How are you?" The sudden shyness he was showing was making my already hard cock even worse.

"Not bad, we'll have to catch up." Dean nodded before he turned his gaze back on my sister. "You too, Helena." He dropped his eyes down her body.

"Stop eye-fucking my sister, asshole," I grunted. "Go find the other guys." I hooked my arm over Matthias's shoulder. "What the fuck took so long? Why didn't you text me?" I demanded the second Dean was gone.

"Flight delay." He reached up to touch my jaw, the pads of his fingers lightly grazing my skin. "My phone died, and I forgot my charger. I was in such a rush to pack everything so

I could come see you that I forgot a few things." His eyes had grown hooded. "This doesn't seem real to me."

Relief flooded my body. "I can't believe you're here. I was worried you'd changed your mind and I couldn't..." I shook my head as I gripped his face with my hands. "Fuck, babe." I caught my sister's raised brows. "What about you? You didn't have a charger?" I asked.

"I left my phone at home." Helena shrugged. "I worked two doubles so I could be here, Kill, and I didn't pack anything because I'm going home after the show. Don't look at me like that." She narrowed her eyes at me.

"You're still convinced I'm going to run?" Matthias asked.

I nodded. "Every damn day." I kissed him again. "God, I missed this face," I whispered.

Helena coughed. "Do, uh, you two need some space? I mean, I'm just your sister, your blood, but by all means, make it about him." A teasing smile slipped up her face.

"Get over here." I released Matthias so I could hug my sister. "It's good to see you, Helena," I assured her.

She hugged me back. "You too." Helena looked up to meet my eyes. "Don't fucking hurt him again, do you understand?" she hissed.

"Helena!" Matthias exclaimed.

"What, I'm only looking out for you, Matty. I want my best friend and my brother to be together and to be happy, but Killian didn't have to pick up all your broken pieces after breaking you the last time. That was me, and I'll be damned if I'm going to let him do that to you again."

My brows shot up. "You think"—I took a step back and popped my jaw—"that's what I'm going to do? After telling the world that I'm with him you think I would just throw that away? I fucking love Matthias." The words tumbled from my mouth. "What I did to him four years ago will haunt me for the rest of my life, and I plan on spending it showing him how sorry I am." I glanced at Matthias to find him watching me with surprise written all over his face. "Did I say something wrong?"

"You said you loved me," he whispered. "Do...do you mean that?" He sounded so hopeful, only his eyes told me he was scared. Would he always be like this with me, or could I convince him just how much he meant to me?

I swallowed hard. "Yes, babe, I fucking mean it," I answered. "I'm sorry that it took me this long to finally tell you. I'm sorry for what I did to you, and I want to spend the rest of my life making it up to you," I promised.

Matthias slammed into my body with his, his hands sliding up the back of my neck and into my hair as I laughed. "Say it again," he begged. "Tell me you love me, Killian." His eyes sparkled with happiness.

"I love you, Matthias. I always have," I whispered. "I always will," I promised.

***

Playing Madison Square Garden to a sold-out stadium was awesome but having my boyfriend with me made it even better. Just knowing Matthias was there, standing to the side of the stage watching me as I gave it my all, made this show one of the best Mulligan Downtown has had in months. Catching Matthias singing along to every single word helped a little, too.

I was completely drained after the concert—mind, body, and soul—so all I really wanted to do was grab Matthias and head back to the hotel to fall asleep; I hadn't been able to do that much. Only when I was with him. I figured it was my manic mind running constantly, or the drugs and the booze that I hadn't touched since that day with Matthias in the church. I hadn't told anyone yet because I was hoping the problem would fix itself. The last thing I needed was to have to start seeing a shrink again because I hadn't been taking my medication or taking care of myself.

I found Matthias sitting with Helena in the VIP room. I stood in the doorway and watched him as he sat talking with my sister, laughing at something she said and shaking his head. All my blood drained between my legs as I took him in: The backwards hat, the way he smiled, the broad shoulders. Just watching Matthias made all the stress I carried disappear. And when he caught me staring? The smile that spread across his face made my heart feel like a shooting star.

I moved slowly across the room before I pulled off Matthias's hat, ran my fingers through his hair, and bent down. "Did you enjoy the show?" I whispered before bringing my mouth to his. Just a slight brush of my lips over his before I heard him sigh softly.

Matthias nodded. "It was awesome. You were great." He tilted his head to meet my gaze, his hazel eyes shimmering like the moonlight.

"Go ahead, babe, don't be afraid."

"Everyone is watching."

I nodded. "That's the point." I grabbed the back of Matthias's head to crush my lips to his. His hands came up, gripping my shoulders, and I lost myself. The way his mouth parted, the feeling of his tongue rubbing against mine, and the soft little groans he let escape were everything I needed.

"Get a room!" someone shouted—pretty sure it was Blake—and I flipped him the bird as I kept the kiss going. Fuck anyone who dared try to deny me Matthias.

By the time we pulled apart, Helena had moved over to start talking to Dean—that fucker—and I had to resist the urge to grab Matthias to go somewhere private. It had been too long since I had touched him or felt his hands on me.

His hazel eyes looked surprised, but happy. "Killian." The way he said my name with lust and want made my breath come just a little faster.

"Babe." I cupped his cheek. "You're it for me." When Matthias leaned into my touch, relief flooded my senses. "Let's go."

He looked confused. "Don't you have to stay?" he asked.

"Don't care."

Matthias shook his head. "No, your fans." He reached up to touch my wrist. "I'm not going anywhere," he promised. "Spend some time with the people who paid to meet you. Smile: pretend you want to be here." He flashed a grin that made my dick jerk in my pants.

"You know all I want to do is take you to bed," I growled. "Feel your mouth on mine while I jerk you off."

Matthias flushed a deep red. "Kill, you can't say things like that. People might—"

"Hear me? Good, I hope they do." I smirked. "I love you, Matthias. Time you get used to that." Just seeing his face light up when I said those words was worth it. "Sorry it took me so damn long to tell you."

The smile that spread across his face was bright enough to rival the sun. "I don't think I'll ever get used to you saying that." He blushed.

"I love you, Matthias." I had to say it again just to make sure he knew. "I love you, Matthias Fuller. I always have, and I always fucking will." My heart beat loudly in my chest as I said the words, but they weren't a lie.

Matthias crushed his mouth to mine. "I love you too, Killian Hampton," he whispered. "Now, go spend some time with your fans before we go back to your hotel room." The desire in his eyes made my blood pressure spike.

"Twenty minutes," I told him. "No, make that fifteen, and then we're out of here," I promised.

Chapter Thirteen

Matthias

"Matthias." Killian's voice was soft in my ear. "Babe, I could watch you like this for the rest of my life." I felt his hand as it grazed my cheek, causing my eyes to pop open. "You fell asleep," he told me.

I blinked up at him in confusion. "I did?" I reached up to drag my hand through my hair, just as I noticed Killian had my hat on. I had to admit, I liked seeing him in my things. "What time is it?" I sat up. "Where is everyone?" I looked around the now-empty backstage area.

"Hotel." He sat down next to me. "I meant to get us out of here earlier, but Lou forgot to tell me about the reporter, and why are you looking at me like that right now?" Killian gave me a lazy smile.

I shrugged. "I don't know what you're talking about." I was just happy to be here. "You don't have to apologize for anything, Kill. You're important, and if I turn into some jealous boyfriend, please tell me," I told him.

"You're my boyfriend?"

Shit, was that not what he wanted me to call myself? "I mean, if you don't want to put a label on it..." I felt doubt mixed with dread creep into my brain.

"Stop." Killian put a finger over my lips. "You *are* my boyfriend," he said again. "Fuck, I like how that sounds," he whispered before his mouth was on mine. God, I missed this. I missed *him*, and now we didn't have to hide. Killian was finally ready to admit who he was. "Oh." He pulled back. "The reporter was asking me about you. About us," he confessed before he dropped his eyes from mine.

I touched his face. "I don't care." Since he had posted on Instagram, a few reporters and paparazzi had shown up at our house, but Helena usually chased them away. I wasn't going to talk to any of them about my relationship with Killian. It was no one's business but ours.

"Uh." Killian gripped the back of his neck. "He asked about the recording," he whispered.

My stomach dropped at his words. "How did they hear about that?" That day, and those months after, would forever be burned in my brain. No matter how hard I tried to forget or to not let it bother me, I was taunted, teased, and humiliated until the day I graduated. Everyone at Canfield High heard me tell Killian I loved him; heard me ask him if I thought maybe someday, he could love me back. When he didn't answer, I got to my feet. "Who, Killian. Which one of your fucking friends did this?" I clenched my teeth so tight I thought they might break.

"I don't know," he admitted. "I didn't stop to consider whether that would come out, babe, and I'm so damn sorry." I watched as Killian dropped to his knees before me and buried his head in his hands. "I can't fucking win, can I? Whenever things start to go my way, I always manage to screw them up." When he looked up at me, his eyes glistened with tears. "I can't blame you for hating me."

I shook my head. "I don't hate you anymore." I got down on my knees next to him on the floor.

"Not even if they print a story about us? About what happened four years ago?"

"I handled it once, I can do it again."

Killian let out a sharp laugh. "I'm going to ruin you all over again, babe. I can already feel it." He ran his hand over his eyes, and I watched as a few tears slipped down his cheeks. "I'm not good enough for your love. You deserve someone who isn't toxic."

"Don't say stupid shit like that." I grabbed Killian's face in my hands. "I've been in love with you since I was fourteen years old." I watched the way his eyes widened. "You're the only one for me, Killian. My first kiss—hell, my first everything. It doesn't matter what everyone else says about us." I stroked his cheeks with my thumbs. I hated when Killian doubted himself like this. How defeated and broken he suddenly looked.

He clutched my wrists. "You're too good for me, Matthias." His voice was barely a whisper.

"I don't see it that way," I told him.

Killian took a shaky breath. "I'm a mess." He gave me a shy smile. "A complete and total disaster, babe. I hope you know what you are getting yourself into, because being with me is not going to be easy."

"I already told you how I feel, Kill," I assured him. "Nothing is ever going to change that. Now, why don't we get out of here so I can put my hands and mouth all over you?"

***

The second the hotel room door shut behind us, Killian was on me, his hands tugging at my shirt to pull it up over my head. "Get out of the rest of these clothes. I need you," he whispered before dropping his mouth down to my throat. He dragged his tongue over my skin, licking my Adam's apple, while his fingers brushing my nipples.

An animal-like sound escaped me as I tried to pull his head back up to mine. "Killian." I moaned his name as he dropped to his knees. I stared down at him as he popped the button on my jeans and yanked down my pants, along with my underwear. I whimpered as Killian's hand gripped my hard shaft, his tongue rolling over the tip.

"I missed this." He stopped for a second to meet my eyes before he wrapped his lips around my cock, swallowing me all the way down to the balls.

My hands went to his hair, knocking off my hat he still had on, my fingers digging into the thick strands as a feral, brutish sound rattled in my throat. I loved Killian's mouth on me, craved it like a drug, and when I felt his finger linger close to my backside, I felt my thighs start to shake.

"How long has it been"—Killian sat back on his feet to look up at me—"since you've had a cock in your ass?" He gripped my ass cheeks with his strong hands.

I swallowed the nerves that were threatening to rise. "Four years," I whispered. "Four years since you. In the treehouse." No one else had ever meant enough to me.

Killian jumped to his feet with a growl. "Mine," he hissed, before slamming his lips back against mine. His arms wrapped around me as he started to walk me backward to the bed. "Every single inch of this body," he murmured before I sat down on the mattress. "Will always be mine."

He pulled back to yank his own shirt off, exposing his ink-colored torso.

"Always has been," I confessed.

Killian pulled his pants off before he climbed up onto my lap to straddle my waist. "That's right, babe." He tugged on my hair to turn my face up. "We'll always be unfinished business, you and me." His teeth grazed my lips.

"Killian." His name came out in a deep whisper as his hands began to wander over my body. "I love you." I needed to hear him say it again. Those three little words I never thought Killian would tell me were all I had ever wanted from him.

He stopped to stare at me, his blue eyes darkened from lust. "I love you, too, Matthias," Killian whispered.

I grabbed his face to bring our lips back together, teeth clashing as our tongues fought for control. "That's all I ever wanted," I confessed as Killian pushed me onto my back. "For you to love me the way I love you." My eyes filled with tears as he began to slide down my body.

Killian's tongue dragged over my nipple before he brought his gaze back up to mine. "I've always loved you. I was just afraid to admit it." He flipped us over so that I was now above him, his hand pushing the hair back behind my ear. "You're always going to be the only one I want, Matthias."

This time when he kissed me, Killian was gentler, his fingers digging into my skin the longer it went on. He kept his blues pinned on me, his tongue exploring my mouth with a softness I had never felt from him. When Killian caught me watching him, I felt a smile spread over his face, and a low growl deep in his chest. I closed my eyes as fire rolled over my skin, his cock pressed against mine.

"Touch me, babe." His husked voice caused me to shiver. "You know you want to, and I crave you like a drug." Killian moved us both onto our sides. "Put your hands all over my body." He nipped at my bottom lip.

I slipped my hands up Kill's abs, feeling the tight and toned muscles flexing beneath my fingers. I trailed my fingers over his skin, admiring the tattoos that covered every inch before I hooked my hands around his neck. "Like that?" I watched the way Killian's eyes darkened.

"Fuck, you're killing me," he confessed. "I'm going to make you come so hard," Killian promised before he reached down to grip my dick in his hand. "You like it when I touch you?" His hand tightened around me.

I nodded. "Yes," I panted as Killian began to pump my length.

"Tell me."

"I like it when you touch me, Killian. I fucking love...oh shit." I groaned when he inched down the bed and his tongue landed on my cock. "God, that feels so good," I murmured.

Killian chuckled softly as he began to slide my tautness further into his mouth. He pushed my thighs aside, his nails digging into my skin as he did, and a wild, raw need ripped through me. Killian kept his eyes on me as he sucked me, and I couldn't stop myself from digging my hands into his hair to urge him on. The blowjobs and hand jobs I had received after Killian first put his mouth on me were forgotten as I spiraled toward my release.

I watched Killian as he worked me over, and realized he liked getting me off: The way he sucked in his cheeks, the feeling of his tongue wrapped around my dick as he moved his head up and down, the way he moaned softly against me. He loved this as much as I did.

"Tell me you're going to come, Matthias." Killian's hot breath blew against my skin. "Tell me you're going to give me what I want. What I fucking need."

My throat grew thick with desire as I pulled harder on his hair and felt my toes curl. I tried to fight the sensation, struggling to hold on just a little longer, but the sweet suction of Killian's mouth was too much. I came with a shuddering cry, and Killian taking it all, not stopping until he was sure I had been milked dry.

He crawled up next to me on the bed when he was satisfied with his handiwork, wrapping his arms around my body to pull me close. "I love when you come." Killian dropped wet kisses against my shoulder. "But I love it more when you come in my mouth." He grinned at me when I met his gaze.

"Let me." I licked my lips. "Let me do the same for you." I would beg if Killian asked me to. He always enjoyed giving me head, but only let me suck him off a few times.

He arched one perfectly sculpted brow at me. "Is that what you want?" he whispered. "You want to put your mouth on me, babe?" He rolled onto his back, his dick hard and ready. "I've thought about doing this with you again for years," Killian confessed. He suddenly reached up to grip my jaw in his hand. "Suck my cock, Matthias."

Chapter Fourteen

Four years ago
Killian

My heart was pounding so loud in my chest that I thought the entire world could hear it. What the hell was I doing right now? Kissing Matthias Fuller, my little sister's best friend, was not what I expected to do tonight. I couldn't resist, though: His plump lips, those hazel eyes, and the perfectly sculpted cheekbones. God, my dick was so hard right now, it hurt. Something changed when I saw Matthias hiding in my treehouse.

He looked different. Broken, but still beautiful, and I wanted nothing more than to know what his lips tasted like; what Matthias felt like in my arms, his body pressed against mine. I had always caught the way he looked at me when he thought I wasn't watching. The hooded hazel eyes, the dusting of beauty marks that covered his face and scattered down his neck... I wanted to know what else Matthias was hiding under his clothes. He looked like he had started to fill out—he had grown taller, with broad shoulders that stretched out his t-shirt—and I couldn't help but want to wrap my hands around him.

I had no idea that Matthias's home life was that bad, but I would make sure he had a safe place to stay going forward. His father would never be able to lay another hand on him by the time I finished with him. What kind of a man did this to his own child?

"You want me to kiss you again?" I asked, letting my fingers graze over his jaw. "How long have you been dreaming about this, babe?" I watched the way Matthias's hazel eyes darkened.

He dropped his gaze to my mouth briefly before he looked back to my eyes again. "A while," he whispered, and I closed my eyes when Matthias reached up to touch my hair. His fingers dug into my curls, lightly at first, but then he gripped me tightly and tugged my face up.

"Don't be gentle, Matthias, I like it rough," I murmured before I covered his mouth with my own again. A deep growl ripped up my throat as I felt his tongue slick together with mine, and I couldn't stop myself from pulling his body down onto the floor with me. "You like me," I hissed between hard kisses. "You fucking want me." I needed to hear Matthias say it before I went any further.

His hands slipped from my hair as he tried to stay upright on his knees. "Yes," Matthias groaned.

"Yes, what?"

"I want you."

Just hearing those words caused heat to shoot through me. "Fuck," I whispered as I nipped at his plump lips. "How long have you felt this way?" I needed to know, but when Matthias didn't answer, I pulled away. "You don't want to tell me? Fine, I can leave." I started to get to my feet.

"It feels like forever." Matthias dropped his eyes from mine when I sank back onto the floor. "I've wanted this, *you,* since I can remember." I gripped his chin tightly between my fingers to force him to look at me.

I felt the smile spread across my face, exposing the dimples I knew all the girls around town talked about. "Was that so hard, babe?" I dragged my tongue over his lips.

"Why are you doing this?" His eyes flashed with confusion. "You're not gay, right?" He grabbed at my wrist.

I shook my head. "For you, I could be, though," I confessed before I shoved Matthias onto his back so I could straddle his waist. "What do you want from me, huh? You want me to fuck you? Suck you off? Or maybe"—I popped the button on my jeans—"you want to get me off instead?" I tugged the zipper down slightly.

"Can I touch you?" Matthias reached for me, but I pushed his hand away. "Killian, don't tease me." His voice shook as he spoke.

Guilt hit me full force, which was a feeling I wasn't familiar with. "Are you a virgin?" I couldn't resist grabbing his shoulders to feel the tight muscles under my fingers. "I bet you've never even been touched by anyone else before, have you?" If he told me he had been, I would break whoever dared touch Matthias before me.

"I've never..." He panted as I splayed my body over his. "I've never even been kissed until tonight." Matthias moaned softly when I grinded myself against him. "Why can't I touch you? Isn't that what you want from me?"

I chuckled. "Babe, you're going to do a lot more than just touch me by the time I'm done with you." I captured his lips with mine, needing to taste him again. I had never kissed another guy before, but Matthias tasted the way I thought he should. Girls always tasted like too much lipstick or cherry-flavored Chapstick, but not him. Matthias tasted minty, warm, and just like home.

"Kill, are you up there?" The voice of my best friend, Dean Frost, filtered through the treehouse.

I shot off the floor so fast I nearly smacked my head on the roof above me, buttoning my pants at the same time. "Shit," I hissed. "Act normal. Sit on the damn chair," I ordered Matthias, who simply did as I told him. "What's up, man?" I quickly ripped the door open.

"What are you doing up here?" Dean asked as he tried to pull himself up into the treehouse. The second he saw who was with me, his brows dipped and he looked confused. "What happened?" He jutted his chin toward Matthias.

Matthias's eyes had gone wide with fright, but before he could say anything, I stopped him off. "He got into a fight." I knew he didn't want anyone to know about his father. "Some kids beat him up, you know, because he's gay." I hated how the lie escaped my lips so easily. "He was hiding out up here when I found him."

"Is that why you didn't come to the party?" Dean asked before sat down to make himself comfortable. Shit.

I nodded. "Yep, I was just helping him out. You know Matthias is friends with Helena." I saw the way Dean's eyes flashed when I mentioned my sister. Someday that fucker was going to tell me what had happened between the two of them. "Do you need something?" I wanted him gone so I could finish what I started with Matthias.

"Keeley's looking for you."

I gritted my teeth. "Keeley and I broke up." I moved to grab a beer from the cooler. "Something she seems to keep forgetting." I popped the top open and took a swig. "Maybe you could help me with her? Take her off my hands. She likes you." I didn't give a shit if he fucked her or dated her. I was over that girl.

"Uh, no. That chick is fucking crazy." Dean shook his head before he held out his hand. "Give me one of those."

Fuck right off, no. "Don't you have somewhere to be?" I demanded. Jesus, what a cockblocker.

Dean shrugged. "What's the deal, man? You don't want to hang out with your best friend tonight?" He looked over at Matthias before turning his head back to me. "Am I interrupting something?" His eyes went wide.

"No!" Matthias and I both exclaimed at the same time, only for Dean's brows to shoot up.

He twisted his lips to the side before he spoke again. "O-kay, so why does it feel like I walked in on my parents having sex for the first time? All awkward and gross? I don't care if you're into guys, man, have at it," Dean insisted.

"Fuck off," I growled before I finished my beer. "Let's go." I jutted my chin toward the exit. "We're making a stop at my place first," I added before I opened the door. "Matthias, move your ass. You're staying with Helena tonight."

***

We dropped Matthias off at my house, and then went to the party I didn't want to be at to begin with. I had no other choice, though, unless I wanted my best friend to start digging where he had no place being. I was pissed off, had blue balls from hell, and then proceeded to get so drunk I could hardly walk. Keeley tried to kiss me more than once, and that was when I decided it was time for me to bounce.

It was nearly two in the morning by the time I made it home. I tried not to make too much noise as I stumbled through the front door, kicked off my sneakers, and then made my way over to the fridge. I yanked the door open, digging around the milk, soda, and orange juice before I found the Gatorade I was looking for. Then I opened the cap, threw back my head, and drank right from the bottle.

That's when I saw him.

Standing in the doorway, right between the hallway and kitchen like a deer caught in the headlights, Matthias looked like a wet dream. He wore nothing but a pair of my old sweatpants which hung off his hips, his bare, chiseled torso just calling out to me.

"What?" I snapped as I wiped my mouth with the back of my hand. "You want to tell me how unsanitary this is or something stupid?" I capped the bottle before placing it on the counter. "Why are you just standing there watching me like a fucking freak?" I had no reason to be angry with him, but I couldn't stop the words from tumbling from my mouth.

Only Matthias didn't even respond. He simply turned so he could make his way back to the guest room that I assumed had been set up for him tonight. I watched him go, heard the sound of the door as he closed behind him, and a fierce want pulsed through me. Before I could stop myself, I was rushing after him. This wasn't Matthias's house, it was mine, and I'd be damned if I was going to let him judge me.

"What's your problem?" I demanded yanking the door open. I watched him shoot from the bed back onto his feet.

Matthias shook his head. "I don't have one," he tried to assure me.

"Oh, but I think you do." I pushed both palms out to slam them against his chest and I shoved him back onto the bed.

Matthias's brows furrowed as he landed on the mattress. "Killian." He held up both hands. "Please don't," he whispered.

I smirked. "Don't what, babe?" I asked before I climbed up over his body to cover it with mine. "Do this?" I dragged my tongue over his chiseled jawline. "Or maybe?" I felt him shiver beneath me as I bit down on his fat bottom lip. I sucked the faintest amount of blood into my mouth. "Or this?" The low moan that escaped Matthias's throat caused my cock to throb. "That's what I thought." I reached down to cup his dick through the sweats. "We need to finish what we started earlier."

"We can't do this." Matthias's hazel eyes flashed with heat.

I chuckled softly as I palmed at his length, my lips inches from his. "Says you," I murmured before I covered Matthias's mouth with mine. "You fucking want me." I wanted to swallow his tongue as I felt it rub over mine. "You jerk off to me at night." I moved so I was straddling his waist. "Say it." I tugged my shirt up over my head.

Matthias looked at me with lust-filled eyes, and I felt the way they traveled up my chest like an electric current. His fingers danced over the new ink that flowed over my ribs.

"Did it hurt?" He was killing me with the way he watched me. I wanted to make Matthias come completely undone.

"No," I lied. "You like it?" I let my lids fall closed as the pads of his fingers traveled over the musical notes permanently etched into my skin. Why had it never felt like this with the girls I had been with before? The kissing, the touching, everything seemed to make me feel alive. As if I wasn't living until right now.

When Matthias didn't respond, my eyes flew back open to find him gazing at me with dilated pupils, lips parted, and his fingers still grazing my skin. "You're right, you know." He dragged his teeth across his bottom lip. "I want you."

I slammed my mouth over his before Matthias had a chance to say anything else. This was a one-time thing. He knew that I was just using him to get off and having a little fun at the same time. This would never be more than that. "Take off your pants," I ordered as I sucked on his tongue.

"Wait," Matthias moaned softly. "Kill, I need you to stop for a second. I can't...I can't do this with you." He tried to shove me off him, but that was next to impossible.

I arched a brow. "Is that what you really think, babe? You want me to find some pretty blonde to finish what you started tonight?" Hurt flashed in his hazels, and I quickly slipped off him. I grabbed the sweats he had on and tugged them down his legs. His cock stood up at attention, thick and ready. "I think your dick is saying something completely different." I wrapped my left hand around his shaft.

"Jesus Christ." Matthias dropped back onto the bed as he wrapped his fist into my hair.

I couldn't help the smile that spread across my face. "That's right, babe," I told him. "You're mine now." I listened to the throaty groan Matthias released as my own dick begged for attention. "You want to help a guy out?" I asked before I dipped my head to run my tongue over the tip of his cock.

"Killian, fuck," Matthias moaned. "Anything, anything you want." He sat up. "Bring it here," he whispered.

He didn't have to tell me twice. I released Matthias so that I could climb to my feet and removed my jeans before I climbed up onto the bed with my head at his crotch and his at mine. "That good?" I teased as I felt his lips wrap around my dick. Fuck, yeah, that was more than good.

Matthias's hot mouth felt like heaven as he flattened his tongue against me and slipped my cock down his throat while gripping my balls. He murmured something I didn't understand as I lapped at his head and then slowly tugged my lips around his shaft before finally taking him completely into my mouth. I had never given a blowjob before, but I had watched plenty of porn in my life.

The soft sigh of happiness I heard Matthias make filled my body with warmth. I'd always known how he felt about me, but I don't think he realized that I saw him, too. The yearning, the wanting, I had always felt that pull and I could never understand why. Right now, I didn't care.

Matthias's hand tightened around my leg, his nails digging into my skin and I whimpered at the sting of pain he caused me. I wanted more of that from him, but in time. "Kill." He popped his head up. "Don't, not yet please." His breathy voice made me stop to look at him, his cheeks pink, and his lips swollen.

Again, I arched an eyebrow in his direction, but then continued sucking him off. Matthias Fuller didn't call the shots for me, and it was time he learned that. I reached down to grip the back of his head so I could push him back toward my dick. He exploded in my mouth with a hot rush of cream, filling my mouth and throat as he did. Guess he was closer than I realized. He stifled his groans against me before I pulled off him with a pop.

Matthias pushed me over on the bed, his eyes hungry and wild. I had enjoyed making him come. The salty taste of him lingered in my mouth, and I realized I wanted to do it again. Matthias stared up at me as he bobbed up and down on my cock, his eyes begging me for assurance, wanting my touch, and I gripped his soft hair between my fingers.

"You're so hot," I whispered. Matthias's watery eyes widened at my words. "You've been dreaming about this moment for years, admit it. Sucking me off, touching my cock, watching me while I come." He nodded, tears slipping down his cheeks. "You're not going to do this to anyone else while I'm still here." I tugged hard on his strands and Matthias gave me a quick nod to let me know he understood. "Good boy. You're my plaything until I've decided that I don't need you anymore, babe." I groaned as he sucked right down to the balls, my own orgasm not too far away. Again, he agreed with me. I believed him. I knew he wouldn't touch anyone else. Not until I proved to him that I was bored with him. "Fuck." My muscles tightened and I held back the scream of pleasure that threatened to rip from my throat as I exploded in his mouth.

He really did give me the best blowjob I'd ever had.

Matthias's fingers ran over my ribs before he dropped down next to me. "I do like the tattoo," he commented without cuddling up next to me, but I couldn't stop my own arms from reaching out for him. I liked how he felt just being near me, but the urge to touch him was too strong.

I turned onto my side. "I knew you would." I slid my lips over his.

He stared at me, searching my face for something I couldn't understand. "I'm glad you came back for me, Killian," he admitted before his eyes closed, and he drifted off to sleep.

I let out a sigh and climbed from his bed, making sure to grab my clothes. I shoved on my boxers and carried the rest across the hall to my room, making sure to lock the door behind me.

Chapter Fifteen

Killian

I watched the way Matthias's hazel eyes darkened to a deep green before he moved between my legs. There was a time that I would worry about this: That I worried about how much I loved his hot, wet mouth wrapped around me. Worried that my friends would find out how much I craved Matthias's hands on me. Realize how much I missed him when we weren't together.

I had been lying to myself.

Matthias pushed my legs apart, his fingers digging into my thighs, and then sat back on his knees. A smirk flashed over his face. "You know, I think about the first time you touched me all the time." He dipped his head and ran his tongue around the tip of my cock. "How you made me come so hard I nearly blacked out." His tongue dragged down my length.

"Babe," I moaned softly. "That moment will forever be burned into my brain. It was one of the most amazing things we have ever shared." I met his heated gaze.

Matthias wrapped a hand around my cock before he slowly began to pump up and down. "I'm pretty sure I've jerked off to you more than normal," he confessed, and I watched as his face flushed with embarrassment.

I leaned up onto my arms. "You have no idea." I hissed as his mouth wrapped around my head before he slid my tautness down his throat. "Jesus fucking Christ." Matthias watched my face as he worked me over, almost as if he was desperate for what was waiting inside.

His head moved up and down the hard length of my erection while my body bucked in rhythm. Matthias sucked hard, and when he glanced up at me with big, trusting eyes, I couldn't help the feeling of warmth that spread through me. He still loved me after everything I had done to him. I had treated him so horribly, so wickedly, yet Matthias still picked me.

"I fucking love you," I told him as he cupped my balls. "I can't live without you in my life." I growled before my release hit me full steam. I came with a shuddering cry while Matthias swallowed everything that I had to give him. Then I dropped back onto the bed, trying to catch my breath.

Matthias climbed up next to me. "I love you, too," he murmured before he pressed his face into my neck.

I wrapped my arms around him to pull him tightly against me. "Forgive me," I begged softly. "Forgive me for every horrible thing I've done to you. I am so damn sorry for being such an asshole when all I ever wanted was to love you freely." My throat felt too tight.

"Hey." Matthias's brows dipped as he pulled back to look at me. "I don't hate you," he assured me.

I nodded as tears shimmered in my eyes. "Thank you." This time, it was me who pressed my face into his chest. I couldn't hold back the sob that suddenly escaped my mouth. I tightened my grip around Matthias, trying to get as close as possible. He could make me better. He would make this feeling I carried around with me disappear. Matthias was all that I needed.

"Jesus, Killian, what's wrong?" he whispered, trying to force me to look at him.

I shook my head. "It's stupid," I told him.

"You're scaring me right now. Whatever this is, it's not stupid."

"I need you to fix me."

Matthias went stiff. "How...Killian, what are you talking about?" he gasped.

"I'm so fucked up and broken," I admitted. "I don't sleep at night. I drink, I smoke, I'll do whatever fucking drug someone throws my way. I can't...I can't live like this anymore. I'm supposed to take my medication daily, but fuck, I hate how it makes me feel. Like some doped-up asshole that can't function correctly." I was afraid to look at Matthias. Scared that if I did, I would see something I didn't like.

Matthias cupped my cheeks with his hands as he tried to force me to face him. "Baby, look at me," he begged, and when I finally met his gaze, I saw nothing but love written all over his face. "You're not broken, Kill, you're just struggling. We can fix this together," he promised.

A fresh set of tears began to burn my eyes. "You mean that?" I asked before crushing my lips over his. "I don't deserve you," I told him in between kisses. "You're so good, so fucking pure, and I'm afraid I'll ruin you again." It was my deepest fear.

"You won't ruin me," he whispered, but I wasn't so sure. I nearly succeeded once.

***

I woke up screaming after what felt like only minutes of being asleep. A sheen of sweat covered my body as I tried to catch my breath. I reached for Matthias, only to find him gone. His side of the bed was cold, almost as if he hadn't been there for a while. I climbed from the bed and reached for my pants on the floor, yanking them up to my hips. Where could he possibly be? Just as I started for the door, it opened, and in walked my boyfriend.

"You're awake." Matthias looked surprised.

I grunted. "So are you." I clenched my teeth. "Where were you?" I demanded.

Matthias looked taken aback. "Talking to your sister." He moved closer. "Kill, are you okay?" He reached up to touch my face, but I slapped him away.

"Don't touch me."

"Baby, what's wrong?"

I squared my shoulders. "I needed you. I needed you, and you weren't here." I felt like such a pussy.

"Helena needed me too. I'm sorry, I just..." He dropped his gaze. "After last night and how you said you haven't been sleeping, I didn't have the heart to wake you," Matthias whispered.

Shit, what was I doing? Treating Matthias like he did something wrong when all he was doing was being there for his best friend. "I...I had a nightmare." I watched the way his head shot back up. "It felt so real, babe, like...like it was really happening and I just..." I pressed my lips together. "I needed you," I admitted again.

"Tell me about it." Matthias took my hand and laced our fingers together.

I swallowed the bile that suddenly threatened to come up and shook my head. "I don't want to," I told him.

"Killian." Matthias moved closer so that there was hardly an inch of space between us. "I want to help you, but you need to talk to me." He gripped my shoulder with his free hand.

I bit down on my lip so hard I tasted blood. "It was the night of the car accident." He knew what one I was talking about: The one that killed my parents. "I was in the backseat, only this time I wasn't sleeping." I felt my body start to shake. I wasn't sure how much Matthias knew about that night because I hardly ever spoke about it. I had been six and Helena was only four; she had always claimed she didn't remember anything, but I could still feel that night like it was yesterday.

Matthias released my hand so he could cup my cheek. "You've never told me about that," he whispered. "Tell me." He tried to coax it out of me, but I shook my head. "Baby, you said you wanted me to fix—"

"I can't!" I shouted, and yanked my hands through my hair so hard I felt pieces coming out. "You have no idea what it did to me." I needed to get out of this room. I felt like I was going to suffocate if I didn't get some fresh air.

"Killian, please." Matthias's voice was calm, nearly soothing, and I knew deep down that he was only trying to help.

I popped my jaw. "I fucking can't," I said again before I shoved past him. "I need to leave," I barked over my shoulder.

"What do you mean you need to leave?"

"Just what I said."

Matthias didn't try to stop me as I shoved my shoes on. Instead, he stood there watching me with fear in his eyes, and his mouth pressed together in a firm line. I wasn't sure if he was going to start crying or if he was going to start cussing me out, but I didn't care right now. "Are you going to come back?" he finally asked.

"Of course," I assured him, but when I finally met his hazel eyes, I saw that he didn't believe me.

"Why can't you just talk to me?" he whispered. "That's all I've ever wanted from you, Kill. Even now—after you've confessed your love to me, promised me you're not going to hurt me, and told me how sorry you are—you won't do the one thing I need from you the most." Matthias turned away.

I watched the way his shoulders slumped, the way Matthias dragged his hand through his hair, and I felt my resolve cracking. "It was storming really bad that night—no, don't turn around," I told him when he began to. "It's easier if you don't look at me, or I might lose my nerve." I took a shaky breath. "Helena was in the back with me, sleeping, and I should have been too since it was so late. I never could sleep in the car, though. Dad was talking to mom, holding her hand as he drove, and he wasn't paying attention. If he had been paying attention..." My voice cracked as tears flooded my eyes. "He started to hydroplane into the other lane, right into the path of a tractor-trailer. He couldn't stop, but he tried. Mom started screaming. She died on impact, but dad was alive for quite some time and talked to me from the front seat. There was so much blood, babe, so much blood. All over my mother, and some even on me." A loud sob escaped my throat and just as I started to drop to the floor.

Matthias caught me, though, his arms wrapping around my waist. We both fell, but I barely noticed.

"I'm so damn sorry, Killian," he whispered into my ear.

I buried my face into his chest. "I see it every single night when I close my eyes," I told him. "I hear my mother screaming and the sound of the metal cracking as the truck hits the car. I can't get it out of my head no matter how much I try. No amount of alcohol gets rid of it," I sobbed.

Matthias squeezed me tighter. "Baby, you should have told me." His lips brushed my skin. "You should have let me know that you were suffering, and I could have taken your pain from you. I would have gladly taken it away."

"This isn't your pain to suffer through."

"If it meant you didn't have to, I would gladly suffer for you. That's what couples do, Killian."

I felt fresh tears sting my eyes, but this time it was because of what Matthias had said. Would I ever feel worthy of his love and of the way he treated me, or would I always be afraid to lose him? "I don't know why you love me, Matthias, but I know I don't deserve you."

"I wish you would stop saying shit like that," Matthias murmured, just as there was a knock on the door.

"Are you two awake?" Helena's soft voice carried through the door. "Decent, too, now that I think about it."

I climbed to my feet. "Do I look like I've been crying?" I hissed, and when Matthias nodded, I rolled my eyes. "I'm going to wash my face. You can let her in."

I shut the bathroom door behind me just as Matthias let Helena in. I couldn't hear what they were saying, but I thought my sister said she wasn't going to stay. Shouldn't she be gone by now? I splashed water on my face before I stared at my face in the mirror. I looked like shit, but maybe she would just think I was tired. I took a deep breath and stepped back into the room, where they both stopped talking.

"What's up?" Helena giggled nervously, but the lie was written all over her face.

I looked between the two of them. "What are you talking about?" I asked, before it hit me. "Dean," I seethed. "This is where you finally tell me what is going on between the two of you. Don't tell me nothing, Helena, because I've felt the angst between you two for years," I spat.

Helena twisted her lips to the side. "I don't really want to have this conversation with you right now, Kill." She blushed.

"Do you know?" I asked Matthias. When he nodded, I closed my eyes, trying to keep from freaking out. "Someone better start talking before I start punching holes in the damn wall."

"Dean and I..." Helena's voice was soft as she spoke. "We've sort of had an on-again, off-again thing for years," she admitted. "He's the one I lost my virginity to."

Chapter Sixteen

Matthias

Four years ago

I didn't see or hear from Killian for two weeks after he kissed me in the treehouse, and then gave me my first blowjob in my room. I thought maybe he was ashamed and most likely avoiding me. I was even starting to think he was trying to make sure that it didn't happen again. It hurt, but I wasn't sure what I had expected. Killian Hampton was not my boyfriend; he wasn't my anything. I had been a fool to think otherwise.

When I got home from work, I thought I would be alone, but I noticed Killian's car parked in front of the house. All the lights were off inside which made me think at first he was out. I didn't hear anything as I stepped inside, dripping wet from the rain outside, and I quickly hurried to my room to avoid any unnecessary confrontation.

After changing into my pajamas, I was sitting in my room—Gram insisted I call it that since I was basically living here now. I was just listening to the storm raging outside and scrolling through my phone when I heard Killian call out for his sister. I wasn't even sure he was aware I was home, so I sucked in my breath as I waited for him to figure out I was here.

"Helena!" Killian cried out as if he was in pain. "Helena, please, I need you!" he begged.

He must not have known his sister had a date tonight, with Dean no less. I chewed nervously on my lip, trying to decide what I should do. Should I tell him? I knew Kill had some sort of issue with the rain, but Helena never offered up the information and I never asked. He didn't like it when I went into his room. Actually, he didn't like anyone but Helena going in there.

"Gram?" he tried again, this time sounding more like a child. My heart nearly broke at how upset he sounded. "Gram, I know I've told you not to come into my room, but this time it's okay. Just this one time." Killian's voice broke at the end, and I felt my throat tighten. Jesus, he sounded desperate.

A clap up of thunder caused me to jump, and at the same time, I thought I heard it: My name on Killian's lips. But that was impossible, right? He wouldn't ask me to help him, would he? I picked nervously at the skin under my nail, assuming it was my imagination, until I heard him loud and clear.

"Matthias, I know you're here. I heard you come home from work."

Before I even realized it, I had jumped from my bed so that I could rush from the room. I stared at Killian's door as I raised my hand to turn the knob, my heart pounding so loud in my chest I wondered if he could hear me.

"Matthias, please!"

I found the door unlocked when I turned the handle. I had only been in Killian's room one other time—when Helena was looking for his soccer jersey a couple of years ago for a Halloween costume—but it hadn't looked like this. There was shit everywhere: on the floor, on the bed, and posters ripped from the walls. Beer cans were stacked in the corner, and take-out containers littered the floor.

"I need you," he whispered, drawing my attention back to him. He was huddled on the unmade bed in the fetal position, his eyes clamped shut. He was wearing nothing but a pair of gray boxer briefs that left nothing to the imagination.

My mouth opened, but then I clamped it shut again as the rain pelted the windows. "Me?" I asked softly. "What can I do? I'm sure if you wait it out, you'll be fine." Sweat broke out on my back as thunder exploded outside.

"Please? I can't. This weather..." He shuddered at the sound.

I took a step closer despite myself. "Just wait it out, it's just a little rain and thunder."

"Fucking hold me, Matthias, that's what I need you to do. Shut the door, turn off the light, and hold me. I'm sure even you are capable of that," he snapped.

"I can't do that."

Killian sat straight up, and I saw it. The fear in his eyes. The way his teeth chattered together, and how terrified he was. "Why the fuck not?" He flinched when he heard another clap of thunder.

Because I'm so fucking in love with you I'm afraid it will crush me. You've already used me once, and I'm not sure I can go through that again. "I just..." I couldn't think of a proper excuse.

"We've already established that you like me," he grunted before curling up again. "I don't care that you're gay,

Matthias, and"—he turned to look at me—"you know I like you too," he admitted.

I took a deep breath before I flicked off the light and moved slowly to get to him. As I climbed onto the mattress, I felt Killian's hand reach for mine, our fingers lacing together. He held on tight as I pressed my body to his. His scent was intoxicating, his warmth overbearing, and I knew that I was going to lose myself in him for good this time.

"Thank you, Matthias," Killian whispered and squeezed my hand. "Helena told you."

I swallowed. "Told me what?" I resisted the urge to bury my face in his neck, press my lips against his skin, and mark him to tell the world Killian was mine. Deep down, I knew that would never happen.

"We were in the car the night our parents died. It was a storm just like this one." A sob escaped him, and when he released my hand, I quickly wrapped my arms around his muscled body.

"It's okay," I assured him. "Kill, it's okay. You're not alone. I'm here with you. You're safe."

Killian's body shook as he cried, and all I could do was hold him. I had never seen him like this before, so vulnerable. He always played the role of the tough guy, as if nothing could hurt him. I wasn't sure how long we stayed there, me holding him while he cried, but when Killian finally stopped, I fully expected him to shove me away. To my surprise, he slowly turned around so that he was facing me.

"Tell me something good," Killian whispered in the dark, his big hands cupping my face. "Something that makes you smile when you're sad." He dragged his thumb over my bottom lip, causing my breath to catch in my throat.

I swallowed nervously as I tried to get my brain to work. "When I was little"—I stopped as I stared into his eyes in the dark—"my mother used to make pancakes every Sunday morning." I could feel his erection pressed against my stomach. "They were special pancakes that looked like animals. Chocolate chip, blueberry, strawberry—every flavor that you can imagine. My favorite was always the M&M's." Why did I have to be in love with Killian? Why couldn't it be someone who could return his feelings without thinking he was doing something wrong?

"That sounds nice." Killian's lips were so close to mine, and I remembered what he tasted like. A bit of nicotine mixed with beer, and breath mints he used to cover up his smoking and drinking. "What was your mom like?" he murmured. "Was she a good mom?" His tongue rolled over my throat.

I groaned softly. "She...she was the best." I hissed as Killian pushed me over on his bed, his hard length digging into mine. When he grinded against me, I reached up to drag my hands through his thick, dark curls. "What if someone comes home?" I watched the way his eyes widened.

"Shit." He shoved away from me, but when I started to climb from the bed, Killian grabbed me and held me down. "Don't go," he begged. "Can you stay until the storm stops?"

I nodded. "I can do that." I watched the relief that washed over his face before he released me and flipped on the light next to his bed. The obvious erection in his briefs did nothing to ease the one between my legs.

Killian opened his mouth just as a clap of thunder roared outside, causing him to grab onto me. He buried his face into my neck and clung to me for dear life. "I'm sorry," he muttered, his lips brushing my skin.

"It's not your fault." I wrapped my arms around him, trying to ease the tremors that racked his body. "You were just a child, Killian," I reminded him, smoothing his hair.

He sniffed softly when he looked up into my face. "I'm sorry that I ghosted you the past couple of weeks, babe." Killian slid his lips over mine.

"You don't have to apologize."

"Just fucking let me."

I pulled back to stare into Killian's baby blues. I'd thought that he might look pissed, but instead he looked sad. Exhaustion riddled his face, causing me to wonder when the last time was that he'd actually had a decent night's sleep. I dragged my fingers over the scruff on his jaw, over his chin, and down his neck before I pulled him into a tight hug against me. "I forgive you," I told him.

"You shouldn't." Killian gripped my shirt tightly. "I'm only going to do it again, Matthias. Tomorrow morning or when I see you at the movie theater or—"

I pulled his head back so I slammed my mouth over his, watching the way his eyes flew wide before he opened his mouth to me. The soft moan that escaped Killian's throat was all I needed to know I was doing what he wanted, and when he pushed me over and caged me in against the mattress, all I wanted was to get lost in him again.

"Right now," I said in between his fierce kisses, "I don't care about any of that." I knew I would regret it, would hate the hurt that came with loving him, but right now I just wanted to pretend it was the two of us.

Killian smiled so big and wide that it lit up his entire face. Those dimples might be the death of me someday. It caused my heart to beat so fast in my chest that I wondered if he could hear it. He was so beautiful, so perfect, and right now, he was all mine. "Stay with me tonight," he whispered. "I'll lock the door," he added before I could object. "Please, babe."

"Alright." I nodded, and then watched as Killian got up. He locked the door before he turned off the light again and climbed back next to me.

Without saying anything, he wrapped his arms around me and brought my head to his chest. "This is nice," he said softly. "You know"—he ran his fingers through my hair—"I've never had anyone sleep over with me. Not like this," he confessed.

It made a strange and funny feeling rip through my body. "No?" I touched his bicep lightly. "Not even Keeley?" I teased. I hated the way she used to throw herself at Killian during the short couple of months they dated. It almost seemed desperate.

"She tried." Killian used his index finger to tilt my face up to his. "But I never cared about her like I do you." He pressed his lips against my forehead. "I know you don't believe me when I say that, but it's the truth," he told me.

I felt hope start to brew inside my heart, and that was a dangerous thing. "I want to believe you." I dragged my teeth over my bottom lip.

"Tell you what, babe." Killian smiled in the dark. "How about I take you on a date?"

My eyes widened. "You want to take me on a date?" I gasped, just as a set of car lights pulled up outside. Speaking of dates, that had to be Helena coming home.

"I do." Kill nodded. "We can go out to dinner, and then a movie. Maybe make out a little." He chuckled softly. "Out of town, of course," he added.

I nodded. "Of course." Shame mingled in my throat as Killian pulled me closer.

"We can make this work, Matthias," he promised. "As long as we keep it between the two of us."

Chapter Seventeen

Five, four, three, two—

"Are you fucking kidding me?" Killian exploded before my countdown finished in my head. "I'm going to kill that bastard." He stomped toward the hotel room door, but Helena touched his arm. "Don't you dare," he hissed at his sister. His eyes swung back around to me. "And you!" He pointed an index finger in my direction.

I was confused. "Me?" I had no idea why Killian would be mad at me. Up until a few short weeks ago, we hadn't spoken in years, and honestly, what we had before this was hardly pillow-talk worthy.

"Yeah, you," he spat. "Why didn't you tell me?" The hurt was written all over Killian's face.

"When was I supposed to tell you?"

"I don't know, when we were...uh...when we..." Killian dragged his hand through his sexy-as-hell bedhead.

I raised a brow. "We weren't exactly in a relationship. We hid in the dark because you were afraid of what people might think. Besides, she's my best friend. I wasn't going to betray her like that."

"Did you two forget I'm standing right here?" Helena asked. "It wasn't a mistake because I was in love with Dean back then, but now? Now I wish I had never laid eyes on the man." Her chin trembled as she spoke.

"That fucking prick," Killian growled before he moved to wrap his sister in his arms. He pressed his hand to the back of her head as he met my eyes. "What did he do? Wait no, don't tell me. Wait, tell me so I can break his legs. He can still play guitar with broken legs." Those blues of his flashed with a darkness I was all too familiar with.

Helena shook her head before she rested her chin on her brother's chest. "Promise me you won't go throwing punches," she begged.

"For that reason alone, I'm going to make sure he loses some teeth," Killian warned.

She untangled herself from his arms. "That's why I never told you," Helena pointed out. "You can't just go hitting people because they hurt the ones you love, Kill. I thought I loved Dean once, but he can't go on treating me like this," she admitted, and I swear all the air disappeared from the room.

"Say that again, because I don't think I heard you correctly." Killian's voice sounded like something other than his own. When Helena moved closer to me, his lip curled over his teeth. "Do not take her side, Matthias." His eyes narrowed into angry slits.

I touched my best friend's shoulder. "I understand how she feels, Killian." The words slipped from my mouth before I could stop them, and if I could have taken them back, I would.

"What the fuck did you just say?"

"Killian, wait a second."

Killian's nostrils flared, only it was the flash of anger in his eyes that scared me the most. "I want you both to leave," he demanded. When Helena and I both stayed where we were, his hands balled into tight fists at his sides. "If you don't leave, I'm going to say things I will regret. Maybe even do things I shouldn't, and I don't want that, Matthias. Helena, please take him out of here." He didn't look at me when he spoke.

"Kill—"

His jaw clenched. "I said I want you to leave. Take your shit and get the fuck out. Now!" he shouted.

Tears stung my eyes as I grabbed my bag, shoved my feet into my sneakers, and slid my now fully charged phone into my pocket. Killian stayed in the same position with his head hung down as I prepared to leave. When I stopped at the door; I couldn't help but turn back to look at him. "That's it then?" I asked softly. I watched the way his shoulders jerked at my voice. "You're just going to kick me out? You're not going to talk to me because I said something you didn't like?"

"Go, Matthias," Killian said again.

So, we did.

***

"Are you going to talk to me, or just sit there looking like a deer in the headlights?" Helena asked once we were seated for breakfast in the restaurant of the hotel.

I was in shock more than anything. "Did he break up with me?" I whispered. "I think he broke up with me, Helena." I felt sick to my stomach. "I don't think that I can do this again." I clutched my hands together so tightly in my lap that I felt like I was cutting off my circulation.

"He loves you." Helena's voice was oddly soothing. "You know Killian is probably losing his mind right now, don't you?" She reached across the table to touch my hand gently. "This is all my fault," she murmured.

I flinched at her words. "Wait, how is this your fault?" I asked.

Helena shrugged. "This whole thing with Dean and hiding it from Kill all this time. If I had been honest with him, you wouldn't have had to lie, and then he wouldn't have gotten upset." Two tears slid down her cheeks.

"No, don't do that." I shook my head. "This is not your fault. Your brother, fuck." I glanced up at the ceiling. "He's only looking out for you because he loves you." I sighed.

"He loves you too, Matty, don't forget."

"I guess." Her words rang through my mind. *Killian is probably losing his mind right now.* "Shit, Helena." I sprang from my chair, and without waiting for the elevators, booked it up the stairs back to the room, taking them two at a time. I was panting by the time I hit floor ten, but by then I was scared about what I would find waiting for me. "Open up." I slammed my fist against the door. The sound of something breaking caused fear to streak down my spine. "Killian." I said his name as calmly as possible. "Please, baby, let me in." I caught movement out of the corner of my eye and turned to find Helena standing there.

"Fuck off, Matthias," Killian growled from the other side. "Go home." Something slammed against the other side of the door, and I couldn't help but take a step back.

"I'm going to get the manager." Helena whispered.

I shook my head. "No," I begged. "If you do that, the press is going to get involved." I sucked my bottom lip into my mouth. "Have Dean call Lou." I had spoken with her only briefly, but she seemed to have some sort of control over him.

"By all fucking means, talk about me like I'm not here." Killian suddenly ripped the door open and yanked me inside, but locked his sister out.

I gasped at the sight of the room. Nothing was left untouched. Every picture was removed from the wall and smashed into pieces on the floor, while the pillows were shredded and thrown across the room. The television was lying face down on the carpet and was covered in some sort of liquid. I was afraid to see what state the rest of the room was in.

"Good, huh?" Killian snarled. "I'm just getting started." I reached over to grab his arm, but he shoved me against the wall. "Don't," he warned, before moving to grab the bottle of vodka from the dresser. It wasn't even nine in the morning, but Killian didn't hesitate before taking a long swig, then hurled it against the wall. "You fucking left." He pointed a finger at me.

I swallowed nervously. "You told me to," I reminded him.

"You promised me."

"I came back."

Killian popped his jaw as he thought about what I said. "You still fucking left." He reached down to grab another bottle. Christ, how much alcohol was in this room? Maybe I should make sure Lou knew not to have any in our room going forward.

"Maybe you shouldn't drink that?" I suggested. I ducked when the bottle came flying at my head.

"Maybe you should fucking fuck off!" Killian screamed. "You fucking promised me!" He dragged his hands over his hair. His blue eyes were wild as he stared at me before his entire face crumbled. "Oh my God." He sank onto the carpet. "I could have hurt you. Oh my God." Killian buried his face in his hands.

I climbed down next to him. "Baby, you're okay, I'm okay," I promised, wrapping my arms around his shaking body. "Killian, hey, look at me." I felt my heart stop when I saw the wetness on his cheeks and the horror in his blues. "I'm here now, I'm not going anywhere. I'm sorry I left," I told him.

"You said you wouldn't leave me." Killian clung to my shirt as he stared at me. At this moment, he looked so much like the young boy that saved me when I was eighteen.

I combed my fingers through his hair, noticing the curls were starting to come back. "I know, baby, and I'm sorry. I'm sorry I left, and I swear to you that I will never do it again." I pressed my lips over his. I knew I wasn't in the wrong and that Killian had been the one that told me to go. At this moment, though, all I needed was for him to stop hurting.

"I'm so stupid," Killian murmured against my mouth. "I ruin everything, babe." His breath caught in his throat. "You should leave. You should run as far away from me as possible." He cupped my cheek with his hand.

"You're my ride or die."

"Am I?"

I nodded as I took his hand to put over my mouth. I kissed his palm, and tasted blood. "Killian, what did you do?" I pulled back to examine his skin. Jagged cuts covered his hands and anger flared in my blood at the sight.

"I'm sorry," he said again. "I had to get it out."

"Explain to me what that means, because I don't understand." I knew exactly what that meant, but I needed him to say it. I tried to keep myself from sounding upset, but I was two seconds from losing my temper.

Killian dropped his blues away from me. "You know that sometimes when I'm upset, I cut myself. It helps get out the anger, the anxiety, and everything I'm feeling in that exact moment," he confessed.

I grabbed his face. "Like the night you sliced your wrist? When you cut yourself so badly you nearly died? Answer me," I seethed.

"Yes, okay? Yes. Deep down, part of me wanted to die because of what I did to you, but I also was trying to release the pain. Normally when I do it, I do it on my upper thighs so that no one notices, but today I just didn't give a fuck." Killian's brows dipped as his eyes filled with guilt.

I felt my stomach clench. "You have to stop. You're going to kill yourself," I warned him.

"You think I don't know that?" he asked. "I told you, I'm fucked up."

I pressed my forehead against his. "Promise me something, Kill, right now." I slid my hands around his neck.

"Anything, babe, anything you want."

"When this tour is over, you'll get the help you need."

Killian's eyes went wide. "I won't take medication," he reminded me.

"I didn't say anything about medication. You need therapy. You need to talk to someone about your parents. About what happened with us. It doesn't mean you need to go inpatient somewhere. You need help, baby, and I can't give that to you." I watched his Adam's apple bob. "Can you do that for me?" I asked.

He nodded. "Yes," he whispered.

I smiled. "Come on, let's go wash you up before we get this room cleaned up. This is going to cost you a fortune," I teased, helping Killian to his feet.

"Do you...Matthias, do you still love me?" His voice shook when he spoke.

My heart broke at the possibility that he thought I could stop loving him like that. "Killian, have you ever known me not to love you? Yes, I still love you. I will always love you, and that's a damn promise."

Chapter Eighteen

Killian

Four Years Ago

When I woke up with Matthias in my bed, I actually took a second to soak him in: The long lashes that brushed his skin, the way his lips were parted just so, and the dusting of beauty marks across his face that just did something to me. I reached up to lightly touch the bigger one on the left side of his nose when I heard the sound of my grandmother outside in the hallway. *Fuck.*

"Get up," I hissed between clenched teeth. I yanked the blanket off him, only to expose his body. God, he was beautiful. "Matthias." I shoved at him with the palm of my hand and watched his eyes fly open. "You need to get up."

Matthias blinked at me in confusion. "What?" His sleepy voice caused my cock to plump in my briefs.

"Get up," I barked. "I need you to leave my room." I climbed from the bed.

He dragged his hand through his hair. "What time is it?" He sat up, oblivious to the fact that we were about to be caught red-handed.

"Matthias." I turned to stare at him. "You need to get the fuck out of my room." Maybe that would light a fire under his ass.

This time, fear ripped through his hazel eyes before hurt replaced it. "Kill, I thought, you know." Matthias stood up slowly.

I tilted my head. "You thought what, babe? That I would just let my sister and grandmother walk in to find you here with me?" I snorted. "Get the fuck out." The way he flinched made my heart hurt, but what did he expect? We couldn't be seen in the daylight together. Not ever.

Matthias didn't say anything as he got to his feet and walked to the door, but just as he unlocked it, he turned to look at me. "Please don't break me," he whispered before he disappeared from the room.

Anger mixed with something else ripped through my body. I grabbed an empty beer bottle from the table just so I could smash it against the wall. "Fuck!" I cried out, not caring who heard me. What was I even thinking when I let Matthias sleep with me last night? Telling him that I would take him on a date? It was stupid and careless, but at that moment, I'd wanted nothing more than to have him close to me. I needed him last night, only it felt like something more buried beneath my skin.

I loved him.

I shook my head. No, I didn't love Matthias. I...I wasn't sure what I felt for him, but it wasn't love. I didn't even love myself, so how could I love someone else? I could hear Helena talking to him now from across the hall. I yanked the door open so I could go take a shower; I suddenly needed to get out of this house before I ripped it to pieces. Maybe I should reconsider taking that medication the doctor had prescribed, but I hated the way it made me feel. Nothing. It made me feel nothing, and even though it helped the manic-depressive thoughts in my head, I would prefer those over walking around like some sort of doped-up loser.

Once I had washed up and shaved, I found Helena waiting for me in my room. "Lost?" I raised a brow at her as I dumped my dirty briefs in the hamper.

"What's going on with you and Matty?" she asked.

"Nothing." I started digging around for some clean clothes.

Helena let out a sigh before she sat down on my bed. "Why are you both lying to me?" She crossed her left leg over the right.

"Make yourself comfortable."

"He wasn't in his room last night."

I spun around to face my sister. "So?" I shrugged my shoulders.

"Matty wasn't in his bed last night, and when I tried your door it was locked." A smile started to spread across her face. "Are you two doing it?" She giggled.

I rolled my eyes. "Mature, Hel, real mature." But I could already feel the warmth spreading over my cheeks. "I need to get dressed. Do you mind leaving?" I felt sick to my stomach.

"Please don't hurt him, Kill," Helena whispered. "He's had a thing for you since we were kids, and I really couldn't stand it if you broke his heart." She stood up. "Promise me." She placed her hands on her slim hips as she waited for my answer.

"Fine, whatever, I won't hurt your little friend," I told her.

"I mean it." She dipped her head. "If you hurt him, I will disown you."

I groaned. "I am not fucking Matthias, so you don't have to worry about me hurting him," I exclaimed. "Now get lost."

I pointed to the door. I uncrossed my fingers when she slammed the door behind her.

***

The look on Matthias's face when he saw me at the movie theater made me hate myself more than normal, but the look in his eyes when he saw Linda Williams hanging off my arm made me want to slit my own wrists. I don't even know what possessed me to ask her out, but then I had to go and bring her to the place I knew he would be working? I was a world-class prick.

"What do you want, baby?" I asked Linda as she leaned against my side. The scent of her flowery perfume made me sick to my stomach, and I suddenly craved the aftershave Matthias wore.

Linda sucked on the end of her long, red nail. "Uh, popcorn." She gazed over at me with her dark eyes, and I hated myself more than life itself right now. I felt nothing for her, my dick even less so, but what else was I supposed to do? This was who I was, not the guy Matthias wanted me to be.

"You heard the lady, Matty." I avoided his eyes. "Large popcorn." I glanced around the theater, which was less than busy for Friday night. "Baby, go grab us some seats. Somewhere private." I pressed a kiss into Linda's dark hair before she walked off. When I finally met Matthias's eyes, they were filled with heated venom and jealousy.

He filled the popcorn tub, and I noticed the way his hands shook as he placed it on the counter. "Anything else?" he grunted.

"I don't know, babe, you tell me."

"Fuck off, Killian."

I clicked my tongue off the roof of my mouth. "Is that any way to talk to your customers?" I teased. Now my dick was coming alive.

"You can't be serious," Matthias seethed. "You brought a date here knowing damn well I would be working, and—what are you doing?" he asked as I stalked behind the counter. He started walking backward the closer I got to him. "Killian, you can't be back here," he hissed.

I raised my brows. "Oh?" I pressed my body against his. My cock hadn't wanted Linda, but right now it liked what it saw.

"You're going to get me fired." Matthias's voice shook with lust. "Why are you doing this to me?" he asked with eyes full of tears.

I dragged my thumb over his fat bottom lip. "Doing what?" I whispered before I covered his mouth with mine. I watched the tears fall from his hazels, tasted them on my lips as his tongue curled against mine, and couldn't stop the smile that spread across my face. "Where can we go?" I needed more. I dug my hands into his shirt to yank him closer before he could pull away.

"Go back to your date." Matthias shoved at my chest, but that only made me smile harder. "I'm serious, go back—" My mouth was on his again, but this time he fought back and bit down, hard, on my bottom lip.

I flashed a wicked grin at him as I wiped the blood from my face. "Oh, you keep that up, babe, and you're going to have those lips wrapped around my cock right here, where everyone can see." My hand shot out to grip his throat. "I need you," I groaned. "Where can we go that's private?" I watched the way Matthias's eyes flashed with want.

"Killian," he gasped as I loosened my fingers.

"Where?" I demanded.

Matthias's tongue dragged over his lips, and I resisted the urge to kiss him again. "There's a room between the bathrooms. It's for employees only, but—"

"Ten minutes after the movie starts," I growled, shoving away from him. "You'd better be there, or I'll take it out on Linda with video to prove it," I promised. I took my popcorn from the counter and stormed off to find my date.

Linda glanced up at me when I slipped into the seat next to her in the darkened theater. "What took so long?" she asked. When I shoved the popcorn at her, her brows dipped. "Something happen? You look funny." She tilted her head.

"I'm fine," I growled as the lights dimmed.

Only I wasn't. I couldn't stop the movement of my leg as I watched the trailers. I ignored the advances of Linda as her hand wandered onto my knee, up my thigh, and started toward my crotch. I shoved her away without even a glance in her direction. I heard her loud sigh, caught the movement of her leaning back in the seat as she gave up, and then I stood up.

"Where are you going?" Linda hissed. "The movie is going to start. I thought we were on a date." Her dark eyes were wide in the dark, empty room.

"I need to take a leak." I headed back up the aisle toward the bathrooms, and then to the room Matthias had mentioned. I caught the back of him as walked in front of me, and I couldn't stop the blood that flowed between my legs. I stopped to let him get there first, took a deep breath, and followed behind him.

His eyes were hooded with need when they met mine, his cheeks flushed, and lips pressed together tightly. "We can't do this here," Matthias tried to tell me, but when I stepped closer, I saw how much he wanted me. His cock was outlined in his black dress pants, hard and ready for me.

"Liar," I hissed before I pressed him against the wall. "You want this as much as I do." I nipped at his bottom lip before I snaked my tongue between the seams.

Matthias moaned softly before he slipped his hands up my chest and hooked them behind my neck. "Don't do this to me again," he murmured.

"What?" I pulled back. "What did you just say to me?" I stared into his face, saw the hurt and anger flash in his eyes. "You don't get to tell me what to do, babe, I call the shots," I reminded him.

Matthias swallowed nervously. "Then I won't do this with you." He sounded stronger than I thought he was.

I yanked his hands away. "Is that what you want?" I asked. "You don't want me to touch you? Kiss you? Suck you off again?" I took two steps back.

"That's not what I said."

"Oh, I heard what you said, babe."

Tears once again filled Matthias's eyes. "What I meant was that I don't want you bringing your dates here and flaunting them in my face when you know that..." He dropped his gaze to his feet and the tears slipped down his cheeks.

"I know what?" I took those same two steps back to him to grip his chin. "What am I supposed to know?" I wiped the wetness with my thumb before I brought it to my mouth and sucked off the saltiness.

Matthias shrugged. "How I feel about you. Seeing you with her, with someone else, hurts. I can't stand there and pretend it doesn't. Not now, Killian, after what's happened between the two of us."

"You expect me to not see anyone else while I'm fucking around with you?" The thought wasn't horrible, but that wasn't who I was. Besides, people would wonder what was going on with me if I didn't have some chick on my arm.

Matthias shook his head. "No, just don't shove it in my face." More tears slid down his cheeks, and I would have had to be an absolute monster if it didn't do something to me.

"Hey." I cupped his head with my hands and forced Matthias to look up at me. "I won't do that again," I promised. "I'm sorry." I slid my lips over his lightly and heard the catch in his breath. "It was wrong, and I didn't...I fucked up," I told him.

Matthias gripped both my wrists. "Killian." The way he said my name, the way it sounded coming off his lips like that, I almost wanted to promise I would do anything for him.

"Listen." I brushed more tears from his face. "Tomorrow night"—I kissed his forehead before I leaned mine against his. " Let's go out." I saw the light come back in his eyes, and that's what I wanted. I never wanted to burn it out the way I had tonight.

A smile tugged at Matthias's lips. "You mean that?" he asked.

"Yeah, I do, babe." I hated hurting him, and even though I couldn't treat him the way he deserved in town, I could take him out and show him off somewhere else. "I should get back." I pulled away.

Matthias nodded. "Sure."

I pressed my mouth over his. "Tomorrow night we won't have to hide this," I promised.

Chapter Nineteen

Killian

I stared up at Matthias in an alcohol- and drug-induced haze from inside the bathtub. "Thank you," I murmured as he turned off the water and began to soap up the washcloth. When his brows went up in question, I dropped my gaze to my knees. "For coming back. For doing this. For not leaving me," I whispered.

Matthias lifted my arm from the water and slowly ran the cloth over my skin, carefully removing the blood that had dried there. "I'll always come back for you, Killian," he told me. "No matter what happens, you're it for me. You should know that by now." He stopped to stare at me before he gently placed my arm back in the water.

Tears burned my eyes. "I hate this." I shook my head and buried my face in my hands. "Fuck, why am I like this?" I murmured into my palms before slamming them into the water. "Why do you want me? I'm such an asshole. I am a fuck up and I'm just...I'm just going to hurt you again." I raised my chin. "You should leave. I won't stop you if you do."

"Stop it." Matthias's nostrils flared as he stopped to stare at me.

I grabbed his wrist. "I'm serious, babe, you should run," I warned him. "Because you know this is only going to happen again. And again. And again," I hissed before he yanked his hand away from me.

"You're drunk."

"You're gorgeous."

Matthias sighed. "I love you, Killian. I'm not leaving, so stop trying to push me away. It's never worked in the past." He started to lean forward for my other arm, and I grabbed him and pulled him into the bathtub, fully clothed. "Are you kidding me right now?" he exclaimed as water splashed onto the floor. I started to laugh at the sight of Matthias half in the tub, half out, with his legs hanging out of the side. "I'm glad this is amusing you." He struggled to get up, but I only held him tighter. "Seriously, Kill, let go."

"Nope." I slid my hand down to cup his cock with my hand and enjoyed how it instantly went hard. He groaned as I squeezed him, pressing his dick into my palm. "Relax, babe, let me make you feel good. It's the least I can do right now."

Matthias glanced in my direction with fire in his eyes before his hand dipped under the water. "Only if I get to return the favor." He found my own length hard and ready for him. "Jesus, Killian." He rocked against me as I jerked him through his pants. "Let me just... fuck." He hissed as I managed to unbutton his jeans so I could wrap my hand around his dick.

"That's better," I groaned as Matthias stroked me. "God, you're so good." I wanted to watch him, but I couldn't seem to force my eyes to stay open.

Matthias bucked his hips. "We should...the water...more, baby, don't stop." He pumped his hand up and down against my flesh faster, urging me on.

A rumble of pleasure tore from my throat before I husked out his name. My body shook as I came. The sound of water splashing over the edge of the tub filtered into my senses just as I felt Matthias shudder above me. His nails dug into my cock, but that only made me groan as he milked the last few drops of cum from me before he slipped into the tub and stared at me.

"Love you," I whispered before I threw back my head and laughed. Then I grabbed Matthias and pulled him over onto me. "I love you," I said again.

He searched my face with those hazel eyes, looking for something, but I wasn't sure what. Then, he eased his weight against mine. "I loved you first," Matthias teased before resting his head against my chest.

"You sure about that, babe?" I asked. When his head shot up, I gave him that smile—the one I knew he liked, complete with dimples. I grazed his cheek with my fingers. "You think I didn't have feelings for you back then? Even though I was horrible to you, it didn't mean I wasn't in love with you." I pulled him closer despite the chill of the now-cold water.

Matthias didn't say anything as he lowered his head back to my chest, and I combed my hands through his hair. "How could you love me when you treated me the way you did?" I heard him ask.

"Because I was fucking stupid," I answered. "I was in serious denial back then, babe, and everyone could see it except me. Helena saw it. Dean saw it. Hell, even Linda knew something was going on the night I took her to the movies knowing damn well you would be there." I still regretted doing that, but not as much as letting out that recording. That would always be my biggest one.

Matthias started to get up and, even though I didn't want him to move, I let him. He climbed from the tub, wet clothes clinging to his body, and when he ripped his shirt from his body to fling it at me, I didn't fight back. The anger radiating from him was all I needed to know what he was feeling. "Don't." Matthias held up his hand. "Don't say another word." He clenched his teeth.

"Wouldn't dream of it, babe."

"Don't call me that, either."

I nodded. "Okay, babe."

"Stop it, Killian!" Matthias exclaimed, and I saw it. The pain was etched all over his face. The horror he had to endure while I pulled him in and pushed him away. "You couldn't have loved me. No, not like I loved you. I would have fucking died for you, and you?" He gave a choked laugh. "You used me."

I stood up. "I never used you," I shouted. "I fucking loved you, too, Matthias. I just didn't know how to tell you. I was fucking stupid. I did dumb shit, and broke your heart, and lied to you. I hid you away from everyone because I was afraid that people would...would..."

"Would what, Killian? Think you were gay?" Matthias finished for me. When I didn't answer, he closed his eyes. "Exactly. Even now you can't admit it. Fucking asshole."

I started to climb from the tub, but when I slipped—and nearly fell because I was wet and still drunk—Matthias was there to catch me. His arms hooked around me, saving me once again from myself. I gripped his shoulders with my hands. "Thank you," I whispered.

"I'll always catch you if you fall," he promised.

I felt shame mingle in my throat. "You know I love you." I hated when he was upset with me. Even back then I hated to hurt him, but now I realized it was because of how I felt. I was afraid to admit it in the past, but not now. "I've never been gay, Matthias."

"Right." He started to shrug me off, but I held on even tighter.

"Listen to me," I growled. "I'm not gay because I like girls too, but with you? Hell, you do it for me, babe, and you know that. I love every inch of your body, your cock, that mouth. So, does that mean I'm bi?" When Matthias's brows went up, I continued. "I'm bisexual. I can admit that to you. I'm into *you,* though. I already told you, I've never looked at another dude and thought shit, I want to suck his cock real bad. Just you."

"Hey," Matthias said. "Why are you crying right now?" he asked.

"What?"

Matthias dragged his thumbs over my cheeks. "You're crying," he said again. "Why?" He reached for one of the towels hanging by the tub and started to dry me off.

"I...I don't know," I admitted as I raised my arms so he could get my ribs. "You...you're not leaving, are you?" I asked.

He shook his head. "Not leaving you, I promise. Stop asking me that, okay?" He stood up to wrap the towel around my waist. "You should probably lie down."

"Will you lay with me?" I couldn't bear the thought of being alone. "Please, babe, I need you."

"Let me dry off and change into some clean clothes." Matthias sounded tired.

I moved into the room, and was smacked in the face by the mess I had made: Glass littered the floor, and pieces of the mattress and pillows were everywhere. We couldn't stay here anymore. I had ruined that just like I did everything else.

"We're going to have to change rooms." Matthias walked past me while carrying his wet clothes, and I admired his body. "Maybe you should call Lou?" he suggested, but when I didn't move from the spot I was standing in, he let out a soft sigh. "Killian?" His brows dipped.

"What?" Was he talking to me right now? Because I wasn't sure what he had said.

Matthias touched my cheek. "Can I use your phone to call Lou for you? Helena has my bag and my phone." His voice was calm.

"Yes, sure. My passcode is your birthday."

He looked surprised for just a second before he took my phone from the dresser. "Hey, no, it's Matthias. Um, so we had a bit of an issue here. No, he's alright. Uh..." He moved into the bathroom, where I could no longer hear him talking. When he returned, he had one of those bathrobes that the hotel provided us with. "Lou is on her way up."

"Good." I nodded.

"Baby." Matthias moved closer. "You want to tell me what's going on in that head of yours right now?" He touched my arm.

I shrugged. "I'm fine," I assured him.

"I'm starting to think it's not all vodka. What did you take?" he asked.

I narrowed my eyes. "Take?" Had I taken something? I might have, but I wasn't so sure. There had been some pills in my suitcase, but what were they?

"Did you take something while I was gone with Helena? Some sort of downer with the booze? A drug, maybe?" Matthias suddenly sounded scared.

"Oxy."

"What?"

I nodded. "I took some oxy." At least I think that's what it was.

"Jesus, Killian." Matthias dragged his hand through his hair before he gripped the back of his neck. "How much?"

I shook my head. "I don't know." It was an honest answer.

"You don't know?" Matthias looked angry. Maybe even more angry than I had ever seen him. "Where did you get it?" He suddenly grabbed onto my shoulders. "Someone in the band? A groupie? Who?" he demanded.

I swallowed hard as I stared at him. "Some guy, a couple of shows ago. I don't remember his name." I watched the hate blaze in Matthias's eyes. "Babe, I'm sorry. Don't be mad." Why did I sound like that? Why was I apologizing to him again?

"Some guy? You got drugs from some guy? Are you trying to kill yourself, Killian? Because you may succeed if you continue like this. I'm starting to think that you don't give a shit about Helena, me, or yourself at all. Everything you say or do is bullshit." He released me just as there was a knock at the door. "That's probably Lou. You had better come up with a good excuse for this, because I'm done making them for you."

I opened my mouth just as Matthias went to let Lou in. She looked just as pissed as she should be. Her dark hair was swept up into a tight bun, her makeup was done perfectly, and she was wearing one of her signature business suits. I watched as her blue eyes moved around the room before she finally introduced herself to Matthias. I knew they had spoken on the phone, but this was the first time they had met in person.

"What did you do now, Killian?" she finally asked me before holding up a hand, shaking her head. "No, don't tell me. I don't want to know. I already have another room for the two of you. Gather your things together so we can get you moved. Just"—Lou sighed—"don't do this again, because you're paying for this mess you made," she glanced over at Matthias. "You two okay?"

Please don't say anything. Don't tell her about my cutting or my drinking or anything. That's between us, I silently begged.

"No, we're alright." Matthias laced his fingers through mine.

Lou looked like she might say something else, but instead she let out a long breath. "Let's get you moved then," she said.

Chapter Twenty

Matthias

Four Years Ago

I glanced at Killian as he drove out of Canfield. He hadn't said a word to me since we left the house. He kept his hands on the wheel, at ten and two, while his eyes were glued to the road in front of him. His jaw was clenched in a tight line, and I watched as he twisted his lips to the left before his tongue snaked out to moisten them.

I looked away before Killian could catch me watching him, afraid of what he would say or do. Then I remembered he was the one who suggested this date. It was a date, too, because Killian called it one. If he had changed his mind, all he had to do was tell me. It might break my heart, but I would get over it. I always did.

The sounds of Nirvana's "Something in the Way" filtered through the speakers. Just as I opened my mouth to say something, I felt Killian's hand on mine, his fingers squeezing tightly. When I looked over at him again, he gave me a cheesy smile, one that flashed his dimples for a second. My stomach jumped at the sight. This was actually happening.

"You're quiet," Killian finally said.

I looked down at my feet. "Nervous," I admitted.

"Really?" He squeezed my hand and then tugged lightly. "Shy again, too?" he teased.

I was glad it was dark, except for the occasional light that flashed through the car, because I felt the blush creep up my neck and over my cheeks. "A little, sure, I guess so." I turned to look at him again as the car slowed to a stop. "Where are we going?" I asked.

"There's a great restaurant in Avon I thought we could go to." Killian pulled my hand up to his mouth, where he then pressed his lips to my hand. "They also have arcade games, go-karts, and all sorts of fun shit for us to do. A fun first date, right?" He smirked at me as he pressed down on the gas once the light turned green.

I felt my blood rush to my cock, and my brain went all foggy. "So, this is actually a date? You weren't messing with me." It wasn't really a question, more of a statement.

"Babe." Killian cast a look at me for a second. "There is one thing you're going to learn about me. It's that most of the time when I take girls out, I don't do this." He waved his hand around the car. "Sure, I want to make sure no one knows us, but it's also because I want to take you out somewhere fun, and somewhere we can have a good time. Other than the movie theater where you fucking work, where can we go in Canfield that's fun? Nowhere," he pointed out.

I hated that Killian had to hide this from everyone, but I was thrilled to be going out with him. "It sounds fun," I admitted. I would go anywhere with him at this point.

"You're going to love it."

When Killian pulled into the parking lot, which was packed full of cars, I saw the look of fear pass over his face. We were about an hour away from Canfield, but that didn't mean we couldn't run into someone we knew. Someone might recognize him from the soccer team or from Mulligan

Downtown. Even worse? They might realize he was with me. The only gay kid in our town.

I touched his arm. "We can leave," I whispered. "We don't have to do this if you don't want to." Dread clawed at my brain when I thought about him agreeing with me, but if he wasn't comfortable with being seen with me, I wouldn't make him.

"I want this." Killian turned to me. "I'm just—"

"Scared," I finished for him. "I know the feeling, Kill, and it's perfectly okay if you want to go home." I had been on two official dates in my life, and this was one of them.

Killian grabbed the back of my neck and slammed his mouth over mine. His tongue forced its way between my lips while his hands were digging into my hair, and his breath came in hot pants. "Not scared. Happy," he told me. "Now let's go inside."

***

Once we were seated at a booth, with Killian across from me, we ordered a couple of burgers and sodas before he leaned back to look at me. I wanted to look away, but this was also the perfect time for me to take in the messy curls on his head, the icy-blue eyes that scanned over my face, and the smile that spread over his features when he finally caught me watching him.

"You like what you see, babe?" He nudged my knee with his foot beneath the table.

I nodded. "You know I do." I reached for the soda when the waitress brought it over. She didn't hesitate to stare at

Killian just a little too long, and it made my blood boil. I couldn't call him mine, but I didn't have to like it either.

"Me too." He chuckled when my mouth fell open. "Not going to deny it, Matthias, I like the way you look." Killian smirked. "You're kind, sweet, and funny, but you're hot, too. I like the beauty marks you have scattered all over your body." He tapped the left side of his nose for emphasis. "Hot," he teased, and my dick jerked in my pants.

I wasn't sure what I was going to say to him, but the waitress came back with our food, and I was happy to have something to busy myself with. I knew Killian liked me, or at least I hoped he did, but he'd just freely admitted it. My stomach was in knots as I poured ketchup on my hamburger, and I wasn't sure I was going to be able to eat.

"You're quiet again," Killian commented as he took a bite of his food.

I shrugged. "This is crazy," I admitted. "All of this. I mean, everything we're doing." I noticed our waitress making her way back toward our table again and gritted my teeth. This would be something I would have to get used to if I wanted to be with Killian. Girls were always just attracted to him, and I couldn't blame them.

"Just wanted to check and see how your meal was." She batted her lashes. "Will you be needing anything else?" She hadn't even looked in my direction since I placed my order.

Killian nudged my leg. "I think we're good," he answered as she placed the bill face down on the table.

"Well, if you need anything else, just let me know." She tilted her head. "I left my number if you want to hang out sometime." She patted the piece of paper, and my mouth dropped open as she walked away.

"Relax." Killian held up his hand. "You're going to burst a blood vessel, babe, and I can't have that." He grinned.

I narrowed my eyes. "She just gave you her number. Right in front of me. Why are you laughing?" I asked. I pushed my food away because I was no longer hungry.

"You're jealous."

"Damn right, I'm jealous. I get enough of this shit back home."

Killian chuckled. "I like that." He flipped the bill over and sure enough, she had written her number, along with her name—which was Gwen—in bright-pink pen ink. "Is she watching?" he asked as he lifted his hip to take out his wallet, dropping a couple of twenties on the table. When I nodded, he grabbed the pen she'd left and scribbled something down next to her number. Then he stood up and held out his hand. "Ready?" He wiggled his fingers at me.

"I thought—"

"Take my hand, Matthias," he ordered. When I did, he yanked me up onto my feet and slid his mouth over mine. "We're on a date, remember?" He then hooked his arm over my shoulders. "No one knows who we are here, so I don't care."

When we had walked away from the booth, I dared look over my shoulder to see if Gwen was watching. She had her eyes narrowed into angry slits. "What did you write?" I asked.

"That I was yours." His voice was soft in my ear.

My heart soared at Killian's words, but then I wondered if the words were spoken in the heat of the moment. I remembered last night at the theater, the things he said to me, and knew he would never truly be mine.

"Hey." Killian stopped walking. "You okay?" he asked.

I nodded. "Never better," I lied.

"Great, let's go play some games."

We spent the next couple of hours playing every single video game in the building. Most of them I sucked at, but there were a few I managed to actually beat Killian at. I liked listening to him as he laughed when I accidentally got myself shot during the Jurassic Park game, or when I was surprised that I managed to do a dunk shot during the NBA game. He would let out a loud belly laugh that shook his entire body, and it was probably one of the first times I had ever seen Killian so happy. He always seemed so stressed or uptight when he was home; never happy or smiling much. It was nice to see him let go and be himself, because he deserved that, and I was the one who was able to give that to him. He kicked my ass at miniature golf, skee ball, and finished third to my dead last at go-karts, though. I had never been the athletic type.

It was nearly eleven o'clock when we decided we should head back, knowing we had an hour drive back to Canfield. As we got closer to the car, Killian suddenly released my hand and stopped dead in his tracks. I watched as his eyes went wide with fear before it turned to anger, and that's when I saw why. Someone had scratched the word "fag" into the hood of his car. I think we both knew who did it.

"Fucking cunt," Killian hissed under his breath before he started walking again. He unlocked the car and then pulled something from his pocket. "Get in," he barked at me before he started carving at the word. "Are you deaf, Matthias? Get in the damn car." He hadn't looked at me, but I could tell by the tone of his voice how upset he was.

This was my fault. If I hadn't been so annoyed with that waitress and had just let it go, Killian wouldn't have told her we were on a date, and this wouldn't have happened. Now he had that horrible word written on his car, and he would never forget it. He would always blame me for Gwen ruining his car. He would never take me out on another date or want to see me again. This was the best and worst date I had ever been on.

"Matthias, where are you going?" Killian called after me as I started back to the restaurant. "No!" He grabbed me by the back of the shirt and yanked me back around. "Don't," he hissed between clenched teeth. "If you go in there, if you start something..." His voice trailed off.

I cupped his face with my hand. "She wins then?" I asked.

Killian shoved me away. "Get in the car." he said again.

"What if I don't want to?"

"Then I'll leave without you."

I stared at Killian. I saw the way he avoided making eye contact with me, noticed the way his lips were pressed together and his jaw was set in a firm line. He was scared. He was afraid that if I went back inside, someone would find out what we were doing: Killian Hampton had been on a date with a boy, and he liked me. Without another word, I climbed into the car and waited for him.

Killian slid into the driver's seat about fifteen minutes later. "Look." He sighed as he started the car.

"Don't." I shook my head. "Just take me home." I couldn't look at him. Not now, maybe not ever. Killian would only be mine when no one could see, and I wasn't sure I could handle that. It made my heart ache in places I didn't know were possible.

Neither one of us spoke during the hour ride home, and when Killian pulled into the driveway, I climbed out of the car without waiting for him. I went to my room thinking he might come find me, but when I heard him drive off, I felt my heart break into a million pieces.

Chapter Twenty-One

Matthias

Killian slept for the rest of the morning, and afternoon. I was thankful he did because not only was I furious with him, but I was also scared shitless too. I told Lou nothing about what happened, no matter how much she asked; believe me, she asked. She stayed to talk with me for a couple of hours after Kill passed out in bed. I couldn't—no, I wouldn't—betray him like that, and I was surprised about how relieved I was when she finally left.

When Helena showed up it was a bit of a shock. She was never supposed to stay the night, and now here she was, still hanging around. I was never happier to see my best friend than in this moment. I engulfed her in a tight hug, not wanting to let go.

"You want to talk about it?" Helena asked once I released her.

I shook my head. "I'm just happy to see you," I assured her as we sat down on the small couch in the room. "I thought you had to go home? Weren't you supposed to go back to work?" I raised a brow.

"Stop." Helena smacked at my arm playfully. "I was worried about Killian, and you," she confessed. "Is he okay? I mean, after everything that happened this morning?" She chewed nervously on her lip. "You don't have to give me details, Matty, but he didn't sound good when we got back to the room. Dean said—"

"Dean said what?" I cut her off. This was none of Dean's damn business. I didn't care how close he and Killian were.

Helena pushed up onto her feet. "Dean said he drinks too much sometimes. Gets angry and hits things. He used to do that when we were kids. Before..." She started to pace. "Before you two started dating."

"We weren't dating back then."

"Matthias, you two were together until Kill fucked it up. He changed for a little while, and no one knew why. When you're not together, he's not okay. He needs you in his life."

I swallowed the needles in my throat when I realized what she was getting at. "He told you," I whispered as I realized what she was talking about.

"Killian's been cutting himself since we were kids, I just had no idea it had gotten so bad that he ended up in the hospital." Helena dropped back onto the couch, tucking her feet beneath her. "I wish he would talk to me. When we were younger, he told me everything, but now he just bottles it all up." She dropped her gaze to her hands.

I gritted my teeth. "Dean had no right to tell you that." I was going to have some words with Dean Frost tonight. I didn't care if he hit me. That wasn't his secret to tell.

"Killian is my brother."

"He's my everything, Helena, and Dean had no right. If Killian wanted to tell you, he would have."

Helena sighed softly. "Aren't you worried about him?" she asked. "Worried that next time he's going to slice too deep or hit something he shouldn't? Do you really think Killian wants to die, or maybe he's trying to get someone's attention?" Her brows dipped. "Don't look at me like that. I'm worried, just like you."

"I'm not having this conversation with you," I growled. "End of discussion." I was so mad right now, my hands were shaking. I could feel the blood rushing through my head. "Why don't you tell me what's going on with you and Dean?" I needed to change the subject before I started screaming at my best friend.

Helena's face went pale. "Uh...could we not?" she asked.

"What's wrong, little sister? You can dish it out, but can't take it?" Killian's voice caused us both to turn around. "I appreciate you sticking up for me, babe." He was wearing a pair of sweatpants that hung loose around his hips. "I'd like to know when it started with my guitar player, why it's still going on, and why you never told me." He moved over to run his fingers through my hair before he pressed his lips against my head.

"Killian." Helena shook her head.

Killian grunted. "It's either you or him," he said. "One of you is going to tell me the truth. Maybe I should go pay my guitar player a visit before the show tonight? I'm sure he would love to talk to me, especially since he opened his fat mouth to you so easily; he probably won't have any problem telling me all about your torrid love affair." He sounded pissed, and I guess I couldn't blame him. "I'm not going to let this go, Hel, so you may as well start talking." He moved to sit on the arm of the couch, grabbing my hand so that he could grip it tightly. When I looked up at him, his blue eyes pleaded with me to stay where I was.

"Fine." Helena dragged her teeth across her bottom lip. "We always sort of had a thing for one another," she confessed. "Don't say anything until I'm finished," she whispered, "or else I might not be able to get this out." She kept her eyes on her hands, which were twisted together in her lap. "I always liked Dean, you know? I thought he was cute, and he was nicer to me than the rest of your friends. He was also around a lot." None of this information was new to me. From their first kiss to when Dean left for California with Killian, I knew all about everything that happened between the two of them. "We never meant—" She stopped to look at her brother. "We never meant for this to happen. To go as far or as long as it did."

Killian's lip curled over his teeth. "Go on," he snarled.

"We went on our first date together the night that Matthias first slept in your room. After that, we sort of snuck around behind your back when you weren't looking. I knew you were going out with Matthias, because you both were never home. Dean thought you were just seeing someone from out of town." Helena dropped her gaze to her feet.

Killian dropped my hand. "Hel, what's really going on? Are you pregnant or something?" When she didn't answer, he stood up. "You're pregnant?" he whispered.

"I was...I *was* pregnant." Tears began to stream down her cheeks. "It was an accident. I was on the pill, but then I caught bronchitis and the antibiotics caused it not to work. Wait, where are you going?" she exclaimed when Killian started toward the door.

Killian turned to look over his shoulder. "To have a few choice words with your baby daddy," he growled.

"Wait." I grabbed his arm. "Maybe let her finish telling the story before you go busting skulls." I watched the way his blues darkened.

Killian tilted his head. "You didn't know about the baby, did you?" His eyes focused in on his sister. "You told Matthias, but not me?" He sounded hurt, but I couldn't blame him.

"I didn't know I was pregnant until I miscarried."

The room went deathly quiet. I felt like I was going to be sick all over again as the words rolled through my ears. Killian and I both moved together to sit down, pulling Helena into a hug. She let out a sigh of surprise before she leaned into us and began to cry. I felt Killian's hand on mine as we held her, and I knew he felt terrible for blowing up the way he did. She had no idea she was pregnant before it was too late.

"Hey." Kill soothed her back. "I'm sorry I got so upset," he said calmly. "I'm an asshole."

She nodded. "Yeah, you are, but I love you." Helena sniffed. "I would have kept the baby," she told him, and I saw the way Killian's jaw tightened. "Look, the last time I came to see you guys on tour, I had no intention of going anywhere near him again. It just sort of happened."

"That was a couple of months ago, Hel," Killian reminded her. "You mean to tell me you got pregnant then?" He climbed to his feet again. "As a medical professional, shouldn't you know better?" he demanded.

Helena sighed loudly. "Yes, Kill, I should, but we all make mistakes. I had no plans to sleep with Dean again when I was here. I thought we were over, since he had been avoiding me. Until Maverick started hitting on me."

"Stop!" Killian held up his hand. "I don't need to know that my bandmates are into you." He released his sister and stood up. "I still think that I should go talk to him. You know, make sure this shit doesn't happen again."

Helena shot me a look. "Did I ever stop you from going after Matty?" she asked.

"What?"

"I asked a simple question, Kill." She patted my arm. "Did I ever stop you from going after Matthias? No, I didn't. I just wanted to make sure you didn't hurt him. Which you did. You ripped his damn heart out." I grimaced at her words, but Helena wasn't wrong. "I made peace with the fact that Dean and I were never going to be together forever. He was good to me though. He was sweet, kind, and gentle. I never asked for more than he could give me." Helena flashed a small smile.

Killian looked between the two of us before he leaned against the wall, then slid down onto the floor. "I'm none of those things," he muttered. "Is that what you're saying?"

"No." I rushed to his side, sliding onto the carpet next to him. "Baby, you're perfect." I brought Killian's head to my chest as I shot daggers at my best friend.

He wrapped his arms around my waist. "Am I?" he asked softly.

I pinned my eyes on Helena. "Yes, always." Killian was still so fragile after this morning that I wasn't sure he could handle much more. Maybe I could talk to Lou about postponing a few tour dates. Get Killian some help, get him rested, and away from the road for a few days. Maybe weeks. It might kill him if he kept this up.

"Killian, I didn't mean to upset you," Helena assured him. "You were different back then." She was just going to keep digging a bigger hole for herself if I didn't step in to help.

I pressed a hand against the back of my boyfriend's head. "What Helena means"—I shook my head as I felt Killian's fingers dig into my shirt—"is that you were unsure about your sexuality." I raised my brows at her, and she nodded. "You didn't know what you were feeling. We were young, and you didn't understand what it meant to like me the way you did. You didn't realize you were bisexual." I watched Helena's eyes widen at my words.

"I am." He nodded into my chest. "But"—Killian struggled against me before he finally turned to look at his sister—"just for Matthias. He does it for me. I don't look at Dean or Mav and think that I'd like to suck their cocks." He suddenly snorted with laughter. "God, could you even imagine how awkward that would be?" He leaned his back against me. "I'm so glad you're here, babe," he murmured, raising his face to look up at me.

"Me too," I assured him.

Helena stood up. "I'll go. Let you two have some alone time." She gave a half smile.

"No, stay." Killian reached his hand out. "Please, Helena, for me. I've missed you." He sounded sad again. I hated this version of Killian—so unsure of himself.

She nodded. "Only if you want me to. It would be nice to spend some time with you." Helena could feel it too: The string that was holding Killian together.

"Please." Killian held his hand out to his sister. "The three of us together again," he said.

Chapter Twenty-Two

Killian
Four Years Ago

I avoided Matthias like the plague after our first night together. I wasn't mad at him; I was mad at myself, but instead I took it out on him. I made sure to come home late when I knew he would be asleep, if I came home at all. I ignored the texts he sent me and took girl after girl with me to the parties I went to with my friends.

I was a complete asshole.

"Wait, do you still live here?" Helena asked one morning when I was sneaking in. I had spent the night at Dean's after I felt uncomfortable driving home. I'd had one too many drinks and decided to crash on his floor, which I now deeply regretted. My neck, back, and head all felt like someone was standing behind me with a jackhammer.

I wrinkled my nose as I gave her the finger. "Very funny." I sank into one of the chairs just as Gram walked into the kitchen.

"Good morning, Killian." She nodded at me. "I was beginning to think you forgot where you lived." She started digging through the fridge, placing food on the counter as she found it. I knew that meant she was going to start making breakfast, and that I should go to my room before Matthias showed up.

Too late. I felt hazel eyes digging into me the moment I started to climb from the chair. When I met his gaze, his eyes flashed with anger, hurt, and sadness. Shit, I really was an asshole. "I can't stay," I heard myself say. "I need to get back to Dean's. We're working on a new song." That was a lie, but no one knew that but me.

"Sit." Gram put a hand on my shoulder pushing me back down. "I haven't seen you in a week. You're going to eat breakfast with us." She moved to the stove with a frying pan in her hand. "Matthias, you too, sweetie. You've been a little MIA lately as well." Which meant he was trying to avoid me as much as I was avoiding him. My hands curled into fists. Where had he been staying if he wasn't here? Was he seeing someone?

I watched Matthias sink into the chair across from me as lust suddenly consumed me. The endless girls did nothing to quench my thirst. Their messy kisses, their teeth smashed against mine as they tried to get into my pants; they weren't the ones I wanted. No, the one I wanted was sitting not even a foot away from me, his eyes glued to the table keeping us apart. I smirked to myself as I raised my leg and nudged his thigh with my foot, watching as Matthias's head suddenly shot up. I raised my brows at him, but he only shook his head and shoved my foot away.

"Excuse me." Matthias jumped to his feet. "I should..." He sounded nervous. "Let me help set the table," I heard him mutter.

Gram flashed him a smile as she mixed together the pancake mix. "That would be wonderful, Matthias. Thank you," she commented.

I watched as Matthias moved over to the cabinets before I scraped back the chair to get up. I pressed my chest against his back, my body flush against his. "You're such a good boy,

Matthias." My tongue flicked his skin before I pushed past him, moving out onto the porch to light a cigarette.

My hand shook as I brought it up to my lips to take a drag, inhaling the smoke deep into my lungs and then letting it out slowly. This was fucked up. I had to get myself together before I completely lost my mind, only I wasn't sure how to do that. I heard the sound of the glass door sliding open, and I figured it was Helena.

"How long are you planning on avoiding coming home? Avoiding me?"

I spun around to stare at Matthias, expecting him to drop his eyes or shrink away. When he didn't, I simply shrugged. "Depends on how long you plan on thinking that we're a thing." I watched the way his shoulders slumped forward. "Look, I don't want to hurt your feelings. What we did was fun, but it's not going to happen—what the hell!" I stumbled back as Matthias swung his fist at me. Shock and pain ripped through my jaw when he not only hit me but lunged forward to do it again.

"Fuck you," he growled. "I despise you." His eyes blazed with hate as I shoved him away.

I couldn't stop the smirk that tugged at my lips. "Liar," I whispered, before I slammed Matthias up against the house. "You want to hate me, babe, but right in here"—I tapped his chest, right over his heart—"you know that's never going to happen." I dragged my nose over his, down his cheek, and then caged him in. "You've wanted me for years. My lips on yours, my cock in your mouth, yours in mine, and you're never going to be able to think about anyone else but me because I was your first." I watched the way Matthias's eyes grew hooded before they darkened with need.

"But not you?"

"But not me what?"

Matthias took a shaky breath before his hands came up to grip my hair, his fingers digging into my curls. "You don't feel that way about me?" he whispered.

"It was a lot of fun for me, but that's all it was." I was surprised at how easily the lie slid from my tongue. I leaned forward so I could brush my lips against his. "Go back inside, Matthias." I took a step back before I turned my back to him. The sound of the glass door sliding shut told me he was gone, and I didn't go back inside until I knew breakfast was over. I didn't speak to him again for another two weeks.

***

I was supposed to be at Dean's practicing right now, but the second the sky opened up and the rain started, I couldn't seem to start my car. I sat there with my hands on the wheel, willing myself to turn in the key in the ignition, but it was no use. Until the rain stopped, I wasn't going to be able to go anywhere except where I was: Trapped inside this tin can like an animal.

"Idiot." I smacked myself in the forehead with the palm of my hand. "God, you're such a damn pussy. It's just rain, Killian," I told myself as tears stung my eyes. "Idiot, fucking idiot." I slammed my hand back down against the steering wheel. I jumped as the passenger door opened and Matthias slipped inside. "Get out," I hissed, but he didn't move. "Are you fucking deaf, asshole? I said get out. And don't touch me." I slapped at his hands when he tried to reach for me, but the second he made contact, relief flooded my senses, and I couldn't stop the sob that escaped my throat. I shoved the seat back so I could yank Matthias against me, and wrapped my arms around him so tightly I was surprised that he could breathe.

He didn't fight me, even though I imagined it must be incredibly uncomfortable. "How long have you been sitting out here, Killian?" Matthias asked calmly as he combed his hands through my hair. "Can't be too long since it just started." He tipped my head up so I had to look at him.

He was straddling me, his legs on either side of my waist. As I searched his hazel eyes, I felt guilt hang heavy on me. "A few minutes." I loved the feeling of Matthias's hands in my hair. "Why are you doing this?" I whispered.

"You know the answer to that," he teased.

"Tell me anyway." I wanted to hear Matthias tell me how he felt. They were the words I could never tell him but yearned to say.

Matthias dragged his thumb over my bottom lip. "Maybe another time, Kill." He started to climb off my lap, but I stopped him.

"Stay."

"Why?"

I gave him a lazy smile. "You know the answer to that." I chuckled, only to have Matthias's eyes grow heavy with sadness. "I'm sorry." I blurted out before I could lose my nerve. "For what I said, and for avoiding you and for...being such a prick." I pressed my face into his neck. "Matthias," I gasped. "I don't know how to do this," I confessed.

"Do what, Killian?" His hands were back in my hair as thunder crashed overhead, and I hugged him closer. "Because all I know is that you're pretty good at pushing me away."

I dragged my eyes back up to his face. "If I don't push you away, will you stay? Will you give me another chance?" I saw the hope in Matthias's eyes; the way the hazel darkened to green as he tried to fight what he wanted. "Say yes, babe." I needed him. It scared me how much. "It still has to be on the downlow."

"Forget it." Matthias once again tried to untangle himself from me. When thunder ripped through the sky, though, he must have felt me tremble beneath him because he sat back so that he could watch me with narrowed eyes. "What are you so afraid of? Huh, Killian? That your loser friends won't want to hang around with you anymore because you're with a guy?" He tilted his head.

"Or maybe it's because it's me. You're afraid of what they'll say because you like being me with me?" He shook his head.

"I'm afraid of losing you for good."

Matthias stared at me for so long I wasn't sure I had spoken the words aloud until his lips crashed down on mine, his hands tangling in my hair. "You can't," he groaned as our tongues fought together. "You can't just go saying shit you know I want to hear so I won't leave." His hips moved against mine, and when I slid my hand up the back of his shirt and down the back of his jeans to grab a handful of his ass, he moaned softly.

"It's the truth, babe," I promised. "Can't lose you when you make me feel like this."

Matthias's hands yanked hard on my hair. I loved how obsessed with it he was; how he wasn't afraid to take control when I needed him to. "Tell me how I make you feel." He ran his tongue over my lips.

"Safe. Normal. Alive. Loved. Happy." I felt Matthias smile against my mouth as our kisses grew wilder. "It's never felt like that with anyone before."

Matthias bit down so hard on my bottom lip that I tasted my own blood, but it sent lust straight to my cock. He knew exactly what I liked. "Don't touch anyone else," he whispered. "If you want to hide this, you don't kiss anyone. Fuck anyone. Look at anyone else. And if you dare bring someone else to the theater again, I will personally make your life a living hell." His hand suddenly reached down the front of my jeans to find my raging hard on.

"Fuck." I groaned as he began to jerk me off.

"Say it," he hissed into my ear.

I nodded my head as Matthias tightened his grip on my length. "No one else. Just you. Just you and me. I promise." I could already feel myself spiraling toward release. "Kiss me." I opened my eyes as his lips found mine again.

Matthias sucked hard on my bottom lip. "Tastes like copper," he teased before he sank his tongue inside my mouth. "Fuck, I love making you come," he whispered before I exploded in his hand and inside my jeans. He brought his hand up to suck the cum from his fingers, and I'd be a liar if I said it wasn't the hottest thing I had ever seen.

"Promise me," I said softly as I reached up to grip his jaw. "You won't touch anyone else." The thought made me sick to my stomach.

Matthias chuckled. "You already know the answer to that."

Chapter Twenty-Three

Killian

I was going to commit murder tonight. The longer I stared at Dean holding Helena's hand, the more I wanted to strangle him. No, that was too good for him. I would slit him from throat to belly and then disembowel him right in front of my sister. That felt more like my style. I didn't care that we had known one another since we were in kindergarten, or that he had been the one to take me to the hospital when I'd cut myself so deep I nearly bled to death. That was my little sister. When I'd said I wanted to spend time with Helena, this was not what I meant.

"Look, man." Dean dragged a hand through his emerald hair. "It's not like we planned this." He glanced at my sister for help, and I gritted my teeth so hard I thought they might snap. "Don't look at me like that. We've been friends for years."

I felt my lip curl up over my teeth. "Yet here we are, having this conversation." I reached for the water before me, wishing it was something stronger, but I had promised my boyfriend I would try to lay off the booze and the drugs for a while. We were supposed to have dinner at the hotel's restaurant, but it was the furthest thing from my mind now.

"Kill." Helena sighed.

My eyes shot over to my sister. "Don't you start with me right now. I'm the last one to find out about this," I reminded her.

"Easy." Matthias's voice was soft in my ear, and I instantly relaxed. "Remember what we talked about." He squeezed my hand, the one that was wrapped so tightly around his I was surprised I hadn't cut off the circulation. He had made me promise to hear them out instead of jumping all over them. Waiting was something I wasn't used to doing.

I brought my chin to my chest, taking a deep breath. "You two, uh, in love?" I muttered before I glanced at Dean. Images of him with groupies flashed through my head, and I knew he could read my mind. He wasn't as bad as Blake, but he'd had his share. None of us were angels when it came to the girls that we had on tour, but if he said he loved my sister, he wouldn't be partaking in that shit anymore.

"It's not like that." Helena surprised me. "Things were different when we were younger, but now it's just sort of a friends-with-benefits thing." She gave me a smile. "Not like you and Matty." She leaned against Dean. "We like each other, enjoy one another's company, but I don't think we're going to get married and settle down together." Helena glanced up when Dean looked down at her.

I grunted. "How do you feel?" I needed to hear it from Dean's mouth.

"I like your sister," he told me, and I felt Matthias's thumb drawing circles over my palm. How did he know just the right way to calm me? "If she hadn't miscarried, if we were going to be parents, I would have married her." He also would have had to deal with me breaking his neck. "But we aren't meant for a happily ever after, bro." Dean leaned forward. "And listen, I'm sorry we didn't tell you sooner."

This time, I felt Matthias grow tense next to me. "You probably wouldn't be breathing if you had." I watched the way his eyes widened. "But it's alright." I couldn't stay mad forever. All that anger was going to push me into an early grave, and I trusted Dean; Maverick and Blake were another story.

"Really?" Helena sounded surprised. "You don't want to hit him?" she asked.

I shrugged. "Give it time. I could change my mind." I snorted, and then wrapped my arm around Matthias's shoulders. "This guy might have something to do with it. He calms me."

"I noticed. He's good for you," Dean commented. "I knew you were a good guy, Fuller. You should come around more often." He smiled.

I pressed a kiss against Matthias's cheek. "I'm hoping he never leaves," I teased, but it wasn't a lie. I was going to ask him to stay with me until the end of the tour, and maybe even come back to California with me afterward, if he wanted. If not, I would be going back to Canfield instead. I couldn't imagine not having him in my life again. Matthias was the eye of my storm.

"You couldn't get rid of me if you tried, Kill." Matthias gave me a shy smile, but before he looked away, I saw it. The confusion and concern in his face.

I leaned in closer. "We'll talk about it," I murmured so he could hear me. "Okay?" I squeezed his arm as I wrapped my arms around the muscle. When he nodded, I felt nothing but relief flood my senses. I couldn't see myself doing the rest of this tour without Matthias.

I wouldn't do it without him.

***

"So, this idiot"—I slammed my hand against the table as I roared with laughter—"strips off all his clothes, runs through the hotel naked, and does a belly flop into the pool." I announced as Helena threw her head back, laughing.

Dean shook his head. "Oh, but don't forget who joined me two seconds later." He pointed his fork at me.

"Me?" I tried to act innocent as Matthias chuckled next to me. "Right, well, what can I say? I don't like someone trying to show me up."

Dean snorted. "Showing you up? You not only jumped into the pool behind me, but you also dared the other two guys to do it too. Which they refused to do," he reminded me.

"Not my fault their dicks are smaller than ours." The table went silent. "What?" I popped a piece of pasta into my mouth. "Oh, because I'm with a guy now, I'm not allowed to make jokes about that? Stop, I've never even looked at your cock, dude. Fucking relax." Christ, was this how it was going to be now? I couldn't make jokes about guys and dicks anymore?

Dean's entire face had gone pale. "I didn't...I wasn't...shit, I'm sorry." He dropped his gaze to his half-eaten plate of food.

"You're the one making it weird," Matthias spoke up, and pride swelled in my chest. "Killian likes me. Did you even suspect he was into guys before?" He raised his brows when

Dean shook his head. "He's still the same Kill he was before. Just dating me now." He nudged my arm with his elbow. "Still a giant pain in everyone's ass." He smirked.

I turned to stare at Matthias, only to hear my sister and Dean start laughing. "That so, babe?" I reached over to turn his head toward me.

"You know I love you," he confessed.

"Not as much as I love you," I whispered.

Matthias's eyes grew dark. "Bet," he answered back.

"Okay, okay, before you two start doing it on the table," Dean interrupted, "Kiss and get it over with."

I gladly slid my lips against Matthias's soft, plump ones, and when he grabbed the back of my head, I couldn't remember a time I felt this happy. I knew I had fucked up again: Pushing him away again, drinking and doing drugs, cutting myself when I knew I shouldn't...but he was still here. Matthias still wanted me with all my crazy, fucked-up ways, and I would do everything possible to keep him here.

"They look so cute, don't they?" Helena teased, and I couldn't help but throw my napkin at her when I pulled back. "I always hoped they would find their way back to one another." She winked at me when she tossed the napkin back.

Dean took a sip of his beer. "I thought something weird was going on the night I found the two of you in the treehouse, but then I figured it was just me. I had no idea you two were fooling around." Well, that was a big fat lie, but I was thankful he didn't say anything else.

"I always wanted him," Matthias blurted out, and I watched as embarrassment crept up his neck. "I mean, I crushed pretty hard on him for years until that night." He glanced over at me. "He kissed me first."

I nodded. "I did." I wasn't scared to talk about it anymore. "Matthias was just...I don't know. I knew he liked me. I could feel him when he was watching me, and there was just something there I had never felt before." I reached for his hand so I could lace our fingers together. "All the songs are about Matthias."

"I figured that out already." Dean sat back in his chair. "Some of the things you wrote about. I was starting to put them together." He didn't look upset, which I guess was a good thing. He opened his mouth just as I realized what he was going to ask.

I shook my head. "Don't." I wasn't going there. That was something private; something I would regret doing until the day I died and would spend the rest of my life making it up to Matthias. I never should have agreed to the recording. Never should have let Maverick give out the recording, and right now I knew my cover was probably blown. When I looked over at Matthias, he had a horrified look on his face. I was going to hate myself forever for doing that to him.

His eyes locked with mine, and it was like the moment we had just shared seconds ago never happened. "I...I have to use the bathroom." He stood up and rushed from the restaurant so fast I didn't even have time to stop him.

"Thanks," I hissed at Dean. "You had to bring that up?" I hurried after Matthias and saw him disappear into the bathroom just as the door slammed shut behind him. "Babe," I called after him. I could see his feet in the one stall as he tried to hide from me, and I sighed softly. "You can't hide from me, Matthias." I chuckled softly as I moved to place my hands over the top of the door, wiggling it. "Did you hurt yourself? Should I break the door down to make sure you're okay?"

When the door opened I nearly fell in, but it was the fact that Matthias tried to shove past me that caught me by surprise. I pushed him back against the stall and pinned my body against his. "What the fuck?" he growled.

I stared down into his hazel eyes as they blazed with anger and lust, which only caused me to press myself further against him. I wanted him to feel every single inch of me against him. My muscles, my weight, and most of all, the raging hard-on I had for him right now. "You love me, babe." I raised my hand to cup the back of his head.

"Yes." I felt the goosebumps that broke out over Matthias's skin.

"You want me."

"Always."

I grabbed a handful of Matthias's hair, and the moan that escaped him was so deep that I crushed my mouth over his. "I want to fuck you so bad," I whispered. "Right here, right now, where anyone could walk in and find us." I nipped at his bottom lip before I moved so that my cheek was flushed against his. "Remember what that felt like? My cock buried inside your ass?" My lip brushed Matthias's ear.

"Oh God," he whimpered.

I chuckled, wrapping my hand around his throat. "I'll take that as a yes. Stop running away from me or I'll never do it again," I promised. I pulled back to look Matthias in the eye. "Understand?" I cocked a brow.

"Yes." Matthias nodded. He started to bring his hand up to touch me, but I slapped it away. Hurt flashed over his face. "Killian—"

The sound of the bathroom door opening caused us both to turn our heads.

"Are you two alright?" It was Dean.

My lips turned up into a smile. "Behave," I mouthed at Matthias before I released him. "We're good. Just making up. Let's go finish our meal." I walked out of the stall without looking back at my boyfriend. I knew he would follow me. He always did.

Chapter Twenty-Four

Matthias
Four Years Ago

I woke up with Killian wrapped around me, as if he was afraid I was going to disappear. After what had happened in his car, when I found Killian frozen in his car because of the store, and when the rain stopped, he'd asked if he could come sleep in my room with me. It was almost as if he'd been afraid I would tell him no. He didn't say much as we'd walked there, but instead stripped down to his briefs and climbed into my bed, pulling the covers up to his chin.

"Can I hold you?" he'd asked softly, reaching his hand out toward me. I liked this version of Killian, and had hoped he wouldn't disappear in the morning.

I'd smiled as I'd started to sit down. "Yes," I'd told him before sliding under the blankets with him. His arms had instantly been around me.

"You smell good," Killian had commented as he pressed his face into my neck. "Your skin, your hair, everything about you smells like coming home." His lips had brushed my skin, and I knew he'd felt my length as I'd grown hard against his thigh. "You ever"—Killian had pulled back to look at me with hooded eyes, and his thumbs had caressed my jawline with a gentleness I wasn't aware he was capable of—"think about what it would be like if we had sex?" He'd dropped his gaze to my lips.

My mouth had dropped open. "Killian," I'd whispered.

"I didn't mean now... I just... I don't know, maybe not. Forget I said anything."

"I think about that all the time."

His eyes had shot back up to mine. "Yeah?" Killian swallowed, and I'd watched the way his Adam's apple moved against his throat.

"You want to be my first, is that it?" I'd moved my hand up to comb it through his chestnut hair, and watched the way his curls had moved under my fingers.

Killian's eyes had slowly closed. "I want all of your firsts, babe," he'd murmured.

I'd smiled as he'd started to drift to sleep. I knew I would give him that, too. It didn't matter that he had ghosted me after our date or that he'd tried to push me away, I would always come back. I loved him. It was as simple as that.

"Promise me." Killian's sleepy voice had drifted through my thoughts. "Matthias, promise me you'll never give up on me," he'd whispered.

My stomach had clenched at his words. "I promise," I'd told him.

"Watching me sleep?" He gave me a lazy smile that had my heart thumping in my chest. Those dimples would be my undoing. "That's not creepy." He chuckled softly before untangling himself from me to roll onto his back. "I think your bed is much more comfortable than mine. I might need to start sleeping here full-time." When I didn't answer, Killian's blues swung back over to me. "You okay?" He leaned up onto his forearms.

I nodded. "Fine." *Just waiting for you to freak out; scream and yell about how you didn't want anyone to find out about us before you slam the door and leave me feeling like your dirty little secret.* I didn't say that part to him though.

"Right." Killian moved onto his side. "Talk to me," he urged, but instead I climbed from the bed. "Matthias." He sounded scared.

I shook my head. "No, it's nothing. I'm fine. I have to shower so I'm not late to school," I said again, yanking on a pair of sweatpants and then a shirt.

"Your body language tells me something completely different, so please don't lie to me. I'm not as stupid as everyone thinks I am."

I spun around to find Killian sitting up and watching me, his blue eyes wide with fear. "Who said you were stupid?" I demanded.

"Why won't you tell me what's going on in that pretty brain of yours, huh? What are you not telling me?" Killian climbed up onto his knees.

I stared up at the ceiling. "I'm waiting for you to freak out," I admitted before I dragged my gaze back to him.

"Waiting for me...shit." Killian fisted his hair before he jumped from the bed. "Babe, no." He started toward me.

I moved away from him. "You can't just touch me and fix that, Kill. You've yanked me around for the past month, and you think that's just going to go away?" I asked. "I get that you're scared, I understand, but you can't just use me when you want to get off. You can't make me feel like shit when it suits you. I'm a human with feelings—who cares for you—and if you walk out the door again, I don't think I can survive." I watched the smile that spread over his face showing me his dimples. "What?" I asked.

"You like me," Killian teased.

"Fuck off." I slapped at his hand when he tried to touch me, but when he shoved me back against the wall, I couldn't stop him from caging me in. "Don't, Killian. I'm serious," I warned.

He only continued to smile at me before he ran his tongue over his lips to wet them. "I'm sorry I upset you." His breath was hot on my face. "Sorry about my morning breath, too. I'm sure it's not that great," Killian chuckled. "I'm not leaving or freaking out on you though, am I?" He reached up to grip the back of my neck. "I'm still here. Still with you, and I promise I won't do that to you again. When we're together, we're together." Then his mouth was on mine, and I couldn't even worry about what his breath tasted like because Killian was kissing me like he needed me to survive.

"What you said last night—" I groaned as he grinded against me. "About being my first." I wanted that so badly, he had no idea.

Killian yanked hard on my bottom lip with his teeth. "Fucking you?" he growled. "That's going to happen, babe, you know that." He dropped a hand to cup my dick. "Soon," he murmured. "Come see the band this weekend." He pulled back to look at me.

"I don't think that's a good idea."

"Please?"

"You won't be making out with any girls?" I asked. "I'll never speak to you if you do that to me again. Like when you brought a date to the movie theater."

Killian chuckled softly. "No girls," he assured me.

***

I slammed my locker shut just as Helena came around the corner and slid her arm through mine. "Is it just me, or has today been the longest Friday in America?" she teased.

"I couldn't agree more." I had struggled through most of my classes this morning, trying not to fall asleep. Maybe having Killian with me last night wasn't the best idea but waking up next to him had been the highlight of my week.

"Are you listening to me?" Helena waved a hand in front of my face as we walked into the cafeteria.

I grimaced. "Sorry." I glanced around the crowded room.

"Spill," Helena hissed as we moved to sit at our regular table. "I know Kill was in your room last night." She started to pull her lunch from her bag. "Don't even try to deny it, Matty, because I saw him. What's going on with the two of you?" she asked.

I chewed nervously on my bottom lip. Killian hadn't told me not to say anything to Helena, but he had said we needed to keep whatever this was a secret. "I can't." I shook my head.

"You know about Dean."

"That's not fair."

Helena dropped her chin to stare at me. "Am I not your best friend?" Her eyes moved behind me, and when I turned around, I saw who she was looking at. Linda Williams was standing with her friends, her dark hair piled high on her head and wearing pants so tight they looked painted on.

"He invited me to come see the band play tomorrow night," Linda giggled to her friends. "I mean, we're not a couple or anything, but it's technically our second date after we went to the movies a few weeks ago."

I felt like I was going to be sick. Killian had said no girls, only here was Linda, talking about going to see Mulligan tomorrow night; the same show that he had invited me to come to.

"God, she's gross isn't she?" Helena hissed as she grabbed my wrist. "That girl is a first-class whore."

"He brought her to the movies when I was working," I answered.

Helena pressed her mouth together. "Why won't you tell me what's going on with the two of you? I can see the pain in your eyes right now." She squeezed my hand. "Matty, no," she gasped.

"No what, Helena?" I wasn't sure what she was talking about.

She once again glanced behind me at Linda. I was trying hard to pretend she didn't exist right now, but the giggles she and her friends kept unleashing were making it incredibly hard. Helena looked back at my face. "You're in love with him, aren't you?" she whispered, just as the banshees behind me exploded into yet another fit of laughter.

"I..." I could deny it, but Helena could see the truth. She knew me better than anyone, and what was the point of lying anymore? "I am." I sighed softly.

"Jesus, Matty, for how long?"

"I don't know. Years, I guess."

Helena stared at me with eyes that matched her brother's. "How does he feel?" she asked, finally releasing my hand so she could take a bite of her sandwich. "Is my brother gay?" She shouldn't be asking me that. It wasn't something I could answer.

"I don't know how Killian feels about me. And no, I don't think he swings that way," I answered truthfully.

"But you two..." Helena made a motion with her hand and mouth as if she were sucking a dick.

I snorted with laughter as I grabbed at her hand to bring it down to the table. "You're terrible," I chuckled. "We've done some things, which I won't discuss with you because he's your brother. Sex is not one of them, though." Yet. Killian's words from last night came back to me, the ones about him being my first. "He invited me to come to see him play tomorrow night, but I can't do it if she's going to be there, Hel. He promised me no girls. He already used that against me once, and I can't handle that again. It will break me."

"Then don't go."

"I want to go, though. I want to be there because he invited me."

Helena let out a long breath before she placed both her hands onto the table. "Come on." She wiggled her fingers at me. "Come on, Matty, I'm your bestie." She waited until I took her hands. "I love my brother, but I know him. He does not know how to be in a proper relationship, and he's going to hurt you. How many times has he already broken your heart?" Her brows dipped.

"Too many." I hated myself for telling Helena that.

Helena nodded. "How did I not see this was going on?" she asked.

"You've been busy keeping your own secrets," I reminded her. One that I was going to take to my grave, because Killian would freak the hell out if he knew. Dean was his best friend, and the guitar player in his band. If Kill found out he was dating his younger sister? It would not end well.

Helena squeezed my hands. "Don't go to the show. We'll stay home, have a movie night—which we haven't done in a long time—and you won't end up with a broken heart again. You know that's how it's going to end." She chewed on her lip.

"How could you say that about your own brother?" I yanked my hands away.

Helena jutted her chin at Linda. "Because of girls like that. Ones that he uses and tosses away. Just like he'll do to you, Matty, and I love you too much to see that happen." She met my eyes.

"I'm going." I stood up, but she didn't follow me.

"I won't pick up the pieces if he breaks your heart," she informed me.

I barked out a laugh. "You won't have to," I promised, but even I wasn't so sure.

Chapter Twenty-Five

Matthias

I didn't speak a word until we went back to our hotel room. I was furious at Killian for the way he'd treated me at dinner after Dean brought up the recording, and he should have left me alone. I was sick and tired of picking up his broken pieces. Why couldn't he do the same for me every now and then? Hold my hand while I cried, or comfort me when I had a bad dream instead of making me feel like it was my fault.

"I know you're mad," Killian commented as he kicked off his shoes.

I ignored him as I yanked the covers off the bed and climbed onto the mattress. Maybe he would get the hint if I didn't talk to him for a couple of days. Figure it out on his own if we didn't kiss or get one another off or—

"You think you're going to just not speak to me?" Killian suddenly landed on the bed next to me, like he'd taken a running start. "Is that it?" He grabbed at the blanket in my hand. "Don't be like that."

I rolled my eyes and tried to shove him away, but Killian held on tight. "Leave me alone," I growled.

"Ah, he speaks." He grinned before he moved to climb onto my waist and straddle me. "Remember what I said before?" Killian asked.

"Go away." I planted both hands against his chest and pushed.

Killian stared down at me. "Shit, you're really pissed at me." He dragged his hand over his hair. "I'm sorry, babe," he cooed. "You don't want to fool around?" His blue eyes landed on my mouth, and I turned my face away before he could kiss me. "Don't do this to me." Killian grabbed my head to force me to look at him.

"I told you to leave me alone."

"I don't care what you told me."

I tried to wiggle out from beneath him. "Get off me, Kill, I'm serious. I don't want this, or you, right now." The pain that flashed through his blues made my heart sink.

"Fine," Killian seethed, "I'll go find someone who does." The second he got to his feet, he started toward where he'd left his shoes and began to slip them back on.

I jumped from the bed. "You wouldn't," I exclaimed.

"I would."

"I hate you."

Killian stopped to stare at me with wide eyes. "I'm starting to believe you actually might, babe, and it scares me more than you know," he whispered. "Honestly, you have every right to feel that way, because I'm a horrible person. I'm no good for you. You should go home and find a good man to love you the way you deserve. One who isn't fucked up on the inside like I am." He turned back to move to the door.

"Wait." Tears began to burn my eyes. "Don't leave, I didn't mean that. I love you. Please, Killian, you know that." If he left me in this room, I would never forgive him. Ever. For a split second, I thought I had him when he stopped, until he opened the door and it slammed shut behind him.

I dropped to my knees as a sob escaped my throat, and I let out a scream so loud I was sure the entire hotel heard it.

I fisted my hair with both hands and pulled on it so hard I felt like I might pull it out completely. This wasn't my fault. I didn't do anything wrong, but as I struggled to catch my breath, I knew I had no one to blame for letting Killian back into my life but myself.

"Fuck!" I cried out as a fresh set of tears hit me. He was going to be the death of me. How could I love someone that continued to bully and hurt me so much? I had to get out of here; I had to get away before it was too late. I yanked the door open, only to find Killian standing there. "What...I thought you were leaving?"

He slammed into me with all his weight, and I struggled not to fall as we tumbled back into the room. "You think I would do that to you." It wasn't a question. "That's my fault. I made you think that." Killian's mouth found mine. "I love you, Matthias. I love you more than myself, and I'm so fucking sorry for hurting you." His teeth dragged over my lips. "I want you to hurt me back. Hit me, punch me, slap me, I don't care. I'll take whatever you throw my way because I deserve it. I'm the worst."

"Killian." I cupped his head with my hands. "No, I won't do that," I told him. I flinched when his own hand came up and he slapped himself across the face. "Don't you fucking dare." I grabbed his hand. "Don't do that," I hissed before I kissed him again. "Don't you ever hurt yourself again, do you understand me?"

Tears slipped down Killian's cheeks. "I hate myself. I can understand why you hate me." He tucked his face in against my neck.

"I don't hate you, baby."

"You should."

I wrapped my arms around him. "Let's sit down, okay?"

Killian nodded and moved with me when I started to walk back to the bed. He sat down on the bed and dropped his gaze to his feet. "I'm sorry," he mumbled. "As usual, I ruined everything."

I stood before him. "Hey." I tucked a finger under his chin so he had to look at me. "The night isn't over." I pressed a kiss to his forehead. "Lift up your arms." When Killian did as I asked, I removed his shirt, and when I asked him to stand up, he did that too. I slipped his pants down to his ankles and he sat back down again so I could remove them. "Lie down, alright?" I instructed. I removed all of my clothes before I turned off the lights, and found him curled into a fetal position under the covers when I returned to the bed.

"Matthias." Killian's hand found mine in the dark. "I'm sorry." His voice sounded pained. "I never...I don't know what I'm doing." He moved closer to me. "Don't leave me. *Please* don't leave me." I heard the sounds of his shaky breathing, and I knew he was crying again. "I want...can I hold you?"

"You have to stop doing this."

Killian choked back a sob, and I folded him against me. "I'll stop," he promised as he held onto me. "My brain doesn't work right." He rested his chin against my chest. "I'm going to talk to Lou tomorrow. I think I should take a break from the tour to get some rest, and maybe do the therapy thing we talked about." Killian pressed himself closer to my body. "Will you go with me?"

"To therapy?" I was surprised he would ask me.

His lips brushed my skin. "I don't think I can go alone, Matthias, and you're the best person in my life. I need you there," Killian told me, and my heart leaped into my throat. My poor, broken baby.

"Of course,," I assured him as I slowly combed my fingers through his hair.

"I love when you do that."

"I know you do."

"I love you, Matthias. You know that, right?"

I know, but you keep breaking my heart, and I'm not sure I can keep putting it back together. "Yes, Kill, I know." I pressed a kiss to his head.

"You love me, too, right?" Killian pulled away to stare at me in the dark.

I reached up to run the tips of my fingers against his face. "Always. You're my ride or die," I reminded him.

Killian moved to press his lips over mine, and I rolled onto my back. "This is okay?" he asked as his hands clung to my shoulders. "We don't have to do anything if you don't want to."

"Touch me," I whispered.

Killian moaned softly as I slipped my hand down between us to find him hard and ready, wishing I had removed his briefs with the rest of his clothes. "I love you," he told me again as I stroked him through his underwear. "It's always been you, Matthias." His tongue slicked together with mine causing heat to streak through me.

I yanked down the briefs he had on with one hand so I could get better access. His cock strained toward me as I pushed him onto his side and moved to wrap my mouth around him. Killian's hands found my hair as my tongue glided over his shaft before I swallowed him whole, his hips bucking forward.

"That's it, babe," Killian urged me on. "So good at sucking me." I saw the whites of his eyes when I glanced up as he watched me. "You my good boy, aren't you?" he purred as I bobbed up and down. "Suck my cock. Make me come like only you can, Matthias." He groaned.

Fuck, his dirty talk was going to be my undoing. I groaned as Killian yanked my head down, and I wished he was getting me off, too. My cock was so hard it hurt right now. I reached down to cup his balls with my hand, and that's when he exploded in my mouth. Thundering into me like a storm, Killian cried out in pleasure as I swallowed everything he had to give me, his orgasm making me even harder than before. When I was sure he was done, I pulled off him, only to have Killian shove me down onto my back and spread my legs with his thigh.

"I'm so fucking you tonight," he growled as he kissed me hard. "I need to be inside of you." His hand dropped down to wrap around my dick. "Fuck, you must be so ready to come." Killian kissed his way down my jaw, my neck, and over my collarbone, before he suddenly stopped. "You want that, right?" he asked. "Because if you don't, I can just suck you off." He sounded nervous.

"Please fuck me."

Killian growled. "God, I love it when you say that." He jumped up from the bed. "I need to get the lube," he told me as he moved toward his suitcase, which was over by the bathroom door. "Babe?" He stopped to watch me over his shoulder.

I felt every nerve in my body begin to tingle with anticipation. "Yeah?" I whispered.

"I love you."

I would never not want to hear those words from Killian. All those years, I had waited for him. Wanted him to say it, and now, when he needed me most, I would always be here for him. "I love you too," I answered back.

"Spread your legs for me." I could see that Killian had the lube in his hand from the faint light of the moon. "It's been a while," he teased, as the sound of the cap being popped off filled the room. "I'm nervous," he admitted to me, and that made me feel closer to him.

I chuckled. "Me, too," I told him. "It's different than having a toy up there." I hissed with pleasure as his finger rolled over my backside and pressed inside lightly.

"Does it hurt?" Killian asked.

"No, feels good," I assured him as he inched it in slowly. "Really good." I closed my eyes.

Killian's hand wrapped around my dick. "Can't help myself," he teased as he began to stroke me. "Just want to make you feel good, all the time, every single day. You deserve that, Matthias. For all the bullshit I've put you through." I whimpered as he eased another finger in.

"Kill," I murmured. "Do you want me to come? Because this is going to make me come—oh fuck, too late." Hot, sticky seed blew out from my cock as Killian continued to stroke me and finger me at the same time. I tried to catch my breath as he dipped down to lick it from the head of my cock and his fingers.

"Not done with you," he promised. "Still going to have my way with you." Killian slid his fingers out and then spread more lube around his shaft. "Ready for me, babe?"

My cock was already hard again. "Ready," I told him.

"Get on all fours," he growled.

Chapter Twenty-Six

Killian

Four Years Ago

Matthias had blown me off tonight. After promising me this morning in bed that he would be here tonight, he never fucking showed up. Was this his way of getting back at me for hurting him? Knowing he didn't come didn't stop me from looking for him the entire show, searching the crowd for those hazel eyes that made my heart burn and my soul come alive. Where was he? Matthias was a man of his word, I knew that.

It threw my entire night off. My voice sounded terrible, I missed every single cue despite having them in my ear, and it was most likely the worst show we had put on since we started. Something was wrong, I could feel it in my bones. The second I stepped offstage, I had every intention of getting to my phone to check it. Dean, Maverick, and Blake called out to me, but I ignored them, only to come face to face with Linda and some of her friends.

"You sounded amazing tonight." She beamed up at me as my eyes took in her makeup-covered face and the dress she wore that covered her body like a second skin. "We really enjoyed the show." She motioned to her friends, who giggled nervously.

Instantly, something changed in me. If Matthias didn't want to spend time with me, fine. Here was someone who clearly did by the way she was staring at me with those big, brown eyes and "fuck me" written all over her face. I didn't bother to stop Linda as she slipped her hands up my chest and hooked them behind my neck. "Thanks, baby." I gave her a half smile. My dick didn't even respond because if I was being honest, this wasn't who I wanted. That didn't stop me from brushing my lips over Linda's, though.

"What in the actual fuck?" Helena's voice interrupted my thoughts. She glared at me with nothing but disappointment written all over her face.

I pulled Linda closer. "Nice of you to show up." I tried to ignore the fact that she was alone. "Weren't you supposed to be here earlier?" *With your best friend, the boy who has my heart.* Wait, no, that wasn't right.

"Yeah, so, there was an accident—"

I shoved Linda away. "What?" I heard the squeal Linda let out as she nearly hit the floor while she stumbled from my arms.

"If you had maybe checked your phone"—Helena's chin trembled—"you would have seen that I tried to reach you, more than once. All of you." She waved at my bandmates, who had moved closer.

I dragged my hand through my hair. "I was busy, Helena. What the hell happened?" I demanded.

Helena's eyes darted between where Linda had climbed back to her feet and then to me. "I don't know the details, just that Matty made a stop before he came to get me. Someone t-boned his car, and—where are you going?"

"To the hospital," I called over my shoulder, before I realized what I was doing. I came to a halt. "Actually, that could wait until tomorrow," I corrected, as if I didn't care. Because I shouldn't care. Matthias was her best friend, not mine, and if people realized I cared about him? That would look really bad. "Come with me." I grabbed my sister to pull her into the small dressing room the club had given the band, slamming the door behind us. "Spill it."

"He has a few cuts and bruises, and a sprained wrist, but he'll be okay. They wouldn't let me in because I'm not family and visiting hours are over. Gram is working tonight, though, so she's keeping an eye on him. He should be able to come home tomorrow."

"Big deal."

Helena's hand shot out to slap me, but I caught her wrist before she was able to make contact. "Don't act like that." She shook her head. "I know, Killian, so don't start acting like you don't care about him."

"You know *what* exactly?" I narrowed my eyes. "He told you?"

Helena nodded. "You're going to break his heart, and you don't even realize it. You asked him to come to this show tonight, so why were you with Linda?" When I didn't answer, Helena threw up her hands in exasperation. "Damn it, Killian, what is wrong with you? Matthias cares about you. Do you even care about him at all?" Her eyes flashed with anger.

"Yes." I did. More than I wanted to admit. I might even love him, if I was capable of feeling that emotion.

She let out a long sigh. "Then stop this. Whatever it is you're doing with him, stop it before you ruin him forever," she begged, only to grab onto my arm. "Oh, no." Helena gasped.

"What?" I asked. I swiped at my face. Was there leftover powder on my nose from the bump I did earlier?

Helena's lips curved up into a smile. "You're in love with him, too, aren't you?" she whispered.

"Whatever." I rolled my eyes. "Did Matthias tell you that he is in love with me?" My stomach suddenly felt funny at the thought of him admitting that.

Helena rested her hand on the handle of the door. "You'll need to ask him that yourself, because it's not for me to say." She pulled the door open. "I'm going back to the hospital so I can be there when he wakes up."

"I'm coming with you." I caught the smirk she threw me over her shoulder. "Shut it," I warned.

***

I stood in the doorway of the hospital room watching Matthias as he slept, wishing I could just disappear. This was sort of my fault, right? I mean, if I hadn't invited him to the stupid show in the first place, he wouldn't have gone out and then he wouldn't be in this mess. He looked pretty banged up from what I could see. A few deep cuts across his face, a bandage wrapped around his left wrist—nope, I couldn't do this. I started to back out of the room.

"Do you plan on coming into the room?" Matthias turned his head to look at me. His hazel eyes looked tired, or maybe it was the drugs they had him on. "You know that you can come closer, right?" He raised his right hand toward me.

My feet felt glued to the floor as everything began to hit me at once. It reminded me too much of when my parents died. The beeping of the heart rate monitor, the IV tube hooked up to his arm and the clear medication dripping from the bag. The scent of the over-bleached sheets and blankets.

"Killian?" His slurred voice drifted through my nightmarish thoughts. "How was the show last night?" Matthias had dropped his hand back onto the bed.

I swallowed down the bile in my throat. "Horrible," I admitted. *One step*, I told myself. *That's all you have to do to get closer to him. It's Matthias. You like him, and he makes you feel better. He calms the demons in your head.* I was surprised when my feet did as I told them.

He looked surprised too, because his hazel eyes went wide as I suddenly got close to the bed. "Why was it horrible? What happened?" Matthias kept his eyes pinned on me as I started to pull the blanket back to climb into the bed with him.

"You weren't there." I wrapped my arms around him, careful not to touch his IV or sprained wrist. "I thought..." I pressed my face into his shoulder and his scent was like coming home, despite the hospital gown that draped off his frame.

Matthias's hand found its way into my curls. "You thought what?" he whispered.

"I thought you changed your mind." I raised my head to meet his gaze and saw what Helena meant; the love that shined back at me was overwhelming. "Babe." I slid my mouth over his without hesitation. "This is all my fault."

"How exactly?"

"You were going to pick up Helena to come to my show."

Matthias yanked hard on my hair, and my cock went hard as steel. "That doesn't make it your fault, Killian. I've come to your shows before. Stop trying to carry everything on your shoulders," he reminded me.

"This time I wanted you there." I didn't care anymore. I wanted Matthias to know. "I kept looking for you, I kept thinking I saw your face in the crowd, but you weren't there. I thought maybe you'd changed your mind; that I wasn't the one you wanted anymore, and I—" I had to tell him the truth, but the words wouldn't form on my lips.

Matthias's smile suddenly fell. "Linda was there." I felt his body tremble. "You promised me." He released my hair as he realized what I was trying to tell him.

"I didn't...I didn't sleep with her, I just..."

"But you would have."

I nodded in admittance. "I would have." I gripped him closer. "Babe, please don't push me away. I'm an asshole, okay? I was wrong, and I know I shouldn't have done that. I don't know what else to say." I hated the way Matthias was looking at me right now. "I'm here, aren't I? In the bed with you, and I want *you*. You're the one I want to be with. I waited all night for you." Tears stung my eyes.

"You can go now, Killian." Matthias rolled onto his back. "Go back to Linda. I can't do this with you anymore. This constant push and pull is too much for me," he muttered.

I stared at him as he closed his eyes and brought the non-sprained wrist up to his forehead. "Babe, please," I heard myself say.

"Please, what?" His eyes flew open, hot and angry. "Just because you say this to me today doesn't mean you won't have some girl sitting on your lap tomorrow. We already talked about this," he snarled. "I told you to go, and I meant it."

"Good morning." We both turned to look at the nurse who had just walked into the room. She was older, maybe closer to my grandmother's age than not, but when she spotted us, she smiled with brown eyes that danced with happiness. "I'm Monique." She wiped off the night nurse's name from the board and added hers in big, swirly letters. "Aren't the two of you adorable?" she commented as she slid her computer into the room on a four-wheeled cart. "My son just came out to me." I suddenly felt Matthias's hand grip mine, like he knew I would need it. "It's so nice to see young boys your age so comfortable with their sexuality." She moved to look at the monitor before she looked at us again. "How long have you two been together?"

Matthias squeezed my fingers so tight I thought he'd break them. "We're not—"

"A couple of months," I finished for him. Matthias was mine, and I needed to prove that to him. Right here. Right now. This lady didn't know us so it didn't matter if she knew we were together. I pulled his hand up to my lips so I could press my mouth against it. "Right, babe?" I teased.

Matthias's eyes nearly bugged out of his head. "Uh, right," he managed to answer.

"I think that Mr. Fuller is going to be released this morning." Monique smiled at us. "How are you feeling?" she asked.

"A little tired, but okay."

Monique nodded. "That's probably the medication, but on a scale of one to ten, what is your pain level right now?" She typed something into her computer.

"A two, or maybe a three. I've had worse." Matthias winced the moment the words slipped from his mouth.

Monique's hands stopped right above the keyboard. "Does that have something to do with the scars and broken bones we found that didn't heal correctly?" she asked.

"I didn't...it's nothing." Matthias tried to back his way out of what he'd said.

I squeezed his hand. "His dad used to hit him," I spoke up.

"Killian," Matthias hissed at me.

I ignored him. "He lives with us now, so it isn't a problem anymore, but his dad would get drunk and beat him. I'm not sure what broken bones you saw, but I know he ended up with a broken nose the last time it happened."

Monique turned to look at me. "You're Barbara's grandson, right?" *Shit, fuck, crap.* "I won't get the cops involved since he's eighteen," she assured me with a wink.

"No cops," Matthias squeaked. "Please, my dad will kill me." The fear in his eyes was enough to make me wish I had kept my mouth shut, but maybe it was time I finally paid a visit to his father. Let him know just what I thought about him putting his hands on my Matthias.

I nodded. "Yes, ma'am, she's my grandmother. Could you..." I flashed the smile I knew all the girls loved, and saw the blush creep up her neck. "Maybe not tell her anything about this? I haven't actually told her yet." I hoped she understood what I meant.

"I'll see what I can do. Let me go check on those discharge papers for you." Monique smiled again and hurried from the room.

Chapter Twenty-Seven

Killian

I watched with hooded eyes as Matthias rolled onto his stomach, climbed up onto his knees, and then turned to look at me over his shoulder while leaning on his forearms. Jesus, if that wasn't the hottest thing I had ever seen in my life. His mouth was open just slightly, his eyes wide with anticipation, and his hips arched just the right away. Yep, I was going to come the second I slid my cock inside him.

"Perfect," I murmured as I stroked my hard length. "God, you are my wet fucking dream, babe. You have no idea how often I've thought about doing this again." I watched as his hazel eyes dropped to what I was doing to myself before they moved back up to my face. "See something you like?" I asked before I raised my hand and brought it down against his right ass cheek. A thought suddenly hit me. I should probably wear a rubber. Even though I always did when I was with chicks, I wanted to make sure I was clean before I had unprotected sex with Matthias. I would never forgive myself if I gave him something.

Matthias groaned as the slap echoed through the room. "You," he told me. "Always you, Killian, but I think you know that already. Where are you going?" he asked as I got up.

"Need to get a condom."

"No, you don't."

My heart thundered in my chest. "Yes, babe, I do." I didn't want to ruin the moment and tell him why, but I knew by the look on Matthias's face that he'd already figured it out. "Only until we can make sure I don't have anything." I removed the condom from my wallet before I ripped it open and rolled it down the length of my cock. Then I made sure to cover that in lube, too. Matthias kept his eyes pinned on me as I moved back to line myself up with him.

I smirked as I began to ease myself inside, my own groans of pleasure turning into heavy pants. I didn't stop until I was balls deep inside him. "How..." I gritted my teeth, trying to calm the blood rushing through my head. "How does that feel?" I moaned as Matthias clenched around me. "If you do that again..." I closed my eyes. "If you do that again I may not be able to control myself," I warned.

"It feels so fucking good."

"You're goddamn right it does."

Matthias wiggled beneath me. "Fuck me, Killian," he begged softly, and when I opened my eyes again, he smiled at me. Those hazel eyes would be my undoing.

"That's what you want?" I gritted my teeth and gripped his hips.

Matthias pushed back against me. "God, yes," he growled into the mattress, and I watched as he stretched his hands up to fist the blanket.

Making a hungry sound in the back of my throat, I began to ram myself home. I groaned as I pulled out a bit, only to plunge back deep inside of him. Rough, hard strokes rocked both of our bodies as I gave Matthias exactly what he'd asked for, and the sounds that he was making told me he liked it.

At first, a hoarse scream of pleasure escaped Matthias's lips, followed by breathy moans as he tried to keep his hands on the blanket beneath him. I reached down to find his hard dick and wrapped my hand around it, not missing a beat as I kept moving above him. When I began to jerk him off, he instantly went off like a cannon.

His hips bucked back, gyrating and grinding as Matthias cried out my name. He spurted out his release beneath him as I fought back my own, but it was too late. The paralyzing feeling of pleasure rocked through my veins as I came, my mind going blank as I filled the condom with my cum. I found myself slumping onto the bed next to him, face up, as I tried to catch my breath. I managed to roll onto my side so that I could slip off the condom before I tied it up and tossed it into the garbage next to the bed.

"I'm..." Matthias suddenly burst into a fit of laughter. "I'm lying in a pile of my own jizz." He snorted before he rolled onto his back. His stomach was covered in it, and I couldn't help but run my finger through it. "What are you doing? Did you...are you writing your name in my cum?" he asked, watching my movements.

I nodded as I scrawled my name onto his taut abs. "Never forget who you belong to," I growled before I splayed myself over him. "Tomorrow, next week, next month, or next year. You're mine, Matthias." I brushed my lips over his as I looked down at him. "I love you," I whispered. "I'm sorry for everything I've ever put you through, and for everything I'm going to put you through—because you know there will be more. I want you in my life. Forever." I reached for his hand so I could lace our fingers together.

"Promise?" Matthias asked.

I smiled as I rolled onto my side, bringing him with me. "On my parent's grave. I need you," I confessed.

"Killian." He reached up to touch my face with his free hand, the pads of his fingers dancing over my skin. My heart beat a little faster with each touch.

I shook my head. "You know it's true. I was a mess until you came back into my life, but I feel like it can only get better now. If you were to leave?" I shuddered at the thought. "I'm not sure I would survive."

"Don't say shit like that," Matthias whispered as I buried my face into his neck. Being with him was like coming home. My safe place. And, when he untangled his fingers from mine to comb both hands through my hair, I couldn't stop the moan that escaped my lips.

I only clung tighter to him. "You're my safe place, babe. My ride or die."

Neither one of us spoke another word, but when I woke the next morning, I was still wrapped in Matthias's arms and finally felt a little hope in my heart.

***

Lou stared up at me as if I had just grown a second head. "So, let me get this straight." She folded her hands onto her lap. "You want to postpone the tour." It wasn't a question though.

"Yes." I wish I had listened to Matthias and had him come in here with me. With the way my leg was bouncing up and down right now, I felt like I was going to burst out of my own skin. Anxiety clawed at my brain as I watched her, and I couldn't help but feel like she could see right through me.

Lou pursed her lips. "Why?" she asked. Her blonde hair was pulled back so tight I wondered how didn't have a headache.

"Why?"

"Yes, Killian, *why* do you want to postpone the tour?"

I grimaced. "I need some time to think." Not exactly a lie, but not the truth. How did you tell your PR person that you felt like you were losing your mind? That you had been living with bipolar disorder since you were fourteen, hated taking the medication you were prescribed—but took all the illegal drugs you were offered—self-harmed just to make yourself feel sane, and thought that maybe your boyfriend was the only thing keeping you alive. That if you hadn't nearly ruined everything years ago, maybe things would have changed for the better sooner.

"Does this have something to do with Matthias?" Lou steepled her fingers. "Does he want you to take this time off?"

I nodded. "It was his suggestion." I saw the way her brows shot up. "Not like that, Lou. Matthias is my anchor," I assured her. "He keeps me sane when I feel like I might go off the deep end." Shit.

"What happened in the hotel room?"

I swallowed the nerves in my stomach. "Do we need to talk about that?" I didn't want to.

"If you want this tour postponed, then yes." She stood up. "Did you two have a fight?" she asked.

I sighed as I gripped the back of my neck. "Not exactly." I was going to have to tell Lou the truth if I didn't want her to think that any of that was Matthias's fault. I bowed my head before I began to tell her the entire story. About Helena and Dean and how they had kept their relationship hidden from me since high school, about Matthias knowing, about what I did to him, and how I had been in love with him for years. By the time I was able to meet her eyes again, Lou's mouth was hanging open.

"Jesus Christ, Killian." She sat back down into her chair. "You were terrible to him. I can't believe he still wants anything to do with you."

I nodded. "That makes two of us. I need to fix it and make up for everything I've ever done to him. I don't deserve Matthias, but for some reason he still loves me. He still wants me, and I—" Tears blinded my eyes and I choked back a sob. "I need to get some help, Lou," I admitted to her.

"Are you talking inpatient? Rehab? We can get you in somewhere that no one will know you," she suggested.

I started to shake my head, but that's when I realized that might actually be a good idea. "No medication," I barked out. "I can't stand taking things that make me feel doped up or dumbed down. I've done that before with my bipolar...fuck." I hadn't meant to admit that to her, but as I stared at Lou's face, she gave me a secret smile. "You knew."

"Of course, I knew," she told me. "I know almost everything about you, Dean, Blake, and Maverick. That's what I'm hired to do." Lou crossed her legs. "When do you want to do this? You have a show tomorrow, then the NASCAR race this weekend."

My brows dipped. "NASCAR race?" I was trying to remember what she was talking about.

"Mulligan Downtown is supposed to sing the national anthem at the race this weekend. I'll cancel that first so they can find someone else."

I shook my head. "No, I want to do that." The last time we did that, I had really hit it off with a couple of the drivers. It would be cool to see them again. "I'll go after that," I told her. "On second thought, can I get a few days to spend with Matthias first?"

"Of course. I'll make some calls," Lou assured me. "I think this is a good idea for you, Kill." She glanced at her phone that was blinking on the table. "Anything else?"

I stood up. "Nope, that's about it. I'm going to go get ready for the show tonight." I started toward the door. "Thanks, Lou. I really mean it." I flashed a quick smile before I left the room.

Chapter Twenty-Eight

Matthias
Four Years Ago

I didn't say a word to Killian on the ride home from the hospital. He made mindless chitchat on the way, talking about the next Mulligan Downtown show and how there were rumors about someone from a record company wanting to sign them, and how he couldn't wait to go to California if that happened. I was so mad at him about the whole Linda thing that I was afraid I would tell him how much I loved him. So, instead of talking, I kept my eyes on the road and listened to him instead.

"I wrote a song. I thought maybe you'd like to see it."

That got my attention. I glanced at Killian to find him smiling as he turned down our street. "You want me to read the song you wrote?" I noticed the flush that crept up his neck.

"I mean, if you don't want to..." He tried to play it off, but I could tell by the sound of his voice he actually meant it. Killian parked the car in the driveway and turned to look at me. "I want your opinion, babe." He reached for my hand. "I know you're mad, because you've been giving me the silent treatment since we left the hospital, and I honestly can't blame you. I'm a first-class asshole." He dragged his thumb over the palm of my hand just as Helena came running out the front door. I went to pull away, but he only gripped me tighter. This was different.

Helena whipped the door open. "God, I'm so glad you're home...what's this?" Her eyes went wide when she saw her brother holding my hand. "Wait, it's official now?" A smile started to spread over her face.

"Fuck off." Killian shoved my hand away. "You say anything, and I mean anything, I'll have your hide." He started to climb from the car before he leaned back in. "It's official, but not official, do you understand?" He pointed at Helena. "He's mine." He grunted before he sauntered into the house.

I don't think I had ever met someone as afraid of his sexuality as Killian Hampton.

Helena giggled softly. "I think that's progress." She started to help me onto my feet.

"Jesus!" Killian shouted before he came sprinting across the lawn again. "Move." He bared his teeth at his sister. "I'll make sure he gets inside safely."

"I can walk."

"Babe, just let me do this."

I saw the way Helena's brows went up as Killian's arm wrapped around my waist, and he eased me against him. Or maybe it was the nickname he used on me. Could have been both. "Thanks," I murmured as he slowly helped me into the house and onto the living room couch.

"What?" Killian bellowed at his sister once I was seated comfortably against the cushions.

Helena only shook her head. "I don't think that I've ever seen you be so gentle before, Kill." She gave him a warm smile. "Are you two hungry? I can make some sandwiches," she suggested.

Killian sat down next to me. "I could eat." He nudged my shoulder with his. "You should too," he added before wrapping his arm around me. "Thanks, Hel," he muttered.

Once Helena left the room, we sat in silence for a few minutes before I turned my head to look at him. Killian had his eyes cast down as he stared at his feet. "You okay?" I asked.

"No," he grumbled. "Why am I like this?" He shifted his gaze to mine, and his blue eyes were filled with pain. "You know what I mean. Why am I such an asshole? Mad at the world. A prick to you, when I just want to be with you. Horrible to my sister, who just wants us to be happy. I don't understand it." His chin trembled as he spoke.

I cupped Killian's face with my hands. "Hey." I stroked his jaw with my thumbs. "I happen to like the way you are." Except when you're *shoving your tongue down some girl's throat or sticking your dick in her*, but I kept that part to myself. Killian was reaching out to me in his own way.

"Right." He scoffed.

I wanted to kiss the shit out of him right now, but I knew with Helena in the other room, he would lose his mind. "I think it's the whole alpha asshole thing you got going on," I whispered before Killian's mouth came crashing down on mine. I was so caught off guard that it took me a split second before I began kissing him back, our tongues and lips fighting to stay in control.

"I don't deserve you," Killian murmured. "You know that, right?" His teeth nipped at my bottom lip.

I chuckled. "Believe me, I know." I only laughed harder when Killian's hands dug tighter into my hair.

"Here." He pulled back and lifted his hip so that he could slide a piece of paper from his pocket. "Read it and tell me what you think." He gave me a shy grin. "Unless you hate it. If you hate it, I don't want to know." His hand shook as he handed it to me.

I knew deep in my heart that I would never hate a single song Killian wrote. "It's my favorite," I said softly.

"You haven't even read it."

"I already know it will be."

Killian watched with wide eyes as I unfolded the lined paper. "You're just going to sit there and watch me read this?" I cocked an eyebrow at him.

"Yep." He nodded. "What, you need me to leave the room or something? Come on, babe, this is my future we're talking about. I've always written with the guys, but this is different. This my heart and soul poured out into words on a piece of paper. I need to know if it's good. You're the only person I've shown this to, so please don't break my ego too much." His voice was full of worry.

I stared down at the words sprawled before me.

"Lunch is all set," Helena called from the kitchen. "Gram will kill me if you eat in the living room." She poked her head into the living room, and Killian yanked the paper from my hands so he could shove it back into his pocket.

"I'll help you." He stood up and then eased me back onto my feet. "You can read it later," he told me when I looked at him.

***

It's crazy how you've got me feeling this way,
You set my heart on fire,
Yeah, there have been others but it never felt this way,
You make me feel like I can be a better man,
It's in the way we kiss,
It's in the way you touch me, babe,
It's in the way you rock my world,
You make me feel like I can be a better man,
With you, I can do anything,
Without you I feel like I can't breathe,
With you, we're two halves made whole,
Without you, I'm missing my soul,
repeat chorus

I had been staring up at the ceiling of my room since we went to bed, thinking about the song and unable to sleep. My eyes blurred as I thought about the words Killian had written. I wanted to ask him if he wrote them about me, but I was scared. Afraid to hear him laugh at me. To tell me no, of course not, how could I even be so stupid as to think that? I started to climb from the bed, only to have Killian's hand find mine.

"Are you alright?" he asked softly. "You've been awake for a while now," he commented.

I turned to look at him in the dark and saw the whites of his teeth as he smiled at me in the dark. "You've been watching me?" I whispered.

"You know I don't sleep much. My brain is always going a mile a minute."

Fuck, I loved Killian. I loved him so much it hurt. Even knowing he was ready to go off with Linda when I didn't show up. I still loved him, and I would probably always love him, no matter what he did to me. I knew it was wrong. My feelings for Killian would never be returned, although I knew he felt something toward me.

"Hey." Killian moved to flip the light on next to the bed. "Matthias, what's up?" He folded me into his warmth, the sound of his heart beating against my ear, and I found it soothing. Killian drew circles on my back with the tip of his fingers as he waited for me to talk to him, but when I was silent, he finally pulled back to look at me. "Talk to me, babe, because you're starting to scare me." He tilted my face up. "Is it about Linda?"

I shrugged. "I guess." I started to untangle myself from Killian's arms, but he only held on tighter. "Let me go." I meant it, too. He was never going to love me the way I loved him. I knew that now. When he released me, I climbed from the bed, but felt his eyes following me around the room while I got dressed.

"You mean that in more ways than one, don't you?"

I tugged my shirt over my head and turned back around. "It's funny." I tried to laugh, but a sob escaped from my throat instead. "The only person I've ever wanted was you, and now that I have you, or at least have a part of you, I realize you're only going to break my heart." I watched the way Killian's eyes went round before he sat up in the bed. "Let me go, Killian," I said again.

"No." He shook his head. "You know I can't do that." He yanked the blanket back from his legs. "What were you thinking about that has you acting like this all of a sudden,

Matthias? Why won't you talk to me? Tell me, what has you trying to push me away?" He got to his feet.

"Who is that song about?" I blurted out.

"Matthias, just sit down for a second."

"No, I won't just *sit down*. Who is that damn song about, huh? One of the many girls you've been with? Keely maybe? Or the one before her? What was her name? Jessica? Jennifer?"

Killian ran his hand down the front of his face. "What does it matter what her name was?" he asked.

"So, you admit it then?" I realized my voice was starting to get louder, but I didn't care. I was sick and tired of Killian using me. Hiding me so no one would know he liked the way I felt in his arms, or that he liked my lips on his. Or that he enjoyed getting me off with his hand and loved the way I used mine on him.

I saw the flash in Killian's eyes and I tried to move, but he was faster than I was, moving to cage me in to shove me against the wall. "Are you really that stupid?" he growled. I could feel the anger radiating from his body as he pressed his chest to mine. "The fucking song is about you, Matthias," he said before his lips found mine.

I wasn't prepared for this kiss though. It was soft, gentle, and unlike anything Killian had ever given me before. "Stop trying to push me away," he whispered. "I know I'm an asshole." He nuzzled my neck as his hands pulled me closer. "Why are you crying?" Killian stopped to look at me again.

"It's really about me?" I asked in a shaky voice, and when Killian nodded, I crushed his body to mine. "I wanted to believe that," I confessed.

Killian soothed the back of my hair. "I thought you would have figured it out. I should have just told you, but I'm not any good with this sort of shit." His lips brushed my ear.

"Killian, I..." It was on the tip of my tongue to tell him that I loved him, but when he looked at me with those baby blues, I couldn't get the words out of my mouth. "Thank you," I said instead.

Chapter Twenty-Nine

I hated that Killian had to do this NASCAR race today, when what he really needed was time off; time away from the limelight where he could gather himself together and not worry about being a rock star. I knew this was important to him. He had enjoyed watching racing with his father when he was a kid, but I never could understand the appeal. Last night's concert seemed to drain Killian of any of the energy he might have had left. He looked more exhausted than I had ever seen him and had spent most of the night tossing and turning next to me. Once I wrapped myself around him, it seemed to settle him into a troubled sleep until the alarm went off at eight this morning.

As we headed through the crowded garage, which was full of NASCAR drivers and their crewmembers working, Killian reached over to squeeze my hand. "This is going to be fun; I promise," he tried to assure me.

I raised a brow. "They won't care that you're with me?" I asked as I followed behind him, the rest of Mulligan Downtown flanking him.

"What exactly do you think is going to happen, Fuller?" Maverick snorted before smacking my arm. "Do you think that they're going to tar and feather you two or something? The sport has changed a lot over the years."

Killian narrowed his eyes. "Knock it off, asshole," he warned, just as someone called out his name. Or at least it sounded like his name.

"Killian!" Yep, there it was.

I watched as a giant man with dark hair and green eyes moved toward my boyfriend with a wide smile on his face. "Man, I heard you guys were going to be here." His voice carried a deep southern drawl, and I watched the way his eyes roamed over the band, past me, and then back to Killian again.

"Shepard, good to see you again." Killian held out his fist for a bump, and then they did that weird bro-hug thing that I hated. "Matthias." He was still holding onto my hand, and he tugged me closer. "This is Rand Shepard. He's one of the drivers. Rand, this is my boyfriend, Matthias Fuller." It seemed to flow so easily off his lips, as if he said it all the time.

Rand nodded. "Nice to meet you, man." He didn't flinch or look like it bothered him, which I guess was a plus. "Dude, Lake was beside himself when heard you guys were coming. Come on." He jutted his chin, and as Killian started walking he dropped my hand, leaving me behind with Dean, Maverick, and Blake. I suddenly felt like this might have been a horrible idea.

"Don't look so terrified, Matthias," Blake chuckled softly. "It's not like Killian, Rand, Lake Mills, Finn Houston, and Mason Pelletier all got black-out drunk the last time we were here and hooked up with some girls. Oh wait, yeah they did." He threw his head back as he roared with laughter.

"Why are you such an asshole?" Dean hissed before he punched his arm. "Ignore him. Kill loves you," he tried to assure me, but as I watched Killian disappear into the crowd and out of my sight, I couldn't help but want to keep an eye on him. "You want to go after him, don't you?" he asked.

I nodded. "Is it that obvious?" I met his eyes.

"Come on." Dean started through the garage, nodding and waving to people who recognized him, stopping to say hello to some of the drivers, and signing a couple of autographs. When we finally caught up with Killian and Rand, they seemed to be deep in conversation with a handful of people I didn't recognize.

I suddenly wished I had paid more attention to NASCAR so I had an idea about who they were.

"They will probably be a while," a soft feminine voice said next to me. I turned to find a petite, brown-haired woman with big, brown eyes smiling up at me. "Rand loves Mulligan," she added. I must have looked even more confused because she touched my arm lightly. "That's my husband, Rand. He's like the biggest Mulligan Downtown fan on the planet. I'm Brooklyn Shepard, by the way," she rambled as a blush crept up her neck. "I'm kind of a fan myself. I don't suppose you could get him and the band to sit for some photos later today, could you?" Her color grew even redder. "I'm a photographer." Brooklyn held up the camera around her neck. "Sorry, sometimes I get all excited and start rambling. You're Matthias, right? I mean, I thought I recognized you from Killian's IG."

I nodded. "I am. Sorry, this is a little overwhelming," I admitted to her.

"I totally get that. When Rand and I got married, his fans went crazy! It was kind of a spur of the moment thing, and let me tell you, when he came back for his first race? I thought they were going to riot." She giggled. "I mean, Rand isn't a Grammy-winning superstar like Killian, but it has to be sort of the same, right?" Brooklyn nudged my shoulder.

I smiled. "Sort of." I watched the way her brows went up and chuckled. "I'm kidding," I told her. "Rand's really your husband?" I noticed how he towered over Killian, the ink that covered his hands as he waved them around while he spoke to him and realized how completely different he was from the rest of the drivers. The words Maverick had said just a few moments ago filtered through my mind, but maybe Rand hadn't been with Brooklyn then.

"Yep, he's dreamy, right?"

"He's okay."

Brooklyn snorted. "Right, he's no Killian Hampton." She laughed.

"No one is," I said before I laughed along with her. I think I liked this girl.

Killian suddenly looked over at me, and my heart stopped like it always did when we made eye contact. "I love you," he mouthed to me, before he winked and went back to his conversation. My gaze found Brooklyn watching me wide-eyed. "What?" I asked.

"That was...that was so sweet," she whispered.

This time it was my turn to grow red. I wasn't used to Killian's open PDA yet, but I liked it. "Rand isn't like that with you?" I tried to change the subject.

"He has no problem telling me loves me in public, but...I don't know. Killian seems more like the closed-off type." Brooklyn grimaced. "Sorry, that was kind of rude. I shouldn't have said that. I don't know either one of you." She placed a hand on my shoulder just as Killian and Rand walked over.

"Making friends, babe?" Killian's voice soothed my nerves as I looked up at him. "You must be Brooklyn. Killian Hampton." He held out his hand.

"I see you met Killian's boyfriend, darlin'." Rand wrapped a thick arm around Brooklyn's shoulder to pull her closer, and I watched the way she lit up. "I've gotta say, I was a little surprised when I heard about the two of you."

Killian's body went tense next to mine. "What the fuck does that mean?" His eyes narrowed as he stared up at Rand, and I lightly brushed the tip of my finger over the top of his hand to try to get him to relax, before I clasped our hands together.

"Nothing, bro, but you know. I just didn't think you were into guys. You've always been with chicks before." Rand never flinched or backed down. I think if I were his size, I would act the same way. "I'm not trying to start a fight with you, Kill. You seem happy for the first time since I've known you. I honestly don't give a shit if you like dick," he added.

Killian's grip tightened around mine to the point I thought he might cut off the circulation. "I'm only into Matthias, no one else," he growled. "It's always been him, got it?" He kept his eyes glued on Rand for what felt like forever, until Brooklyn pressed a hand to her husband's chest and started talking in whispers to him.

"Hey." I did the same thing to Killian with my free hand to try to calm him down. "I don't think Rand was trying to upset you. Only making a point." I could feel the anger radiating from his body as he clenched and unclenched his jaw.

Killian's nostrils flared. "He doesn't know me. Why does everyone think that they know me?"

"Did I say I did?" Rand shot back.

"Okay." Brooklyn sounded nervous. "Maybe we should, uh, take this outside? People are starting to stare."

I had completely forgotten we were standing in the middle of a NASCAR garage filled with hundreds of people. "Kill, baby," I murmured, and that seemed to finally get his attention. His eyes drifted over to me, his features softening in the process, and he loosened the death grip he had on my hand.

"Shit." He dragged his hand up through his hair. "I'm sorry, Shepard." He glanced over at Rand, who gave a curt nod. "I'm still...this is all still new to me. I love Matthias, but I'm still sorting my shit out. Surprised you didn't knock me out." He met my eyes again, and I smiled at him. Hearing Killian say he loved me would never get old. I wanted it written on my grave.

"Thought about it, but then I'd be the asshole who punched Grammy-winner Killian Hampton."

Brooklyn was the first person to giggle, and I snorted with laughter. By the time Killian joined in, it felt like all the stress and anger had been lifted from the moment. Maybe I had been wrong about this race after all.

***

The crowd went crazy when Mulligan Downtown sang the national anthem. They did an amazing job too, and I might have even teared up a little bit. I was proud of Killian. He had accomplished everything he had ever wanted at twenty-four, and I knew he would achieve so much more in the years to come.

I wanted to be with Killian during the race, but since the band had some interviews and marketing to do after, I let Brooklyn convince me to hang out with her instead in Rand's pit box. She was currently trying to explain some basic rules of NASCAR, but it was hard to concentrate. I had on a pair of headphones to drown out the noise of the cars but could still hear Rand yelling at his crew chief every few seconds about how shitty his car was.

Speaking of his crew chief, Hutch Kelly was currently trying to talk his driver down off a ledge, and I couldn't help but think he was the biggest saint in the world. His voice was calm, soothing, and reassuring as he told Rand that as soon as he could pit, they would make any adjustments he needed.

"He's amazing, right?" Brooklyn shouted at me as she pointed to Hutch, who was a few inches away from us. "Believe it or not, they're besties." She grinned.

I turned to find Hutch watching us. "That's a bit of a stretch, don't you think, Sully? My best friend is currently on bed rest until the birth of our son." His brows dipped before his eyes landed back on me. He gave a quick nod before turning back to the race.

Brooklyn rolled her eyes. "He's shy," she mouthed. "His wife Jillian is very pregnant. I think he misses her." She giggled.

"I can hear you," Hutch growled. "Ah, shit," he muttered as Brooklyn suddenly jumped to her feet. "How's the car? You hit anything?" he barked.

"No, it's fucking fine. But you tell number eleven that if he doesn't watch himself, I'm going to punt his ass into next week," Rand warned.

Brooklyn looked as pale as a ghost as she eased back into her seat. "Sometimes I remember why I hate racing," she murmured before she flashed me a quick smile.

"Darlin'." Rand's voice was suddenly different through the headset as he spoke to his wife. "I'm okay," he assured her, and I saw the light come back into her brown eyes once again.

I suddenly had the urge to find my boyfriend, kiss him until neither one of us could see straight, and hold him until we fell asleep in each other's arms. I missed Killian something fierce right now, and wished he were by my side. What was it going to be like while he was in rehab? The thought made my heart nearly stop beating. We could survive that, right? We had been through much worse. A flash of light brought me back to reality, and I found Brooklyn smiling at me from behind her camera.

"Sorry, Matthias, but you looked adorable. I thought maybe Killian would like it," she teased.

I felt a blush warm my skin. "Adorable my ass," I muttered, only to have her nudge my foot.

Brooklyn giggled while she stood up and removed her headphones. "Come on." She held out her hand. "I'm not going to bite, Matthias. Take off your headphones so we can go find your man. I can see how much you miss him." She winked.

I followed her lead, and once we were on the ground Brooklyn slipped her arm through mine. "You'll have to tell me how you met," she said as we weaved our way through the crowds of people.

So, I told her how I met Killian, leaving out the part about him breaking my heart. When we finally found the band, I almost wished we hadn't. Because when I saw Killian sitting with some random girl on his lap, and a beer in his hand, it felt exactly like that same day four years ago.

Chapter Thirty

Killian

Four years ago

I knew Matthias was bored of his mind right now watching the NASCAR race, but I appreciated him sitting here with Helena and me while we did. He knew how much it meant to us, since our father and grandfather both had been huge fans. I just wished he didn't look like he was ready to fall asleep.

"Come on!" I exclaimed as Rand Shepard was sandwiched in between two other cars.

Helena snorted. "You're just pissed because Mason is out front," she teased.

"Bullshit. If it wasn't for bad luck, Shepard wouldn't have any luck at all." I smacked my thigh before nudging Matthias's with my own. "You're bored, huh?" I asked.

He shook his head. "No." He made a raspberry noise with his lips. "Whatever gave you that idea?"

"Liar." I grinned before I grabbed the back of Matthias's neck to bring his face closer to mine. "Thank you," I whispered before I slid my mouth over his. I watched the way his pupils dilated, and I nipped lightly at his bottom lip.

"Killian," he gasped.

I smirked. "Yeah, babe?" I asked as I caught my sister staring at us with her mouth hanging open and her eyes wide. My stomach clenched as I realized I had just kissed Matthias in front of her without even thinking twice about it. *Shit.*

"Hey." Matthias cupped my face with his hands. "Don't freak out on me." He pressed his forehead against mine. "It was a kiss, and that's Helena. She's not going to judge you," he assured me. I felt the way his fingers just lightly touched my scalp, his breath warm against my skin.

I felt a smile start to spread across my face. "I'm alright," I assured Matthias as he watched me with those hazel eyes that drove me crazy. My gaze moved to my sister, who had turned her attention back to the television, but I could see she was trying to keep her reaction down to a minimum. "Helena." I tried to sound as normal as possible, but my heart was beating like a drum in my chest.

"Yeah?" She turned to look over at me.

"What, you can't face me now?" I asked.

Helena slowly turned back toward me with her lips pressed firmly together. "I saw the look on your face, Kill. I saw how scared you were when you realized that I had seen you kiss Matthias, and I just..." She bit her lip. "Don't hurt him, okay? He's my best friend, and he's already been through so much." Her voice was strong as she spoke. "I love you, you're my brother, but I love Matty too, and you're not the relationship type." She raised her chin.

"Okay, thanks." Matthias shook me off. "You don't have to do that, Helena," he hissed. "I'm perfectly capable of handling this."

My brows shot up. "Handling what exactly?" I asked.

"This, you, whatever."

"How do I need to be handled?"

Matthias shook his head. "You know what I mean." He leaned toward Helena. "Killian cares about me okay? So you don't have to worry about that. I'm not going to end up hurt," he tried to tell her.

"Answer the damn question, Matthias," I grunted. "How do I need to be handled?" I was slowly starting to lose my cool.

Matthias glanced over at me for a second before looking back at Helena, and then his head swiveled right back to me. "Why do you look so mad right now?" He swallowed nervously.

"Because you said you were capable of handling me, and I want to know what the fuck that means!" I roared, jumping to my feet. "What am I? Some fucking charity case? Some problem that you can solve? What the fuck!" I didn't care that my grandmother was trying to sleep for her night shift at the hospital. Matthias did not get to control me. I was in control of me. No one else.

Matthias must have realized what he'd said, because he climbed to his feet. "I didn't...Kill, that's not what I meant. Calm down." He tried to sound convincing, but I saw the panic in his eyes and the fear written all over his face. Fuck, why was I such an asshole?

"Explain it to me then. What did you mean?"

"I just meant...what I meant was that I could handle it if you broke my heart. I would be okay if you decided you didn't want me anymore."

I felt the blood drain from my face. Did Matthias think that's what I was going to do to him? That I was just going to push him away when I was done? Honestly, I wasn't sure I would ever be done with him. I wasn't sure what it felt like to love someone, but maybe what I felt for him was that.

"This is what I was afraid of," Helena muttered.

"Shut up," I barked at her before I gripped Matthias's shoulders. "I'm not going to do that," I told him.

He nodded. "Right, but if you did, I would be okay."

"I'm not. I promise." I yanked him into a hug against my chest, shooting daggers at my sister over his shoulder. "I won't break your heart, babe, so you don't have to worry about handling me or any shit like that." I hugged him so tight I thought I'd break him in half.

Helena rolled her eyes as she crossed her legs. "If you two are done, the race is still on. Maybe Eli will pull off this win." She tried to sound annoyed, but I saw the way her lips turned up. Was she happy for us? I hoped so. I meant what I'd said, too.

I wasn't going to hurt Matthias. I was starting to think I might be in love with him.

***

"What's wrong with you tonight?" Blake Duncan, the bass player for Mulligan Downtown, asked as I stumbled over the lyrics for "Wild at Heart." Again.

I glanced over to where he stood, bass slung over his shoulder and his blonde hair slicked back from his face. "Nothing." I lied.

"Right," Blake grunted. "You've only gotten the words wrong to Wild how many times?" He jutted his chin at Maverick

Maverick spun the drumstick in his right hand. "Five," he answered before he narrowed his eyes. "You're not thinking about Linda, are you?"

"What?" I exclaimed. "What the hell ever gave you that idea?" I scoffed. "Dean, help me out." I needed all the help I could get right now, because the person I was thinking about was Matthias, and I couldn't let any of them know that.

Ever.

Dean's eyes went wide as placed his guitar next to his amp. "Uh, well." He dragged his hand through his bright-green hair. I wasn't sure why he had dyed it that hideous color, but when he'd walked into the Blakes' basement tonight, we were all too shocked to say anything.

"It's not Keeley, is it?" Blake grimaced. "Because, well, you know." He made a circle with the thumb and forefinger of his right hand before shoving the index finger of his left through it.

Maverick made a gagging noise. "Gross, dude, sloppy seconds? What about bro code?" He thumped out a quick beat with the drums. "Was she any good?" he asked.

"Jesus Christ," I growled. "It's not Keeley; you're all welcome to her. Could we just drop it?" I had to get out of here. I felt like I was suffocating. It was hot in this room, and if I didn't get out—

"Knock, knock," A cheerful voice called out just as Linda burst through the basement door with the rest of her friends. When she started toward me, I took two steps back. "What's wrong, Kill, you look like you just saw a ghost," she purred.

I gritted my teeth. "What are you doing here?" I snapped.

"I invited them." Maverick came out from around his drum kit. "Thought it would be a nice distraction after we were done practicing," he told me.

I needed to keep my cool about this. "Who said we were done?" I asked.

"You're clearly off your game, bro. Maybe a little pussy will help you relax," Blake chuckled.

Linda placed her hand on my arm, and I couldn't help but pull away. "Don't," I warned.

"Come on, baby, you know I can help you with whatever's going on." She batted her lashes at me.

I looked around the room at my bandmates who were waiting for me, and I realized I had two options. I could push Linda away like I wanted; tell her to fuck off because I wasn't interested in what she was offering, and go home to the boy I really needed. The one that made my heart race, my life feel complete, and the one who calmed all of my demons. Or, I could keep pretending to be the guy they all thought I was. The Killian Hampton who could have any girl he wanted, and usually did, before leaving them on the side of the road and moving on to the next one.

"I'm not doing this tonight." I started to gather my shit together. "Maybe another time." I shoved my notebooks of lyrics and music into my bag. "What? Why is everyone staring at me like that?" I shouted.

Dean squared his shoulders. "Look man, you've been acting kind of weird lately," he told me, and the others nodded. "We just thought maybe you could use a little fun, help you unwind. You hardly ever hang out with us unless it's practice or a gig." He pressed his lips together.

"I'm fine."

"Are you though?"

I spun around to glare at Maverick. "Fuck you." We had never really gotten along. He was only in the band because he was Dean's older brother, and a damn good drummer.

"You'd like that, wouldn't you, Hampton." Maverick smirked.

I don't remember launching myself on him or hitting him, but the next thing I knew, Dean and Blake were pulling me off of him as the girls screamed behind me. Meanwhile, Maverick held his hand up to his nose, which might be broken.

"You're crazy." Maverick pointed at me with his free hand.

"I want you out," I yelled back. "You're fucking done." I struggled against Dean and Blake, but they held me back. "You're out of the band, do you understand?"

Dean yanked hard on my arm. "That's not just up to you, Kill. We're a team, remember? Just because you and Mav have a disagreement doesn't mean you can kick him out of the band," he hissed.

"Then I'm out." I raised my chin.

Maverick grinned at me with blood slipping down his face. "Don't let the door hit you on the way out, asshole." He spat onto the floor.

"No one is leaving the band," Blake hollered. "What has gotten into the both of you tonight?" he demanded.

"It's either me or him," I shot back. "I will have no damn problem walking out of here."

Dean let out a frustrated sigh next to me. "Jesus Christ," he muttered. "Girls, you should leave. Maybe another time," he added when they started to protest. Once they had left, he moved to face me. "You are not to touch him, go near him, or look at him right now. Do you understand?" he asked as his green eyes flashed angrily.

"Whatever."

Dean poked me in the chest. "Say it, Killian. I'm not playing games," he growled.

"Fine, I understand." I folded my arms over my chest.

Dean turned to look at his brother. "Is your nose broken?" he asked. When Maverick shook his head, he looked back at me. "Same goes for you. You leave one another alone until we get this shit sorted out."

"I understand." Maverick stuck his middle finger up at me and when I started to move, Dean spun around. "Sorry." He held up his hands.

"Prick," I seethed.

"Fag," he shot back.

"What did you just say to me?"

Maverick chuckled. "You heard me, Killian." He looked proud of himself, too. "You think I don't know about you and Matthias—" He never finished because I shoved Dean out of the way to knock Mav to the floor. I climbed onto his chest to keep him there and wrapped my hands around his throat.

"Jesus Christ!" I heard Blake scream.

"You ever fucking say his name again I will fucking kill you!" I watched as Maverick's eyes began to bulge from their sockets and his face turned a shade of blue. "You don't ever say that name, do you understand?" I felt hands on me, dragging me off Maverick again, just as I realized I was crying. Tears streamed down my face as I watched Dean get to his brother, who was now coughing and gagging while trying to catch his breath.

"You're fucking crazy!" Maverick's voice came out in a hoarse whisper.

"Call me that again," I warned. "See what happens when you do. They won't be able to save your ass," I promised.

Dean turned to stare at me. "Is it true? Are you gay?" he asked. "I'm not judging you, man," he added.

"Do you really have to ask that?" I bared my teeth.

Maverick let out a bitter laugh. "Someone saw you and Fuller together a couple of weeks ago. Holding hands." He smirked when I narrowed my eyes at him.

"They're lying." I couldn't breathe as I watched Blake's eyes bounce between the two of us. "Who told you that, huh? Which one of your friends?" I demanded.

Maverick waved his hand at me. "Right, like I'd tell you. So, what? You can go kick the shit out of them or choke them like you did to me? You're fucking nuts, Hampton." He climbed to his feet.

"What about..." Dean stopped when I looked at him.

I could see his brain working, and I didn't like it. Was he remembering the night he found me in the treehouse with Matthias? "What about what?" I sneered.

"Nothing." Dean shook his head.

I growled. "Fuck you." I pointed at Maverick with my middle finger before I waved it around the room. "Fuck all of you." I told them. "We're supposed to be a team, right? If you think your friends saw something, come to me. Ask me. Don't go around spreading rumors. How are we supposed to make it as a band if we can't trust one another, huh?" I had to get out of here before I broke someone's neck for real.

"So it's not true?" Blake asked. "You're not into guys?"

"Have you ever seen me into dudes, Blake?" He shook his head. "Right, so there's your answer. Thanks for ruining my damn night," I grunted. "I'm going home."

Maverick held up his hand. "Wait," he called to me just as I put my hand on the door.

"Wait for what?" I swung back around to look at him to find him with his brows dipped. "What? What do you want now?"

Maverick took a step forward. "Prove it."

"Prove what?"

"Prove that there's nothing going on between you and Fuller."

I rolled my eyes. "My word is my proof." I opened the door.

"Your word is shit, Killian," Maverick snapped back. "Prove it or you're out. You decide by next practice." I didn't even bother to turn back around, but instead slammed the door as hard as possible behind me.

Only by the time I got to my car, my hands were shaking, tears were streaming down my face again, and I felt like I might throw up. What was I going to do about Matthias now?

Chapter Thirty-One

Killian

I'm not sure how it happened. One second Mulligan was doing an interview with some local radio station, and the next someone handed me a beer, which I drank without thinking about it. I figured one wouldn't hurt, but that turned into two, which became four, and then I didn't remember much after that.

The girl? Hell, I don't know where she came from, but all I could think about right now was the look on Matthias's face when he saw me. "Wait!" I started after him, not caring that I was so smashed I might fall flat on my face. I was surprised when he stopped and slowly turned around.

"Why? So, you can come up with some excuse that you think I'm going to buy? Not happening. Not this time. I'm done with your lies and bullshit, Killian." Matthias glared at me.

I felt my stomach drop. "What does that mean?" I whispered.

"It means I'm leaving." He turned around, but I reached out to grab his arm and spun him back around. "Let go," Matthias growled.

I shook my head. "Don't go," I said. "I can't...please don't leave." Fear began to claw at my skin. "You know I need you," I reminded him.

"You? You need me?" Matthias barked out an ugly laugh. "That's funny, considering two seconds ago you had some girl on your lap and you looked pretty happy." He grabbed my hand to pry my fingers off. "Let me go, Killian. I don't want you anymore." I watched the way his jaw tightened.

"I can't do that, babe."

"You have no choice."

I felt tears sting my eyes. "Matthias, I love you." My throat was so dry I could hardly talk. "If you leave..." I swallowed trying to loosen the tightness and shook my head. I was afraid to finish the sentence.

"If I leave, what?" he hissed through clenched teeth. When Matthias met my eyes, I watched his pinched face soften. "Don't do this to me, Killian. It's not fair. Let me walk away," he begged.

"Talk to me," I begged him, and when he gave a curt nod, I felt hope rise inside of me. "Here." I reached for Matthias's hand, only to have him push me away. So much for hope.

He followed behind me as I tried to find somewhere we could talk; somewhere no one would bother us. I found a quiet spot behind the garage away from prying eyes. When I turned around to face him, Matthias folded his arms over his chest and narrowed his eyes at me.

"It's not..." I closed my eyes, trying to gather my thoughts as the beer I consumed washed through me. "It's not what you think," I told him.

Matthias snorted. "Right, there wasn't a random girl on your lap. You weren't drinking after you promised you would give it up. It was all in my head. Okay, Killian." He sighed loudly. "I'm sick of this, you know? I'm not as stupid as you think I am. Do you even love me?"

"Are you serious?" My eyes flew open to find Matthias watching me with pain written all over his face. "Yes, I love you Matthias. I would rather die than live without you. I would give up my entire career for you. I hate myself for everything I've done to you. I'm nothing without you. You're my ride or die." I felt like the walls were suddenly closing in. Why was this happening? Why did I keep fucking everything up with him?

Matthias stared at me, searching my face with his hazel eyes before he finally spoke again. "Why did you do it, Kill? Tell me why you gave that recording out to everyone when you knew how it would hurt me." Tears began to slip down his cheeks, but when I tried to touch him, he simply took a step away from me.

"Why won't you let me hold you, babe? Why are you doing this?"

"Why won't you answer the question? I want the truth for once."

I swallowed the bile in my throat as I dropped my gaze to my feet. "Please, Matthias." My voice shook.

"Tell me. Goddamn it!" he shouted into the night.

The truth would not set him free. The truth would rip us apart forever.

I dragged my gaze up to Matthias's beautiful face, knowing this might be the last time I ever saw it again once I told him what he wanted so badly to hear. I sucked in as much air as I could before I let out a shaky breath. "I love you," I murmured. "Since that night I found you in the treehouse, Matthias, it's been you." I was going to lose him after this.

"I knew you wouldn't tell me." He started to turn around.

"I did it because Maverick told me someone saw us together." I watched as Matthias stopped. "I had to prove to them I didn't like you. Not like that." I felt my heart cracking in my chest and Matthias slipping from my fingers as the words fell from my lips. "I couldn't let them think I was into you like that."

Matthias's shoulders slumped forward before he turned back to look at me, his eyes full of hurt and hatred. "You did it for the band?" He sounded just as horrified as I felt.

"Yes, but—"

"I hate you."

It felt like someone was tearing my heart out when Matthias said those words to me. "Babe, you don't mean that." I needed to touch him, but he only moved further away. "Matthias, please," I begged.

"No, you don't get to fix it this time," he snarled. "I'm going home. We're over, and you're not going to contact me again. Understand?" Matthias raised his chin.

I shook my head. "I thought we were past this." I needed to touch him. If I could wrap my arms around him, he would feel how much I loved him; how much I needed him. Matthias felt the same way.

"Goodbye, Killian."

I dropped to the ground at his words. "Matthias, please," I croaked out, yanking my hands through my short hair, but when I looked back up, he was already gone.

***

"Do you think he's dead?"

"No, he's not dead, idiot. He's breathing."

"Why is he outside in the middle of the grass?"

"Probably passed out. I've been there myself. Not fun."

"Should we wake him?"

I opened my eyes to find two of the drivers, Mason Pelletier and Lake Mills, standing over me. "If you touch me, I swear to God I will punch you," I grunted before I leaned up onto my arms. "Fuck, where am I?" I dropped back onto the grass.

"Uh, you're in between my RV and Shepard's. What's the last thing you remember, man?" Lake ran a hand through his signature long, blonde hair.

I closed my eyes trying to think. "Shit." I shot back up. "I need to find Matthias." Everything began to turn before me, and I might have gone down again if Lake and Mason hadn't been there.

"Whoa, you're not going anywhere," Mason exclaimed. "Everyone is looking for you, dude. You have no idea how upset your PR person is." He gave Lake a look. "Don't you have a phone?" he asked me.

I patted my hips but couldn't find it. "Must have lost it." I didn't have time for this. It was daylight now. How long had I been here? Where was Matthias now? I had to get to him. I struggled in their grip before I realized it was no use. I was too hungover and too exhausted to fight them.

"Why don't we get you hydrated?" Lake suggested. "You have that look about you, Killian." He grinned at me as we started to walk through the rows of RVs.

I had heard the rumors about Lake Mills. In fact, the last time I had seen the guy, he was three sheets to the wind—but something told me he didn't remember that. "What look is that?" I asked him as I saw Lou standing with a few uniformed cops. *Fuck.*

"Where the hell have you been?" She came marching toward me. "Do you have any idea what the hell I've been going through for the past eight hours?" Lou smacked me in the chest before she hugged me.

I kept my arms at my side. "Where is he?" I asked when she pulled back to search my face.

"He went home, Killian," Lou told me. "Mason, Lake, where did you find him?" She turned away from me to look at the two NASCAR drivers who flanked me.

Mason chuckled softly. "Passed out next to Shepard's RV," he answered.

"Passed out...Killian! What is wrong with you?" Lou looked like she wasn't sure if she should hit me or hug me again. "Where are you going now?" she asked as I started walking.

"Canfield."

"Killian, stop. Stop right now."

I ignored her. I had to get to Matthias. I had to fix this mess that I created before I lost him for good. Thoughts of him cutting down the tree shot through me and I stumbled, only to have someone catch me. I looked up to find Hutch Kelly, Rand's crew chief, watching me. I knew very little about him since he took over the job. Only that he was camera shy, was good at his job, and loved his wife.

"Careful," Hutch muttered.

I nodded. "Thanks." I started walking again.

"Matthias isn't in Canfield."

"How the fuck do you know where Matthias is, surfer boy?" I shot back. I clenched my fists as I stared him down.

Hutch didn't even blink an eye at me. In fact, I'm pretty sure I saw his lips twitch as he tried to repress a smile. "Because he and Sully got pretty friendly last night. She took him back to the Shepard house. You could get a ride home with Rand. But, then again, I'm just the surfer boy." He grinned.

"Matthias is at Rand's?" I grabbed Hutch's arm before he could walk away.

He looked down at where I held onto him. "Don't," he whispered, and I quickly let go of him. "Yes, and if you hurry, you can get a ride there too." Hutch's brown eyes swam with something I couldn't read. "I don't know what you did, but he was pretty upset. You might want to bring flowers. That usually works with my wife when I screw up." He nodded before he walked off.

Flowers, fuck. Should I bring Matthias flowers? Did he even like flowers? Did dudes want that sort of thing? "Mason!" I called out to Rand's best friend. "Is Shepard still here?" I prayed to God he was. I had to make this shit right.

Mason jutted his chin behind me. "Right behind you."

Rand gave me a little wave when I saw him. "Been looking all over for you, man. Where did you sneak off to? Actually"—he slipped his phone from his pocket—"I think your guy is at my place. What the hell did you do last night? Matthias was pretty upset." He tilted his head.

"I fucked up," I blurted out. "Can you take me to your house? I need to talk to him."

Rand shook his head. "I can't do that. I was given specific instructions by my wife not to let you anywhere near our house. I know, you can call me pussy whipped. But if I want to keep her happy, I do what she tells me." He shrugged his shoulders.

"I can't...Shepard, I can't do any of this without Matthias. Please, you have to get me to him."

Rand's brows dipped. "You don't look good," he commented.

"Because I'm not," I told him. "I'm begging you," I added, hoping he could see the pain I was in. "I have to fix this. I fucked up something fierce."

"I'll take you," Hutch said from behind me.

Rand popped his jaw. "No, you won't," he grunted.

"Yes, I will. We can talk on the way there. I think we might have more in common than you think." Hutch ignored Rand, who called out to him when he started walking. "Come on, Killian, before you get left behind."

I sprinted after him without a second thought.

Chapter Thirty-Two

Matthias
Four Years Ago

I shivered inside my fleece-lined coat as I followed behind Killian through the backyard. "How much further?" I called out to him. I watched the puff of smoke that trailed out from my mouth. "It's cold as a witch's tit out here." I had forgotten my gloves at home, but then again, I hadn't expected to be outside right now. It was a bit chilly for late March, but the weather here was always iffy.

Kill glanced over his shoulder to throw me his signature grin. The one that made me, as well as all the hot-blooded females in town, weak in the knees. "Don't act like such a pussy, babe," he sneered, only to come to a halt so he could yank my hand from my pocket. "To keep you warm," Killian murmured as he laced our fingers together. He tugged me closer before he began walking again.

"Are you taking me somewhere to murder me?" I teased, trying to get that smile directed in my direction again. It was what I lived for, especially when we were alone. When he flashed that smile, those dimples would appear, and then he would pin me down so he could have his way with me. I never put up a fight. I wanted it; no, what I wanted was Killian.

Killian snorted. "You still think I want to do that?" His grip tightened before he yanked me against his chest. "Matthias, what am I going to do with you?" His lips slammed against mine, catching me off guard. His teeth pulled on my bottom lip before his tongue slicked together with mine. I opened my mouth, needing more, and closed my eyes as Killian consumed me. He seemed different tonight, but in a good way.

God, I loved the way he kissed me. The way he found a way to make sure I knew he was in charge. I couldn't stop the moan that escaped my throat. I reached up to drag my fingers over Killian's cheek with my free hand as our mouths mated, teeth and tongues savage with desire, before he shoved me away. "Did I do something wrong?" I blinked up in confusion.

"You know the rules," he reminded me before he started walking again. "Come on, or I'll leave you behind." It felt like a slap in the face. I thought we were past that. Killian had started to act as if he wanted me, and if he was going to say he would leave me here and find someone else to fuck with, I wasn't going to just be his toy.

He stopped to look over his shoulder at me. "Babe," Killian said softly.

I rushed after him because he knew me so well, but most importantly because I wanted Killian's touch again. I didn't reach for his hand in case someone saw us; in case someone thought we were something other than just friends. Killian didn't like to touch or kiss me out in the open. He wasn't gay.

I was.

"Here." Killian pointed to a giant Sycamore tree.

I stopped to stare up, and up, noticing the small treehouse nestled in between the branches. "Holy shit," I gasped, tugging my hat down around my ears. I couldn't feel my toes anymore. How long did it take before hypothermia set in?

The memory of Killian finding me here just a short time ago, crying after the last time my dad beat the shit out of me after coming home drunk, ran through my brain. How he had fixed up my cuts before surprising the hell out of me with our first kiss.

"Thought it was only appropriate to bring you back here," Kill answered before reaching into his pocket. I watched as he removed a small switchblade, which he popped open. I might have taken a step back as he grinned at me. "Not killing you today, babe, I told you that already." He chuckled.

"Then what *are* we doing here?"

Killian leaned forward to start carving something into the trunk of the tree. I watched as my heart beat loudly in my ears, the cold temporarily forgotten as I realized what he was writing in the bark.

K+M

He flipped the blade shut and turned back to face me. "You think I don't want you? That I use you for my own selfish needs?" Killian's blue eyes blazed with heat. "Okay, maybe I do that, but I care about you Matthias," he confessed.

"You have a strange way of showing it," I blurted out. His hand shot out to grip my jaw. "You already know how I feel about you, Kill." I grabbed his wrist as his fingers tightened.

I watched as his tongue flicked out to wet his lips. "Babe, you have never been able to hide it from me. The first day you came to the house and caught me coming from the shower...shit, I wanted you then, too." Killian's lips slid up into a sexy smile. "Only you were there for Helena."

"Do you still want me?" My breath caught in my throat when Killian dropped his hand. I knew that it would never be out in the open for us. Jerking each other off when he snuck into my room in the middle of the night. Stolen kisses that never held me over when he left. Blowjobs that left me wanting more. And there had been plenty of times I thought I should break it off with him.

Killian's nostrils flared. "Climb up into the treehouse and find out, Matthias." His eyes landed on my lips. "Kiss me first though, because I miss that fucking mouth on mine," he growled.

It was on the tip of my tongue to say no, but I never could. Killian had me by the heart, dick, and throat, and the bastard knew it. The look in his eyes when I stepped closer, lifted my chin, and opened my mouth to him before he captured my lips with his own was enough to make me explode on contact.

Killian was never gentle with me. I wasn't sure if that was how he was with the girls he was with, but as his teeth grazed my lips and his hands dug into my shoulders, I realized I didn't care. I liked the rough way he manhandled me. How he kept me as his dirty secret, knowing I would come whenever he called and I would do whatever he wanted, *when* he wanted.

"Treehouse," Killian growled, cupping my head between his hands. I enjoyed the warmth of his gloves for a moment before he shoved me back. "Now, Matthias," he demanded.

I began to climb the ladder nailed into the tree and pushed open the door to climb up inside the house. I blinked in confusion as I let my eyes roam around the small space. Gone was the usual mess of beer cans and garbage, and it was replaced with white twinkle lights glowing against the walls, a large mattress pressed against the far wall with blankets and pillows, and what looked like a bottle of champagne on the floor. I turned to look up at Killian, who had joined me and he gave me a shy smile. This was something I had never expected from a man like him.

"What do you think, Matthias?" He dropped his gaze to his boots as a blush crept up his face. "I used to hate it here. My dad built it before the accident." Killian swallowed nervously as he reached up to remove the knit hat on his head, and I watched as his dark curls sprang out from beneath. "But you changed that for me with just one kiss."

I swallowed nervously. "You did this?" I felt the hairs stand up on the back of my neck. "For us?" I dared ask.

"Fuck yeah I did." He finally met my gaze again. "I know I'm a prick. What we've been doing over the past few months has been better than anything I've ever done with anyone. I hope you know that I'm into you, babe." His dimples appeared as our eyes met. "I fucking like you," he confessed.

I felt warm all over. "I like you, too." But he already knew that.

"I think"—Killian took a step closer—"you sort of more than like me, Matthias." He slowly pulled the zipper down on my coat, then ran his hands up my chest before he dropped my coat onto the floor.

I always liked that we were the same height—six foot one—but right now, I wished I could shrink away from his heated gaze. "Don't make me tell you anything that I don't want to, Kill," I whispered. I couldn't tell him I loved him without him feeling the same. Not to mention I was afraid he would use it against me at a later date—when he decided he no longer had a use for me and threw me away like trash.

"You don't have to."

I noticed the way Killian's hand trembled when he began to unbutton my shirt. "What are we doing here?" I asked, and closed my eyes when his fingers grazed my skin. His touch was heaven on my body.

"What do you think, Matthias?" Killian's voice was against my ear now. "I plan to have my way with you, the way we always talked about." He bit down on my lobe, causing me to groan. "You want that, too, right?" He sounded unsure of himself.

My eyes flew open to stare into Killian's hooded blues. "I'm yours." I dared reach up to grip his neck, and when he didn't push me back I slid my lips over his. "You have to know that by now, Kill." My heart, body, and soul belonged to no other. They never had.

Killian's mouth found mine as he tugged open the rest of my buttons, and then my shirt joined my jacket on the floor. His nails dug into my skin as he wrapped his arms around me, his breath coming faster. "Take off your pants," he growled as he pulled away. "Boxers, too," he instructed.

I kicked off my boots, slid off my jeans, and glanced up to find Killian's eyes pinned on me, his shirt halfway up his chest. "What?" I felt a smile slip over my face. "You see something you want?" I sucked my bottom lip into my mouth.

"You."

My cock jerked at the single word. How long had I been dreaming of this moment with Killian, thinking it would never happen? "Yeah?" I slowly dragged my briefs down my thighs, but kept my eyes on his face. When my length sprung free, Killian's eyes widened.

He nodded. "Yeah, babe." He smirked before his shirt was off, and he unbuttoned his jeans.

I let my eyes move over his muscled chest and the few dark lines of ink sprinkled across his pecs before I faced him again. "Pants and boxers too," I repeated, only to have him chuckle softly. I liked this playful version of Killian. My heart pounded against my ribs.

"Of course." Killian nodded. He removed his boots, jeans, and underwear, which left us standing naked, just staring at one another. He was the most beautiful man I had ever seen, and he was mine. At least for tonight.

"Do you—"

"I think—"

Killian's dimples appeared. "You nervous?" He reached up to tuck a piece of hair behind my ear.

He knew I was a virgin where it counted, only having his mouth and hands on me. I flushed. "A little," I admitted in a hushed voice.

"Matthias." Killian's voice made goosebumps break out on my skin. He gripped the back of my neck tightly. "Lie down, get comfortable, and get ready." He kissed me hard and then released me.

I moved over to the mattress, where I sat down and then pulled my legs up so I could ease myself back down. "How did you get this up here?" I tilted my head as Killian stalked over to me. Heat curled in my stomach as he fisted his cock. "Let me touch you." I sat back up, only to have him push me back down.

"I want to make *you* feel good, babe." He climbed up onto the mattress so he could splay his body over mine. He buried his face against my neck, his tongue darting out to lap at my skin. "You're beautiful, Matthias," he whispered before slipping down my chest. He stopped to lick and suck at each nipple, my hands instantly folding into his curls.

"Killian," I moaned, and for the first time I realized we didn't have to hide right now. We could do whatever we wanted, make as much noise as we needed, and he wanted me. At least for tonight. Killian's hand suddenly gripped my dick and I cried out with pleasure. "God, yes." I bucked my hips as he pumped me, wanting more.

He made a sound deep in his throat. "I love your cock." Killian's tongue ran up my length and around the tip. "So thick, long, and hard, just for me." He wrapped his lips around the head but didn't move. Instead, Killian stopped to lock eyes with me before he took me all the way down his throat.

I loved his mouth on me. I craved it like a drug. "That feels so fucking good." I pulled on his hair, the curls soft and silky against my skin. "Don't fucking stop, please, don't stop." I arched my hips trying to keep him close.

"So ready for me, aren't you Matthias?" Killian reached down to cup my balls in his hand as he stopped to pin his dark gaze on me. "You want to come? You want to shoot your cum right down my throat and watch me take it?" His mouth hovered over my tip as his tongue darted out to lick lightly.

I whimpered. "Yes, please, make me come," I begged, and twisted my fingers into his curls so I could pull on them the way Killian liked.

"Mmmmm," he hummed over me, causing the need to explode to build further. "You look so hot just spread out, watching me. So full of need, ready to pump me full." He swirled his tongue over me before he swallowed me whole.

My sudden eruption was violent and virile, leaving me gasping for air as I screamed out Killian's name. I yanked on his hair, my hips almost moving on their own, and I swear I saw stars. He took it all, every single drop. When he was done, he slithered over me and pressed his mouth against mine.

"Taste that?" He dragged his tongue over my bottom lip, nipping and biting. "You taste so damn good. I could eat you all day." Killian grasped my head between both hands. "I brought lube." His cheeks burned pink.

I touched his wrists. "Let me get you off first." I loved sucking Killian off. His cum was salty but sweet, like a forbidden fruit, and it left me wanting more.

"There will be time for that later." He rolled off me to reach for his pants. I watched as he produced a small black bottle before he smirked at me. "I'm so fucking hard for you, Matthias. I need to be inside you." He pushed my thighs apart. "You want that, don't you?"

I was instantly hard again. "Yes," I whimpered. We had talked about it for a couple of weeks, but I never thought it would happen.

"Then get ready, babe, because I'm going to make both of our dreams come true," Killian promised.

Chapter Thirty-Tree

Killian

Four Years Ago

I stared down at Matthias as he lay spread out before me. His eyes were hooded with need, full of want and desire. Fuck, he was beautiful, and I suddenly hated myself for what I was going to do to him. I wanted this—fuck did I want this—but after? After we had fucked, and I had left for California? I would come back, but maybe by then he would find someone else. I wouldn't blame him if he did.

"Hey." Matthias broke the silence in the treehouse. "Are you okay? Do you not want to do this? We don't have to." He leaned up onto his forearms.

I tilted my head. "Babe, I want this more than you realize," I assured him, and popped open the bottle of lube in my hand. "Have you ever put anything in this tight little ass of yours?" I groaned as I squirted a little of the slippery liquid onto my finger and slowly began to ease it inside of him.

Matthias's eyes clamped shut. "Just—" He whimpered softly. "I have a couple of toys that I've used on myself. God, Killian." His breath began to come out in heavy pants. "That feels so good." He wiggled against me.

"I know, babe." I reached for the condom I had placed on the bed and carefully ripped it open with my teeth as Matthias's eyes flew back open.

"Kill, you don't have to...not with me."

I wished that was the truth, but I always had to be careful. Especially with Matthias. "I know, but I want to make sure we're both safe. Just for now." The lie slipped off my tongue so easily that I couldn't help but feel guilty. Would Matthias always feel this way about me? Would I ever be able to tell him just how much he meant to me?

I rolled the rubber down my shaft before I coated it with the lubricant. Then I moved closer to where Matthias was on the bed, his mouth open and his eyes wide. "Touch your cock, babe," I ordered. "Stroke it slowly and gently for me." I pressed his thighs down as I watched him do as I instructed.

Matthias wrapped one hand around his dick. "Kill, if I do this, I'm going to come again," he whispered. He groaned when I pressed the head of my cock to his opening.

"Do it," I said again. "Jerk yourself off while I fuck your ass." I slid just the tip in, and we both let out low grunts of pleasure.

Matthias's hand slowly slid up and down his hard, thick cock. I stifled a groan as I watched him, while molten desire seeped through my body. I resisted the urge to shove my dick all the way to the hilt inside of Matthias, to fuck him so hard he came in seconds. I didn't want to hurt him, and I wanted us both to enjoy this as long as possible.

"More," he begged as he tried to take what he wanted from me. "Give it to me, Killian. I can take it." His free hand dug into his thighs as I slipped all the way in, and his quiet groans turned into loud cries. "Oh my God." Matthias's hips bucked up. "Holy...Killian, that's so fucking good." His hazel eyes landed on me.

I couldn't speak. I couldn't even think. He felt so good wrapped around me that I was afraid I might have actually been dreaming. Instead, I leaned down to cover Matthias's mouth with my own. "It's the two of us against the world, babe," I murmured against his lips, wrapping my arms around his body. I watched the way his eyes rolled back with each thrust and the way he arched his back to meet me. As I gritted my teeth to fight my impending release, I realized that I not only cared about Matthias Fuller, I loved him. He was everything I would ever need or want in my life.

"I'm going to come." A tortured moan squeezed past his lips. "I can't...I can't stop it." Matthias cried out as his release shook his body. I felt the hot spatter of his cum against my stomach and listened to the sounds of his pleasured screams as they filled the treehouse.

I followed behind him, my own climax filling the condom with such a force I thought I might blast a hole through it. I came harder than I ever had as I pounded into Matthias, and that's when I realized he was still jerking his cock, the sounds of another orgasm on his lips. He clenched around me as his eyes clamped shut, and I groaned as Matthias came again.

"Fuck," he whimpered, dropping both hands against the mattress.

I watched as I carefully slipped my cock out, breath slowly returning to normal. I removed the condom and tied it up before I dropped it on the floor. I had brought some baby wipes to clean up with, but right now all I wanted to do was wrap myself around Matthias and hold him. I started for the bag I had brought, knowing cleanup was more important.

"Killian?" His sleepy voice made my heart stutter in my chest. I glanced over my shoulder to find him watching me. "Are you okay? You're not having second thoughts are you?" Matthias sounded scared.

I held up the container. "Babe." I gave him my biggest smile and watched the way his cock grew hard again. "My, my," I teased. "Are you ready for another round, Matthias? Three orgasms weren't enough?" I moved to sit down next to him, popped open the wipes, and began to clean him off. "Are you sore? Did I hurt you?" I asked as I gently ran the cloth over his backside.

"No." His hazel eyes were wide. "You didn't answer my question," he murmured.

I carefully cleaned off his ass, then used more wipes to clean off his cum. After I had completely taken care of Matthias, I cleaned off myself before I dropped the wipes onto the floor. "Let's get under the covers," I said. Matthias stood up so I could pull back the blankets, and together we climbed back onto the mattress. Once we were wrapped up tightly, I tucked my face into his neck. "No, Matthias, I'm not having second thoughts," I whispered.

Matthias let out a content sigh, his hands finding their way into my curls like they always did. It was so cathartic for me, and I had grown to crave it like a drug. It was the little things like this that I would miss the most when I left. "Did you like it?" he asked softly.

"Did I like it?"

"Yeah, did you like having sex with me?"

I pulled back to stare Matthias in the face. "You're not seriously asking me that question right now, are you?" I growled.

"I just...I've never done it before, and you've been with plenty of girls. So I'm not sure if I did it right." Matthias dropped his gaze.

I cupped his face with my hands. "It was the best sex I've ever had," I assured him. "I swear." I slid my lips over his, and suddenly found Matthias straddling my waist. This was new; He'd never tried to take control like this. I felt his hard cock pressed against me, and I couldn't resist reaching down to wrap my hand around him. "It was so fucking good." I stared up into his face. "Feeling you wrapped around me, the way you came a third time when I did. So hot, babe." I groaned when Matthias's hand found my own length. He gripped it tightly in his hand. "You want another round, is that it?"

"No, not yet. This is good, too." His head dropped back as we slowly jerked each other off.

I stared up at Matthias, watching the way his Adam's apple moved and the panting of his chest, and couldn't resist grabbing his throat to bring him back down to me. "Tell me how you feel about me." I dragged my tongue against the curve of his neck as he groaned. "I need to hear you say it." My teeth grazed his skin, and he shivered against me.

"Killian, don't," Matthias whimpered.

I flipped him over onto his back. "Tell me you need me." I shoved his hand away from me so I could get us both off. "Tell me it's only me. Tell me it's only us." I groaned at the feel of skin against skin. At first I thought he might try to fight me again, but when he finally spoke, it was like the world stood still.

"I love you Killian. I've always loved you, and I hope that someday you can love me back. Do you think that's possible?"

Warmth spread through my body at Matthias's words, and when I met his heated gaze, I felt my eyes fill with tears. I couldn't do this to him. This boy loved me, and I...

I kissed him then, because I couldn't answer that question. I knew that what I was going to do to him in a couple of days would break him, break me, and stomp out any feelings Matthias ever had for me. Any chance at happiness the two of us might have had would be over, and I would hate myself for a little while, but I would recover. I was afraid Matthias might not.

***

"I'm leaving for California in a couple of days." I brushed strands of hair back from Matthias's face as he turned to look at me. "With the band," I added.

Matthias sat up. "What, since when?" His voice dripped with fear. "What about...what about us?" he asked. "I mean, I don't want to assume that there is an us or anything." He stumbled over his words.

I reached for his hands. "There's an us, trust me. I want you to come out there with me. Once you graduate in June." I tugged on him lightly, hoping Matthias would lie back down, but when he didn't I climbed up to touch his face.

"Hey, we can be together out there. We can be whoever we want and no one will care," I assured him.

"You want me with you?"

"I wouldn't say it if I didn't mean it."

Matthias's brows dipped. "What about Mulligan? What will the guys think about you being with me? If you get a record deal, you'll have all these new fans that won't want you—" I pressed a finger over his lips, but he pushed my hand away. "Killian, are you sure?" he whispered.

I was sure enough to know I wasn't going to give that recording to anyone. Maverick could eat a dick. And I would tell him that when I saw him tomorrow. "Yes," I whispered.

"The two of us against the world, right? That's what you said before?" Matthias dragged his thumbs over my cheeks. "Is this real? Is this actually happening?" He sounded so unsure of himself. That was my fault for treating him the way I had, and I wasn't going to do that anymore. Matthias deserved someone who would treasure him, take care of him, and not treat him like some dirty secret.

I reached down for my pants that were on the floor and tugged my phone free. "Yes," I told him. "Here, let's take our first official picture together. I'll send it to you." I waited until Matthias was snuggled into me, my arm around his shoulders and his head tucked next to mine before I snapped a selfie. "Cute," I teased as I turned my phone so I could show it to him. We both looked thoroughly fucked with our bedhead and pink cheeks. I sent it off to Matthias before I put my phone back.

"You're really leaving Canfield?" Matthias asked.

I nodded. "It's only for a few months. We can talk and text. I know it's sudden, but the guys and I were talking about it last night. We decided it was the best thing for the band. It's sort of why I planned this for tonight. I wanted to do something special for you." I hated lying to him, but now that I knew I wouldn't be giving Maverick that recording, it didn't matter. I wouldn't hurt Matthias. I would kill myself first.

"Why did you wait so long to come for me, Kill?"

"I was afraid, babe, but I'm not afraid anymore."

Matthias looked at me with such love in his eyes that I felt my throat grow dry. "It'll be weird without you here. I'll miss you." He gave me a shy smile.

"Not as much as I'll miss you," I murmured.

Chapter Thirty-Four

Killian

We had been in Hutch's car for ten minutes, and the dude hadn't said one word to me. I honestly didn't want to make small talk, but by the vibe he was giving off I could tell he didn't like me, and I couldn't figure out why. I had never met Hutch Kelly before. The last time I was at a NASCAR race, Shepard had another crew chief. The only things I knew about Hutch were that he was the silent type and didn't like attention brought to him, was super awkward during interviews during races, and his wife was some insanely talented ballet dancer.

"Are you on medication?"

I was so surprised that Hutch had actually spoken to me, I almost thought I had imagined it. "Excuse me?" I exclaimed.

He rolled his eyes as he slowed down the car. "Medication? Are you taking any for your depression?" Hutch glanced at me for a second, his brown eyes dark with something I couldn't figure out. Curiosity, maybe, or possibly something more.

"Why would you ask me that?" I grunted. "You don't know me." I felt my blood pressure start to rise, along with my anger. "You know what? I don't have to listen to this—"

"You're wrong, I do know you." Hutch stopped me before I could get any further. "Because I am you." He pulled the car into the parking lot of a nearly deserted diner and twisted his body to glare at me. "You're going to lose

Matthias if you keep this shit up," he warned. "Get out of the car. We're going inside to eat, and talk," he growled before climbing from the vehicle.

I sat there for a second, trying to gather myself together. I didn't have to do anything Hutch told me to. I could call an Uber and go back to the track, or maybe...I jumped when someone knocked on the window, and frowned when I saw it was Hutch. "Fine," I snarled, removing my seatbelt.

Once we were inside and seated, I felt like I was sitting in the principal's office. There was something brewing beneath Hutch's eyes that I didn't like, and once the waitress had taken our orders—although I honestly wasn't very hungry—and poured us coffee, I remembered what he'd said back in the car. "What...what did you mean when you said you *are* me?" I dragged my hand through my hair, chewing on my lip.

"I was a mess when I met the woman who is now my wife. I was depressed, hardly ever spoke at all, and full of so much self-hatred I wanted to die," Hutch confessed. "I saw a therapist back then, and I still do now. I also took medication, but Jillian—that's my wife—she was the person that saved me. Brought me out of the darkness again. I don't deserve her, and I spend every single day making sure she knows how much I love her. You want to end up alone, Killian? Because if you keep going down this road, I promise you that you will." He popped his jaw.

The thought made me sick, or maybe it was the fried food. "Matthias wouldn't do that to me," I whispered. I had to have him in my life, because if I didn't? I was scared of what might happen.

"It's not about what Matthias would do. It's about what you would do for Matthias." Hutch asked, "Would you fix yourself? Get your head on straight enough so that you can be the man he deserves? Sober up maybe? Get clean? I'm not here to judge you, man, but I can see something might be slowly eating you alive." There was something about the way Hutch spoke to me that made me realize he might have been in my situation before. "Like I said, Jillian helped me with my darkness, and I have a feeling that Matthias will do the same for you."

I pinned my gaze on the silverware on the table. "I'm not on medication," I told him. "I never liked the way it made me feel." My chin quivered, but I couldn't stop it. "I was diagnosed with bipolar disorder when I was a teenager. My grandmother tried to get me to talk to someone, but I wouldn't. I said I was fine, and I was. For a little while." When I looked back up at Hutch again, he was looking away, as if he knew I needed some privacy.

"What do you do to relieve the pain? Drink?"

"Sometimes, or I'll take whatever drug I can get my hands on."

Hutch placed his hands palm down on the table. "What else?" He tilted his head. "Girls? Because you couldn't admit that you are gay?"

"I'm not gay."

"Bullshit."

That familiar prickle of fear began to creep up my spine; the one that meant someone might find out the truth about who I really was. That I liked the way it felt when I was with Matthias, that he made me feel like a real man, and that he made me feel safe. When the overwhelming urge to knock Hutch into next week didn't hit me, I took a deep breath. "I cut myself," I heard myself admit to him. "Usually in places no one can see, especially my family and friends. It's helped more than anything else, except the one time I went too deep and nearly killed myself." I shook my head. "No, that's a lie. I tried to kill myself. I broke Matthias's heart and I couldn't live with it anymore. All I could see when I closed my eyes was his smile; the way his eyes lit up when he saw me, and I swore I could hear the sound of his laugh at night when I was trying to sleep." I hung my head in shame.

Hutch's chin dipped down to his chest. "Does he know that?"

"Matthias knows everything about me." I held out my arm. "I tried to cover it with tattoos." Hutch watched as I dragged my finger down the jagged scar. "That would make four people that know about this now, including you." I didn't know why I told him. I barely knew the guy.

Hutch didn't say anything for what felt like forever, and just when I thought the silence was overbearing, he began to talk. "I swallowed an entire bottle of sleeping pills." He let out a forced laugh. "Not my finest hour, but I felt I had no other choice at the time. Jillian and I weren't together, I had married someone I wasn't in love with, and even though I had a beautiful daughter, I felt I couldn't be the father I wanted to be. Jillian saved me, just like she always did. But it wasn't until I got the help I truly needed that I was able to become the man she deserved. I think, Killian, what you need to do is take a step back from your relationship and get some help. I see a lot of myself in you, and if you love

Matthias the way you say you do, he'll wait for you. He'll be there when you're ready, and you can have your happily ever after." The waitress walked back to the table with two plates piled high with food, and I felt sick to my stomach.

"I'm not gay," I said the moment she was gone. "But I guess I could be bisexual." I saw a smile tug at Hutch's lips. "I don't find myself attracted to you, or Shepard, or any other guy. Just Matthias. He's always been it for me."

Hutch chuckled. "You ever want to hit someone like you wanted to hit me earlier when I called you gay?" he asked as he began to cut up his pancakes.

"I didn't want to hit you, but yes, all the time."

"He makes your demons go away, doesn't he?"

I closed my eyes. "Yes," I whispered as tears burned behind my lids. "Matthias makes me feel normal, if that's possible." When I looked at Hutch again, he nodded at me. I reached for a piece of bacon and popped it into my mouth.

"Fix yourself for him, Killian. He's your person, and if you lose him, I don't want to find out you bled out on the bathroom floor of a hotel room." He smirked when my eyes went wide. "I think you're an alright guy," Hutch teased. "That if things were different, we might have been friends." He took a bite of his breakfast.

I washed down the food I had managed to swallow with the bitter coffee. "Yeah?" I asked. "Because we're both fucked in the head, or because we both found the person that quiets our demons?"

"Both, I suppose." Hutch shrugged.

I chuckled softly. "We could still be friends, right? I mean, if you want." I didn't have a lot of friends in my life, other than Matthias, Dean, and my sister. Maybe I should try to make some more. It couldn't hurt.

"I'm a horrible friend. I never text back, and I never want to hang out. I'd rather be with Jillian, although Shepard drags me out with the boys sometimes. I last about two hours before I head home."

"I don't really have any, so I guess that makes two of us."

Hutch swallowed the mouthful of pancakes he had before he spoke again. "Maybe we could be friends." He grinned at me.

"Maybe." I went back to my omelet as he dug his phone from his pocket, saying something about his wife being pregnant. My heart ached at the thought of Matthias thinking I left him, and I suddenly had the urge to call him before remembering that my phone was missing.

"I should warn you, Sully is going to be pissed when we get to the Shepard house." He wiped his mouth. "I have a feeling she isn't going to be your biggest fan right now. She gets pretty protective when she likes someone," he warned me.

I was pretty sure I could deal with whatever Brooklyn Shepard tried to throw my way. "I can handle her," I assured him.

"Yeah, I'm not so sure about that." Hutch grabbed the check from the waitress just as I went to reach for it. "Mason is married to her sister, did you know that?" He raised his hip to slip his wallet from his pocket, then dropped some cash onto the table.

I shook my head. "Wait, Mason Pelletier?" Things had really changed since the last time I was around these guys. "He's married? For real?" I was more than surprised.

"Let's just say things did not go well when that first happened, since Mason is not known for being a one-woman kind of man." He stood up. "Ready?" he asked.

I was still trying to wrap my head around the fact that Mason Pelletier had settled down as I followed Hutch back out to the car. He had been one of the biggest players. "Next thing you're going to tell me is that Lake has settled down, too." He turned to stare at me. "No fucking way," I gasped.

"Yep." He grinned. "He's married to Brooklyn's best friend. And"—he climbed into the vehicle once the doors were unlocked—"stone cold sober." Hutch started the car. "Buckle up, Killian, because it's going to be a bumpy ride once Brooklyn has her way with you. Trust me on that."

I might have noticed or asked last night about all of the things Hutch had just told me, if I hadn't been so caught up in my own world. I really was a horrible friend. Maybe it was finally time I got myself together and made myself a better person.

Chapter Thirty-Five

Matthias

I sat on the Shepard's front porch, holding my now-cold cup of coffee and staring out onto the front lawn. I liked it here. It was quiet, calm, and most of all, there was no drama. Or rather, there was no Killian to cause the drama. Flashes of the man I loved went through my brain.

When he first kissed me.

When he first broke my heart.

When he first jerked me off.

When he broke my heart again.

Tears filled my eyes as I thought about all the times Killian had broken that same heart after he'd promised that he would never do it again. Was I just that stupid, or was he just that good at manipulating me?

"Hey." Brooklyn's voice interrupted my thoughts as she stepped out onto the porch. "How are you holding up?" She sat down next to me.

I shrugged. "The same I guess." I glanced over at her to notice that she was wearing one of Rand's shirts with his number and car on it. "Do you and your husband fight?" I asked. "Sorry, that's not really any of my business. You don't have to answer that." I dropped my gaze to stare at my feet.

"We don't really fight now, but..." Brooklyn giggled as she crossed her legs. "Sweetie, I hated his guts when we first met. He was the most egotistical, stuck-up a-hole I had ever met. He hit on me in front of his teammate—and my good friend, Finn Houston—who had asked him not to. Rand

287

had the reputation of being a playboy, so I wasn't interested. Not to mention I had already dated a driver." She patted my arm. "But I was the bigger asshole because I kept our son hidden from him after we separated for a while."

I nearly snorted coffee out my nose. "You what?" I gasped.

"I told you I was the asshole, right?"

"Yes. I mean, no. It's not any of my business."

Brooklyn started to say something else just as a car started to pull up the driveway. "That looks like Hutch's car," she murmured. Sure enough, once the vehicle had stopped, Hutch Kelly climbed out of the driver's side. I think I was more surprised when Killian climbed from the passenger side.

"No." I shook my head. I wasn't ready to talk with him yet.

"Son of a bitch," Brooklyn hissed before she shot down the stairs, straight toward him. "Get out." She pointed at him. "You're not welcome here, Killian. And you," she exclaimed, turning to Hutch. "How could you?" She crossed her arms over her chest. She was feisty as hell, and I suddenly realized how much I liked her.

Killian simply ignored her as he headed straight toward where I sat. "I need to talk to you," he said as he got within earshot. When I stood up, he sprinted up the stairs. "Matthias, wait."

"No, you wait," I shouted back at him. "I am done having my heart broken, Killian. Do you have any idea what that feels like? Did you walk in on your supposed boyfriend with some random woman on his lap? I can't trust you any further than I can throw you, and I'm not doing this with you again. You're free to do whatever you want, whenever you want. I want nothing to do with you." I watched the way Killian's eyes went wide, witnessing the hurt that flashed over his face, and how his shoulders slumped forward before he took one step closer.

He dropped his head, and then got to his knees. "Please, Matthias." His voice was low, nearly a whisper. "I need you." When Killian looked up at me, tears clung to his lashes and cheeks. "You calm my demons, silence the darkness, and without you, I have nothing." He took a shaky breath. "If I get the help I need: go to rehab, take medication, all the things that will fix me and make me the man I need to be for you, will you still have me?" he asked.

"Killian, I thought you didn't want to take medication?"

"If that's what it takes, babe, I'll do it."

I glanced over to where Hutch and Brooklyn stood before I met Killian's eyes again. "You don't have to do that," I whispered. "I don't want you to do it for me, I want you to do it for yourself. You're the one that needs the help," I reminded him.

"I can't win, can I?" Killian asked. "No matter what I say or do, it's not going to be the right thing." It broke my heart hearing him say that. "I want to be the man you deserve. I want to fix myself so I can be there for you. Whenever I picture my future, you're there. Please, give me one more chance, Matthias." He dropped down onto the grass.

I placed my cup of coffee on one of the vacant chairs before I moved down the steps, and then I was on the ground with him. "You think of me in your future?" I asked as I cupped his face in my hands, and tilted his head up so he had no choice but to look at me.

"It's always you, babe."

"What do you see?"

Killian gripped my wrists with his hands. "Happiness. You and me, with a house of our own." His eyes sparkled, but with happy tears this time. "Would you want that with me? Would you want to...would you want to get married?" he asked.

"Are you proposing to me?" It felt like all the air was being sucked from my lungs.

Killian blushed. "Matthias, when I propose to you, I promise it won't be like this. I'll do it right with a ring and getting down on one knee, and I wouldn't do it here," he assured me. "But would you? Want to get married, I mean?" he asked again, almost shyly.

"Yes." Hope began to bloom inside me again, but I was almost afraid to accept it. "Yes to everything. I'll wait for you. I've always wanted to marry you, so yes, Killian. But I swear to God, if you fuck this up one more time, I won't take you back. I will leave you behind without ever looking back," I promised.

He moved to slide his lips lightly over mine. "I won't," he murmured.

***

Killian clung so tightly to my hand as we left the Shepard house that I thought he might cut off the circulation. He kept his gaze down and away from me so that I couldn't see his face, but it didn't matter. Exhaustion clung to him like a second skin, but it was the anxiety I could feel radiating from his body that hurt me the most. If I could take his place, help Killian get over whatever he was going through at this exact moment, I would in a heartbeat. I hated seeing him like this. We might have stayed longer, but it turned into mass chaos that I could see Killian didn't want to deal with when Brooklyn's sister, London, showed up. I think it was the kids that did it for him. So we, after thanking her for her hospitality and exchanging phone numbers, grabbed an Uber and left.

"I was telling Lou what is going on." I nudged his shoulder, but he kept his blues cast down to his feet. "Hey, you okay in there?" I asked.

Killian nodded. "Sure," he answered. "You're texting with Lou now?"

"She said she tried you, but you didn't answer."

"I lost my phone last night."

I gave him the side-eye. "I'm not going to even ask how you did that," I grunted and sent off another text before I got a reply. "Lou has your phone," I told him.

"Well, that's good. I was afraid someone might have found it and spread my personal shit all over the internet by now, dick pics and all." Killian stared at me.

My eyes went wide. "Are you serious? Kill, you can't—why are you laughing right now?" I couldn't believe he found any of this funny. "You can't have pictures of your dick on your phone. That's just asking for trouble."

"I'm kidding, Matthias, relax." That's when I saw it. The fear he was desperately trying to hide from me. I knew

Killian was scared. Scared of what might happen while he was in rehab. Afraid of what the tabloids would say once they got wind of the situation, but none of that mattered. The only thing that did was getting him healthy. "It's going to be okay, right?" he whispered softly. "I mean, us, me, everything?" His brows dipped as he chewed nervously on his lip.

I nodded. "Yes," I told him, because I knew that was what Killian needed to hear right now. I wasn't sure myself, but I wanted it to be. I wanted us to have our happily ever after. I wanted Killian to be healthy, both physically and mentally. Most of all, I needed him to be okay. For him to stop cutting himself. To stop drinking, doing drugs, and to stop beating himself up over everything. "I can't come with you, you know that, right?" I asked, and watched the way Killian's eyes filled with doubt. "You're going to be great. You're Killian Hampton." I reached for his hand again. "You're going to move fucking mountains, just like you always do."

"What if I can't?"

"What if you can?"

A smile pulled at the corner of Killian's lips. "How can you still love me, Matthias? After all the bullshit and everything else I've put you through?" he asked, without even glancing at the Uber driver. "I ruined your life, and yet you're still here." I watched the way his blues filled with tears.

"I've always loved you, baby, and I always will. You saved me when I needed you, and now it's my turn to do the same for you." I reached up to touch his face with the palm of my hand.

"I like it when you call me that," Killian confessed.

I nodded. "I know you do," I whispered.

Killian moved to bury his face into my neck, and I held him against me. Neither one of us said another word the rest of the drive to the airport, but I knew he was still scared. I was too, but I wouldn't tell Killian that. I needed to be strong for him now, and I would be, no matter what.

"I can't." Killian shook his head the moment we stepped inside the airport. "I don't...I can do this at home," he tried to convince me. "Back in Canfield. You'll be there, and as long as I have you, I can do anything." I felt the way his body trembled when I touched his elbow, but I saw the doubt written all over his face.

I stepped closer. "Baby." Killian's face softened. "We both know that's not true, or else you wouldn't be here right now," I said calmly. "You wouldn't be in this situation right now." I dragged my hands through his hair.

"I'm scared." There it was. "Don't forget about me." His eyes searched my face.

I wrapped my arms around Killian and held him against me. "I've been in love with you ever since I can remember. I don't think you're going to get rid of me easily," I teased, only to have him pull back to stare at me with fire in his eyes. "Hey." I slid my lips over his.

"Don't joke about shit like that, babe. As long as I know you're waiting for me when this is over, that's all I need." Killian whispered before his mouth landed on mine.

Chapter Thirty-Six

Killian

Four Years ago

I couldn't sleep in this car. It was too cramped with the entire band shoved in here, and all I could think about was Matthias. He hadn't responded to my calls or texts since yesterday. Had he changed his mind about us already? About me? I gripped my phone in my hand and stared down at the picture of us that I had set as my background. Maybe Helena had an idea what was going on. I started to text her but was quickly interrupted.

"Are you going to just sit there staring at your phone?" Dean asked, and I quickly shoved it back into my pocket.

Maverick snorted from the passenger seat while Blake drove. "You still think he's going to answer you?" he asked.

"Of course, why wouldn't...wait. Why wouldn't he answer me?" A sheen of sweat broke out over my skin. "Did you do something?" I would have yanked him into the backseat if I could have. "Mav, what did you do? I told you to let it go. We talked about this," I exclaimed as fear began to rip through my body. "I will slit your throat while you sleep," I threatened.

Maverick spun around with his eyes narrowed into angry slits. "We can't have the lead singer of our band tied down the second we hit California, Killian. Not to mention sucking dick like a homo—"

I slammed my fist into the side of his head before the rest of the sentence could escape his mouth. "You're a piece of shit, Maverick." I raised my arm, but Dean grabbed me before I could go at his brother again. "Let go." I struggled against him.

"It's done, Kill, there's nothing you can do about it." Maverick grinned at me with blood dripping down his chin and smeared over his teeth. It gave me creepy Joker vibes. "The entire school already knows. Hell, I'm betting the whole town knows."

My stomach dropped. "What do you mean? I didn't even record anything." I wanted to rip his damn head off.

"You didn't have to. I set up my own recording device. Nice touch with the lights, dude. Very romantic. It seems like you might have actually cared for the guy, so maybe I did you a favor. Getting attached is a bad idea."

I launched myself over the seat, not caring if Blake crashed the car into a tree at this point. "You're a dead man," I cried out as Dean tried to haul me into the backseat.

"Dude, what the hell!" Blake slammed on the brakes and pulled the car onto the side of the road. "Are you trying to get us all killed?" he asked.

"Just him." I straddled Maverick without a second thought and wrapped my hands around his throat. "You know I'll do it." I watched as Maverick stared back at me, and a sick smirk spread across his face. Blake and Dean were blurred noises in my ears. "You want me to hurt you? Is that it? Are you just as sick as I am, or do you just want me to end up in jail so you can find another front man?" I tightened my grip on Maverick and watched the way his eyes bugged, the color of his skin turning blue.

Hands gripped my wrists, trying to pry me off. "Killian, enough." Blake tried to loosen my grip. "You're going to regret this if you actually succeed," he warned.

I turned to look at him. "He ruined my life."

Arms wrapped around my waist. "You can't do this, Kill. He's an asshole, but he's my brother." Dean's voice drifted through my mind. "Imagine if someone wanted to hurt Helena."

My head spun around at his words. "Never," I whispered, and I felt myself letting go of Maverick, who began coughing and gasping for breath. I raised my arm and punched him in the nose. "Fuck you," I cried out, right before I did it again. "I will never forgive you for this. Do you hear me?" I shoved Dean away so I could climb from the car, not caring that he landed on his ass on the damp grass on the side of the road. When I pulled my phone from my pocket, I tried to call Matthias, hoping that he might have mercy on me. This time, instead of going straight to voicemail, I heard the words I never wanted to hear.

"The number you have dialed has been disconnected."

It would take four years before I would be able to speak to the boy I loved again. But in that time, I would I try to kill myself, nearly ruin my life, and almost lose my mind in the process.

***

Killian
Present Day

The moment I stepped foot into the Depression and Anxiety Center, I had to resist the urge to flee from the building. It was the same place Hutch had come to after he tried to commit suicide, but what worked for him might not work for me. I felt like an animal in a cage as they checked both me and my bags for drugs, took my vitals, asked me questions about my life and my diagnosis of bipolar disorder, and then proceeded to poke and prod me until I was sure I didn't have any blood left in my body.

"When can I see my boyfriend?" I blurted out when I finally felt I had a minute to breathe.

The doctor, who had introduced herself as Megan, stopped to look at me. "No visitors for the first thirty days," she told me as she tucked a piece of silver hair behind her ear.

"Fuck this, I'm leaving." I stood up, only to have two giant security guards appear out of nowhere.

Megan shook her head. "Mr. Hampton." She placed my paperwork onto her desk. "Hutch spoke very highly of you. It was because of him that I agreed to take you on as a patient. We have a waiting list of six months here." She waved the guards away. "Hutch was one of my favorite patients, although I'm not supposed to admit that, so I'm going to give you the benefit of the doubt. I know who you are and that you have a reputation for being difficult. I'm going to just tell you this now." She sat down and leaned back in her chair. "If you screw up, even once, you're out, and you're not coming back. Do you understand?"

"I need to see Matthias. He's important to me," I growled, ignoring everything she just said to me.

Megan nodded. "You can call him once a day for fifteen minutes. That's it. Once you've completed thirty days, he can visit you once a week, and you can speak to him for thirty minutes a day. But only if you don't fuck this up." She folded her arms over her chest.

I snorted with laughter. I think I liked this chick. "So, uh, you know Hutch?" I asked as I dragged my hand over my hair before I gripped the back of my neck.

"I can't talk about him, but yes."

"Good dude."

Megan stood back up. "He called me about you; said you needed my help, and *only* my help. Hutch doesn't take to too many people." She stopped to look at me again. "Would you like to call your boyfriend before we continue?" She pushed her desk phone toward me. "Five minutes," she whispered, holding up her palm.

I had never dialed a phone so fast in my life.

"Hello?" Matthias sounded confused when he answered.

"I miss you."

"Are you serious? How are you calling me right now? Are you breaking the rules already?" he hissed, and I couldn't stop the smile that spread across my face. "I miss you, too," he added.

I sighed contently as relief flooded my senses. "I was given permission to call you, babe, so you can relax," I assured him. "Just needed to hear your voice." I glanced at Megan to find her smiling into her paperwork. "I love you, Matthias." My voice tightened at the thought of not seeing him for a month.

"Not as much as I love you," he shot back.

"Liar." Tears stung my eyes. "I'll call you again as soon as I can, okay?" I hated to hang up, but I didn't want to press my luck. "I'll write to you, too." I met Megan's eyes when she looked up and nodded.

Matthias sniffed on the other end. "I'd like that, baby," he whispered.

"Goodbye, babe."

"Goodbye, Kill."

Megan tilted her head as she looked at me. "It's always the tough guys that fall the hardest," she teased as I sat back in my chair.

"Matthias saved my life. I need to get my shit together so we can be together."

She nodded. "I'm going to ask you something, but I don't want you to get upset." Megan tapped her fingers against the desk. "Are you bisexual? Remember, whatever you tell me stays between the two of us," she reminded.

I looked down at the dirty carpet beneath my feet. "I think so," I muttered softly. "I mean, I've never looked at another dude in the same way I look at Matthias. Before him, I was always interested in girls. And when we weren't together, I slept with girls too." Nerves stormed through my stomach.

"You two aren't together now?" she asked.

My head shot back up. "No, we are. There were just a few years that—" Shit, I was going to have to tell Megan about what had happened. "Do we have to talk about this now?" I wasn't ready to get into that quite yet.

"No, not if you don't want to, Killian." Megan gave me a brief smile. "Why don't I show you to your room so you can get some rest? We can talk more tomorrow." She stood up.

I followed behind her through the quiet halls and passed the closed doors. When she pushed open the one that led to the room that would be mine for at least the next ninety days, I couldn't stop the anxiety that threatened to shake me. Megan flipped on the light and turned to look at me. "We like everyone to have their own room here. That way it's more like home." She waved me inside. "I know it's scary, but you're doing the right thing, Killian."

I stepped inside, only to feel panic hit me. I shook my head. "I don't...I can't do this." I backed out of the room while taking giant gulps of breath.

"What if I told you that inside your suitcase, Matthias packed something of his that might make you feel like you were at home?"

My head shot up. "What?" I gasped out.

"A couple of his shirts that smelled like him?" she asked.

I moved so fast that I nearly pushed Megan out of the way to get to my suitcase. As I unzipped it, I found a plastic bag placed on top, and inside there were two shirts that I immediately recognized as Matthias's. I brought one up to my nose and inhaled his sweet, musky scent. "Shit," I whispered with tears in my eyes. My throat tightened as I thought of how he did this for me, and I knew I had to get my shit together.

"He told me you might need that." Megan leaned against the doorway. "Does this mean that you're going to stay?" she asked.

I nodded. "Yes," I assured her.

"Good. Breakfast is at seven, so make sure you're up or you'll miss out." She shut the door behind her, but I was lost in my boyfriend's scent.

I had no idea it was possible to miss someone so much just from his smell. I quickly changed into my pajamas, climbed into the bed, and tucked the shirt against the pillow so I could keep Matthias next to me. I wasn't sure if I would actually be able to get any sleep, but at least it would feel like he was with me.

Chapter Thirty-Seven

As expected, I slept like absolute shit without Matthias next to me. The scent of him helped, but without the warmth of his body to wrap myself around, I tossed and turned until I finally dragged myself into the tiny room they called a bathroom to take a piss and shower. I stared at myself in the mirror, hating the man that I had become.

Dark circles of exhaustion hung under my blue eyes.

Deep frown lines clung to my lips.

Who even was I anymore? Certainly not the Killian Hampton I once was. I was a shell of the boy I was growing up, the teenager I was in high school, and nothing close to the young man who fell in love with Matthias Fuller.

Matthias. Fuck, I missed him. I held up my arm to drag my finger over my jagged scar to remind myself why I was here. Because of what I had done. Okay, maybe I hadn't done it, but it was because of me that it happened. I had to atone for my sins and get better so I could be with him. So we could get our happy ending.

I smirked at my reflection in the mirror. Our happy ending. What did that even mean?

I moved back to the small bedroom to change into some fresh clothes before I put my fist through the mirror, and then made my way down the hallway by following the sounds of soft talking. I was surprised to find everyone up, but it was when they stopped to stare at me that I started to feel uncomfortable. I ignored them and moved to the coffee station so I could pour myself a cup. I drank the cup's entire black contents before I realized no one had started talking again.

"What?" I growled.

"Killian, maybe you want to introduce yourself." Megan seemed to appear out of nowhere.

I refilled my cup and brought it to my lips again. "No thanks." I spoke into the mug before I drank down the rest of the bitter java. "By the way everyone is watching me, I'm pretty sure they all know who I am." Besides, I wasn't here to make friends with anyone. Just needed to get my head on correctly.

"Hey, I know you," a guy with bright-red hair exclaimed. "You're the singer in Mulligan Downtown."

Thanks, Captain Obvious. I pinned my eyes on him. "So, what if I am?" I placed my empty cup down so I could fold my arms over my chest, wishing I could disappear. I never had a hard time with crowds, but right now, I wished the floor would open up and swallow me.

"Easy," Megan whispered. "We're all friends here, Mr. Hampton," she warned. "Jacob, why don't you introduce yourself first."

This was going to be hell on earth, wasn't it? I was going to have to play nice and—oh my God this guy was seven feet tall. He towered over my six-foot-one frame and stuck out his hand. "Jacob." He flashed a set of teeth as he smiled. "Big fan," he added.

"Uh, thanks." I took his hand, and Jacob shook my arm so hard I thought it might fall off. "I love meeting my fans," I added. I relaxed a bit after that when everyone began to talk to soft murmurs around me.

"It gets easier, Killian, I promise," Megan told me. "We have a session at ten, and then we can go over your plans for while you're here." I opened my mouth, but she cut me off. "You can call Matthias later. We'll work out a schedule for that, too." She smiled and patted my arm. "I think you're going to like it here."

***

I hated it here.

Megan brought up the subject of medication, which had upset me so badly that I had a panic attack in her office. I ended up wrapping my arms around my legs and rocking back and forth in the chair while muttering about how if I was bigger, I could have saved them. Yeah, not my finest hour, but when I finally snapped out of it, Megan asked me who I'd been talking about. I refused to answer; told her there was no way in hell I was going to take any fucking medication and stormed from the room. Only to return five minutes later, apologize, and tell her about my parent's car accident. She didn't press me for anything after that, but I knew she would as the week went on, and I knew I needed to prepare myself for that.

I would rather have a root canal than sit through group therapy again. I didn't want one person knowing my business, never mind a room of nine. I had to introduce myself, tell them why I was here, and what I hoped to achieve. If I was struggling, I could only imagine how Hutch had handled this situation.

Then there was the redhead with the burn scars named Josie that wouldn't stop following me. She suddenly attached herself to my hip in group therapy, joined me at dinner, and sat next to me while we were forced to watch *American Idol*—a show I despised more than anything, by the way—and the girl never said a word to anyone. I wasn't sure what her deal was, but when I was finally given permission to call Matthias, I told her I needed alone time and she simply stayed on the couch without arguing with me.

I had so many thoughts about Josie as I made my way to the small room where the phone was. Did she not realize I was taken? That I wasn't interested or into her like that? I liked that she didn't talk to me, she just seemed content sitting there as we ate dinner or I ignored the television, but she didn't talk. Not to me, or anyone. I wondered exactly what Josie was here for and how she got those horrible burns on her face.

"Hello?" Matthias's voice soothed me like nothing else could.

My body instantly relaxed the moment I heard him, and I leaned back in the chair. "Hey, babe," I whispered back. "Miss me?" I gripped the phone tightly in my hand.

"Yeah." He sounded almost relieved. "How was your first official day?"

I let out a long sigh and stared up at the ceiling. "All that matters is that I'm talking to you," I said before I sat up. "Horrible," I confessed before telling Matthias what happened. "I hate this place," I hissed.

"It's the first full day, Kill, you have to give it a chance."

"I know, but...fuck, I just miss you and all I want to do is hold you."

Matthias was so quiet on the other end I thought he hung up. "You're not going to leave yet, are you?" His voice shook as he spoke.

"What, no, why would you ask me that? I'm doing this for us. So, we can be together." I would spend forever in this place if that's what it took. "How are things in Canfield?" I had to change the subject before the tears in my eyes slipped down my cheeks.

Matthias chuckled. "Boring," he admitted.

We made small talk for the next few minutes before my fifteen minutes were up and I had to say goodbye. Standing outside the small room, waiting for me like a stalker, was Josie.

"You need to stop whatever"—I waved at the space between us—"this is." I started to walk past her, and then stopped. "What's your deal?" I turned back to look at her, but she simply blushed and dropped her gaze. "Why don't you talk?" I pushed.

Josie's eyes shot back up to mine, full of fear, and I watched as her chin trembled. Shit, now I was going to make her cry.

"I'm sorry, I shouldn't have asked you that."

Josie shook her head before she reached into her pocket, pulled out a notepad and a pen, and began to scribble something down. *My husband is a huge fan.*

"You're married?" she nodded. "You don't look old enough to be married." I watched her blush again. "You're following me because of your husband?"

Josie began to write again. *His name is Jameson. He and his friends are dying to see Mulligan in concert. I won't tell him you're here, though.*

I gripped the back of my neck. "Thanks, Josie." I wasn't sure what else to say, but now that I realized she wasn't some crazy fan, I felt a little better. "Does he come visit you? Maybe I could say hello sometime," I offered.

No. She scribbled so fast. *I don't want Jameson to see me like this.*

I could understand that. "Well, I'll sign something for him," I offered instead.

Josie beamed up at me with such happiness on her face that I couldn't help but feel terrible for being so mean earlier. "You can hang with me or whatever, if you want." I swear her smile got even bigger. We started walking back to where everyone was sitting around, still watching *American Idol.* Once we sat back down on the couch, I glanced over at Josie to find she wasn't even watching the show. She was staring down at her hands in her lap and chewing nervously on her lip.

"Do you talk to your husband?" I asked. She simply shook her head. I nudged the notepad in her hand. "Why not? I've been here for a day and I miss my boyfriend more than life. I bet Jameson would be over the moon if you called him."

Josie's cheeks reddened. *He put me here.* She stopped, and then continued writing. *My sister, brother, and Jameson did. I can't put all the blame on him.*

"Did you need to be here? I know I do." Shit, why was I telling this girl my business? Maybe because I could feel that she was just as broken as I was.

She stared at me, her eyes searching mine. "Yes," Josie whispered. and I watched as tears filled her eyes before she looked away again.

Before I could stop myself, I wrapped my arms around her and yanked her tight against my chest. "It's okay, we all have our demons," I whispered. "Your family did what they had to do, and that's why I'm here, too. Matthias is my reason for living, and without him, I have nothing. I need to get my shit together for him. So, we can be together." I heard her sniffle softly. "Your family must really love you," I added.

Josie pulled away with a look of embarrassment on her face. She started to reach for her notepad, but I stopped her. When she shook her head, I let her start writing. I knew she could talk just fine, but if this made her feel better, I'd let her go with it for now. *It's a long story, but maybe I'll tell you sometime,* Josie had scrawled out in her big, girly writing.

I think I liked this chick. "You're really married?" I asked. When she nodded, I smiled. "I'm going to ask Matthias to marry me when I get out of here. Do you think I should give him a ring? Did your husband give you one?" When Josie shook her head, I had even more questions, but I let that go too. "How old are you?" I changed the subject.

Yes, give your boy a ring, she scribbled down. *I'm eighteen, but I'll be nineteen in December.*

She was the same age as Matthias when I finally gave in to temptation. "You should call your husband." I touched Josie's hand. "Even if you're not ready to see him in person, at least call him and tell him you love him." I stood up. "I'm going to head to bed."

To my surprise, Josie jumped to her feet to hug me. "Thank you," she whispered, and then rushed off. I hoped maybe she was going to reach out to her husband.

Chapter Thirty-Eight

Matthias

The first week with Killian in rehab was hard, but after the first initial day, he seemed to be doing better. He didn't tell me too much about it, but he said that he was working through some of his problems and was even thinking about taking medication. That surprised me the most, even more than Killian telling me he had made a friend: a girl named Josie who mostly listened to him, hardly spoke, and that her husband was a huge fan of Mulligan Downtown.

"A girl?" I asked skeptically.

Killian chuckled softly from the other end of the line. "Relax, babe, although I do like the jealous side of you. She's married and knows all about you," he assured me. "She doesn't talk much. She writes down her comments on a notepad."

"What happened to her?"

"I'm not sure. She seems like she might be more fucked up than I am."

I liked that Killian seemed to be making progress, but I was still uneasy about this girl. Just because she knew about me didn't mean that she wouldn't try to make moves on my man. It was what I was thinking about on the trip to the center on Saturday afternoon. Helena was working so she couldn't come with me, so I was making the eight-hour drive all by myself. When I pulled into the Depression and Anxiety Center, I parked my truck and stared at the sprawling building in front of me.

It looked innocent enough. More like a college campus than a rehab facility. I wasn't sure why I was so nervous as I climbed from my vehicle, only to stop and watch as a sleek, black SUV slid into the space next to me. Out of the truck passenger side climbed a nervous-looking, dark-haired boy, who couldn't be older than nineteen. From the back, a blonde-haired boy and a purple-haired girl got out. The three of them appeared to be oblivious of me as they spoke in hushed whispers. The blonde wrapped his arm around the girl as they moved to the building, and I realized I was missing out on Killian time as I stood here.

Once inside the center, I gave them my name, why I was here, and who I was visiting. Then I was shown to the visiting area, where the three kids who'd parked next to me were waiting. The girl saw me first, flashed a brief smile, and then went back to talking to her friends. I couldn't sit down though, instead choosing to pace the room as I waited for Killian. I couldn't wait to see him, wrap my arms around him, and feel his lips against mine again. It felt like a year instead of a month.

"Babe."

I stopped at the sound of Killian's voice before I slowly turned around and came face to face with him. His hair seemed longer than before, his dark curls back in full force. If it was possible, he looked refreshed, like maybe he finally was getting the sleep he so desperately needed.

"You're staring at me like you're not sure if I'm not real or not, Matthias." Killian's lips turned up slightly. "I can assure you that I am. You want to come closer so I can prove it to you?" He flashed a smile, and those dimples I loved so much appeared.

I took a step closer, then another, and then I was in Killian's arms with his mouth on mine, and I was lost in him. I didn't care who was watching or in the room; the only person who mattered was Killian. I wrapped one arm around him while I dug my fingers into his hair and opened my mouth for him, his tongue slicking together with mine. I loved him. I loved Killian. I always had. I always would.

"I missed you," he whispered as he pulled back. He cupped my face. "Convinced I'm real now?" Killian teased.

I nodded. "I am, yes." I gripped his wrists. "Want to sit down?" I asked.

We moved to a vacant table, Killian grabbing my hand so he could lace our fingers together. "I love you," he murmured, pushing a piece of hair behind my ear.

"I love you," I answered back before the door opened again, and a red-headed girl peaked her head in. Her eyes moved from where I sat with Killian, to the group of three sitting at the other table. She gave a nervous smile before she moved further into the room, and the dark-haired boy was quick to jump from his seat to get to her.

"That's Josie," Killian told me. "I can only assume that's her husband." He used his free hand to move my face back to him. His fingers danced over my skin as his eyes searched mine.

I smiled. "You look good." I moved to drag my thumb over his bottom lip.

"You think so?"

"You're sleeping."

Killian shrugged. "Eating, too. I think I might have gained ten pounds." He reached for my other hand. "I'm taking some meds, and I think they're helping." He dropped his eyes to where our hands were joined together. "I don't know, Matthias, I just...I want to get better. I want to be better, and I feel like this place is doing that." He glanced up at me with hope in his baby blues. "I haven't had a cigarette since I got here either," he confessed.

"I'm so proud of you," I whispered, and that smile was back on Killian's face: The one that made my insides feel like they were going to explode and my heart beat so loud I thought the entire world would hear it.

Killian untangled our fingers. "That's all I want in this world, babe, is for you to be proud of me." He reached up to cup my cheek. "When I get out of here, we're going to get our own place." He stroked my skin. "I know you like living with Helena, but I think we should get something we can build new memories in. Would you like that?" He looked almost shy as he spoke.

I hadn't really thought about what would happen once Killian came home, but it would make sense for us to do that. "I would." I nodded.

"We can talk more about that later, but I just wanted to let you know that I was thinking about us, our future, about you. You're all I think about, Matthias."

I opened my mouth to answer him but sobbing from the table next to us brought our attention away from one another. I didn't want to eavesdrop or be too nosy, but they were all hugging the redhead, so I hoped that that was a good thing.

"Hey." Killian's husked voice was in my ear. "It's okay if this is too much for you," he told me.

I shook my head. "Never," I assured him.

"Good, because I have something else I need to tell you." His brows dropped, and his eyes moved away from me. "About that recording—"

"That's not something I want to talk about," I cut him off.

"Too fucking bad, babe, because we're talking about it."

Killian looked pissed, but there was no way he could ever be as angry as I was. The shit I went through, the bullying, I thought we were past this. "Why? Why now, Kill? I forgave you. Why do we have to rehash this?" I demanded.

"Because it wasn't me." He stood up. "It was supposed to be me, but I told Maverick that I wouldn't do it. I confessed that I wanted you and I was going to be with you, and there was no way I would hurt you like that." He stopped to look at me again. "Apparently that wasn't good enough. Maverick didn't like the fact that I was into you—that I am bi or whatever—and so he planted the device in the treehouse. He recorded us, he sent it to everyone, and he let me take the fall for it."

I stared at Killian. "You're telling me that Maverick did all that, not you? All this time...you let me think it was you? Why?" I felt sick. "The years we lost...the time we could have spent together..."

"I don't know."

"You don't know?" I stared up at Killian with confusion. "What kind of an answer is that? You picked your stupid fucking band over me, is that it?" I climbed to my feet. "I can't do this."

Killian grabbed my arm. "I can't do this without you." His brows dipped. "Please, Matthias, don't go. Not like this. I'm trying to fix things, and if you leave now..." His voice trailed off.

"What, Killian? You'll leave, too? You'll go back to drinking and snorting all the drugs you can get your hands on? Cutting yourself? That was going so well for you before, right?" I shot back.

"Stop!" I spun around at the sound of the voice behind me to find Josie staring at me. "Killian loves you; don't you see that? He does nothing but talk about you day and night, Matthias. How happy you make him, how much he wants to be a better man for you, how he wants to marry you and have a family with you." Her voice shook as she spoke. "But right now, I don't see why."

"Josie," the purple-haired girl hissed. "This doesn't seem like any of your business."

Josie waved her hand in the air. "If it wasn't for Killian, I wouldn't have asked my husband to come see me. I've been here for two months and haven't spoken to my family. Not my husband, sister, or brother. But today? Today Jameson, Cash, and Brett are here. Why? Because Killian convinced me to call them and invite them. He loves you so much, Matthias. How can you be so mean? How can you say those horrible things? He wants to get better for you. Not for himself. I honestly don't think you deserve him." She folded her arms over her chest, and that's when I noticed the burns over her face. She was dressed in oversized sweatshirt and sweatpants, but her face was beautiful despite the scars.

When I glanced over at Killian, he was watching me with hope written all over his face. "Maybe you're right. I don't deserve him." I swallowed nervously. "He really convinced you to call your family?" When Josie nodded, I looked back at Killian again. "You should have told me." I felt my throat tighten. "Baby, all those years…" He yanked me against him before I could say anything else, and the sob that threatened to escape me disappeared as he held me close.

"I'm sorry," Killian whispered as he held me. "I'm a giant fuck up." His nails dug into the back of my shirt.

I covered his mouth with mine so he couldn't say another ridiculous thing. I would forgive him, just like I had forgiven him for everything else. We had lost four years, but we were together now, and that was all that mattered. Killian loved me. He was no longer afraid of who he was, who we were, and what the future might bring. I would follow him wherever he went, and he wanted to marry me.

"Baby, I'm sorry," I whispered. "I will never use those things against you when you're trying to get better for us. Ride or die, right?"

"Ride or die, babe," Killian answered.

Epilogue

Killian
Six months later

Twelve weeks

Three months

Ninety days.

It was a long time to spend locked up in that place, even if it was voluntary. There had been a few days that I thought I might actually lose my mind, but after the first couple of weeks. I felt confident that I was actually going to be okay.

Seeing Matthias felt like a reward. Sure, talking on the phone to him was great, but seeing him? Touching him, smelling his scent, and feeling the warmth of his skin? That was what made me feel like I was doing something good. The way Matthias's hazel eyes lit up when they saw me, how easily he melted against my chest when I wrapped my arms around him, he was like coming home no matter where I was.

Thirty soon became sixty. Sixty turned into ninety, and then before I realized it, I was ready to go home.

Josie was still there when I left rehab, just like she was there when I arrived. She was better, but not one hundred percent. We had gotten close, which felt strange to me since the only girl I had ever felt close to before her was my sister. In a way, I think we were good for one another, as fucked up as we both were. She confessed to me that she always used her body when it came to men, and I realized I did the same when it came to women. She told me about her scars, I showed her mine, and I hoped like hell Josie got her head together so she could go home to her husband. Jameson seemed like a good dude.

We spoke only once, and I could tell it was because he didn't exactly trust my intentions. I couldn't blame the guy, though. If I were in his shoes, I wouldn't trust me either. The rest of the Knights—that's what Josie called them—sat back as we spoke, but I realized when we were done that he wasn't in charge. No, that would be Easton, the giant, tattooed boy that only came to visit her once. They couldn't have been older than eighteen, the group of them who kept one eye on me, and the other one was his wife, Brett. She was Josie's sister, and the one with purple hair. Josie had explained her family tree to me, but it was a lot to take in all at once.

The morning I was packing up my things, I gave Josie my cell phone number and told her to call me anytime she needed. I also told her that when she was home, I would get her, and the rest of her group of misfits, tickets to see Mulligan Downtown. She said her goodbyes to me before Matthias came to pick me up, but I saw the tears in her eyes after a quick hug.

I gripped Matthias's hand in mine as I led him through the woods. He had to know where I was taking him. There was only one reason we ever came back here, and that was the treehouse. Since Helena had sold the house last week, it wouldn't be here for us to visit much longer. My sister was moving to a smaller, one-bedroom house that she couldn't wait to redecorate and make her own. She wasn't dating, but I think that a part of her was waiting for Dean to come around and realize what he had left behind. I hoped that wouldn't happen, because it wasn't something I wasn't ready to deal with, but if the time came? I wouldn't break anyone's face over it.

When I stopped at the base of the tree, I reached out to trace my fingers over the initials I had carved with my free hand.

"Think the new family is going to keep it?" Matthias asked softly.

I shook my head. "No." I hadn't told him yet, but I had already made arrangements with the new owners. I had bought the treehouse from them, and it was going to be moved to our home in North Carolina.

We had bought our own place not too far from the Shepard's when I finished up with rehab and so far, we really enjoyed the South. I thought I would find myself hanging out with Rand a lot, but it turned out Hutch and I were more alike than I thought possible. We didn't really talk much, but we enjoyed fishing together when he had some off time, and we would just sit around in the boat in silence for hours. Weird, right? That didn't mean I didn't spend time with Rand, too, but it was Hutch that I went to when I needed someone to talk to about issues. Hutch had also talked me out of cutting more than once, and it was Hutch who convinced me that buying a house here would be a great new start. After all, it worked for him and his wife Jillian—who, if you were curious, had a healthy baby boy not too long after I landed in rehab. He was the cutest little thing, too, and almost made me want to have a kid. Babis were something Matthias and I hadn't talked about, but I had seen the way he was with Hutch's baby, as well as the rest of the NASCAR kids. I'm sure that talk would happen soon. Would I be a good father? I wasn't not sure, but I knew Matthias would be the best one on this planet, if not in the universe.

I also found out that Brooklyn's little sister, London—who was married to Mason Pelletier— a songwriter, and we worked on a couple of things together. She was super talented, and was going places. The next Mulligan Downtown album was going to feature a couple of the songs we'd written together, and I was hoping to convince her to sing with me too.

"Come on, babe, let's go up one last time." I tugged on Matthias's hand before I dropped it. "You first." I indicated for him to climb up the ladder. Mostly so I could let him witness the surprise I had inside, but also so I could check out his ass on the way up. He and Brooklyn liked to go to the gym together, and all that time working out was paying off.

Matthias kissed me before he started to climb up the ladder, and when he pushed the door open to climb inside, I heard his gasp of surprise. Once again, I had decorated the treehouse with white twinkle lights, but this time I had also gotten silver balloons that spread out saying "Marry Me?" in big letters. "Are you serious right now?" he asked when I finally got inside. "Killian, don't fuck with me, because—oh shit, you're not kidding." He watched as I got down on one knee.

"Marry me, babe." Tears burned my eyes as I looked up at him. "It's always been you, whether I realized it or not." I smiled nervously at him. "I've loved you forever, needed you longer, and wanted you my entire life." I laughed at the surprise in Matthias's eyes. "Let's start a life together and surprise them all." The tears began to slip down my cheeks as I opened the ring box so Matthias could see the unique, smooth finish on the black rhodium-plated band I had picked out. "If you hate the ring, we'll find you something else you like. I just saw it and thought it was perfect." I glanced up at him. "Say something, Matthias, say yes." I was suddenly deathly afraid he would say no.

Matthias climbed down onto the floor with me. "Yes, Killian." His breath was hot against my face as he smiled. "I will marry you, spend the rest of my life loving you, and prove everyone wrong." He reached out to run a hand over my curls.

I grabbed that same hand so I could slip the ring on it. "I fucking love you so much," I said, before I tackled him to the floor. "Oh, by the way, this is coming home with us." I kissed his nose and watched the surprise in his eyes. "I worked out something with the new owners of the house. I couldn't let someone else have our treehouse."

Matthias broke into an easy smile. "Really?" He looked ridiculously happy right now.

"Babe, this is our place," I reminded him.

Matthias's smile grew even bigger. "Our first kiss," he whispered.

"Our first time," I added.

"I love you so much, Killian."

"Not as much as I love you, Matthias."

THE END

A Note From the Author

I just have to say that this is the darkest book I've written to date. It drained me in ways I've never felt before, and more than once I had to step back, read some funny rom-com books, watch a movie or television show...anything that helped me keep my sanity. That didn't stop me from writing, though. This book made me cry, a lot, more than once, and that isn't something I do easily. Killian and Matthias consumed me during the entire writing process, which is a first for me. I hope you love them as much as I do. I've had book hangovers before (the Devil's Night series by Penelope Douglas and the After series by Anna Todd are the two that did me dirty) but I always snapped back after a few days. Nothing I've ever written has ever done this to me, until now.

Maybe I didn't want to let Kill and Matty go. It's not my longest book, but it took me the longest to write. I started it in December of 2021 and finished it in May of 2022. Maybe pieces of them are threaded into my heart while I left pieces of me inside the lines of this book.

If you're interested in reading Hutch's story you can find it in my book *Out of the Dark*. Josie's story starts with *Piece of Cake*, the first book in the Kingston High series. Or, if you want to meet Rand and Brooklyn, their book *Picture Perfect* is free on all digital platforms.

Acknowledgments

This part is right up there with writing the blurbs of my books. I'm always afraid I'm going to forget something, someone or just royally screw it up. Big thanks to everyone for their support, leaving a review, making art out of my words, and sharing the teasers, cover reveals, etc. It means so much to me.

My amazing husband— Thank you for being my rock, my soulmate, my biggest supporter through life. Without you I wouldn't be here, I wouldn't be doing this or putting out my SEVENTH book (omg, how is that possible?). I love you so damn much. You're my absolute reason for living, *my ride or die.* No one else would put up with my shit, my moods, and thank you for everything. I don't deserve you. **Real love is forever.** IOYAT.

Steph— Bestie, this time you and I aren't represented in this book, but it can't always be about us, right? Thanks for being the Sam to my Dean, the be to my fri, the Harper to my Brooklyn. I miss your face!

Amo Jones, Meghan Quinn, and Helena Hunting— You three amazing authors helped me so much while I was writing this book without even realizing it. Amo, the queen of dark romance, girl, how do you do it? Spill the tea because I was seriously *fucked* after this book. Thank you for being such a huge inspiration. Meghan thank you for releasing *Those Three Little Words* right when I needed an amazing rom-com while I was working on this. This book was the darkest I've ever written, and there were times I questioned my own sanity. Eli and Penny were there to pick me up and make me laugh. *"I ate an apple"*. Your books are always the best, but this was one came out when I needed it the most. Helena, *Pucked*! I have never laughed so hard reading a book in my life. I was crying, snorting and trying to explain to my husband why the puck pillow was so funny will never not make me giggle. Again, TLT took me places I've never been, and you helped dig me out of that hole right when I needed it. I was looking for something to make me laugh, and it was suggested to me. I have since finished all of the books in the series as I write this so just know if I ever start watching hockey it's because of you.

Peachy Keen Author Services— Thank you so much for helping me with the promotion of this book. You have gone above and beyond with helping me reach new readers with everything you have done.

You, the reader— Thank you for reading Killian and Matthias's story as well as promoting it. Whether this is the first time you've read something of mine or you've been there from the beginning, none of this would be possible without you. I want you to know that I appreciate every single one of you. If you loved reading this book as much as I enjoyed writing it, please consider leaving a review so others can find it. This story started out because of the song Chainsaw by The Band Perry and turned into so much more. These two mean more to me than you will ever know.

Also by Sundae

-Wide Open Series-
Picture Perfect
Gravity

-Kingston High Series-
Piece of Cake
Cakewalk
Triple Layer

-Standalone-
Out of the Dark

Watch for more at SundaeLeighton.com

About the Author

Sundae Leighton writes romance novels that are sweet with a dark twist.

She got her start writing fan fiction with her friends in school, but didn't take the plunge to publish her first book *Picture Perfect* until 2020. Born and raised in Connecticut, where she currently resides with her husband and their cats. She sometimes scares herself when she writes things darker than intended, considers coffee the nectar of the gods, and once ran the NYC marathon (OK - *half* marathon). When she isn't writing down what the voices in her head tell her to, she likes watching murder shows, auto racing, and reading romance books with a lot of dark angst.

Read more at SundaeLeighton.com.

www.ingramcontent.com/pod-product-compliance
Lightning Source LLC
Chambersburg PA
CBHW071408200726
48294CB00002B/317